28

GOING IN BLIND

BROTHERHOOD PROTECTORS WORLD

KRIS NORRIS

Twisted Page Press LLC

BROTHERHOOD PROTECTORS

ORIGINAL SERIES BY ELLE JAMES

OTHER BOOKS BY KRIS NORRIS

SINGLES

Centerfold

Keeping Faith

My Soul to Keep

Ricochet

Rope's End

SERIES

'TIL DEATH

1 - Deadly Vision

2 - Deadly Obsession

3 - Deadly Deception

BROTHERHOOD PROTECTORS ~ Elle James

1 - Midnight Ranger

2 – Carved in Ice

COLLATERAL DAMAGE

1 - Force of Nature

DARK PROPHECY

1 - Sacred Talisman

2 - Twice Bitten

3 - Blood of the Wolf

ENCHANTED LOVERS

1 - Healing Hands

FROM GRACE

1 - Gabriel

2 – Michael

GRIZZLY ENCOUNTERS

1 – Iron Will

THRESHOLD

1 - Grave Measures

COLLECTIONS

Blue Collar Collection

Into the Spirit, Boxed Set

RE-RELEASING SOON

TOMBSTONE

1 - Marshal Law

2 – Forgotten

3 – Last Stand

WHAT REMAINS

1 - Untainted

2 - Wasteland

3 - Mutation

4 - Reckoning

For my mum.
For loving without prejudice and always seeing beyond the
scars—whether visible or hidden.
I miss you.

CHAPTER 1

Bainbridge Foundation, Seattle, Washington.

Kent "Rigs" Walker was going to kill Hank Patterson. Not quickly. No, Rigs was going to draw it out. Nice and slow. Make the man suffer, just like Rigs was suffering, now. He'd made a deal with the ex-veteran. He'd join Hank's company—Brotherhood Protectors. Do his best to work his way out of the funk he'd been in since being cast out of his MARSOC unit with the Marines. Left to reassemble the shattered pieces of his soul—the ones the IED had missed when it had taken just about everything else. His career. His honor. Half his fucking face. All Rigs had asked was that Hank, known as Montana to his men, kept Rigs in the shadows. Any dirty job no one else wanted—Montana gave it to him.

Rigs wanted the security details that didn't involve Hollywood starlets or influential CEOs. He didn't want hotel rooms with posh interiors. Dinners in five-star restaurants. Backwoods cabins? Hiding out from the mafia in places so ugly no one would ever think to venture there? Rigs was there.

And for six months, Montana had kept his word. He'd given Rigs every questionable job that had come across his desk—ones Rigs knew the man might have otherwise turned down. Not the usual honorable missions. In fact, some of the people Rigs had shadowed were no better than the people hunting them. But it had kept him off the grid. Out of the limelight, and best of all, isolated.

So, what the hell was he doing at a star-studded charity auction, dressed in a fucking tux, complete with a tie, vest, and what Montana had called a pocket square —was Rigs supposed to blow his nose with it? Because he had visions of using the stupid folded cloth to wipe up Montana's blood. The blood he was going to spill just as soon as he could head back to Eagle Rock and murder the bastard in the very office where he'd shook his hand.

Rigs grinned to himself. Oh yeah. He could get behind that. Or even better, set a few charges around the man's home. Get him when he least expected it. Of course, Rigs wouldn't. Hank had a wife, a pretty little girl. No way, Rigs would ever harm either of them. And he couldn't rightly kill Montana when the guy had tossed him a lifeline. A Hail Mary when Rigs had been just about ready to wire himself up.

But fuck, he wanted to. He hated this. Hated the feel of the starch white shirt against his skin. The way it caught on the raised scars across his chest whenever he turned. How he knew you could see the long keloids through the fabric, which is why he'd kept on the vest and jacket, despite the warm temperatures. It was bad enough his face was in full view—right out there. On display like a freak at a sideshow. If the guests had been able to see how the scars continued down his torso—yeah, the auction would have been a bust because everyone would have turned and run.

Instead, they only turned and ran from him. Okay, they walked extremely fast in another direction. It didn't matter. Their reactions hurt, even if he had braced himself against it. Known from the start how it would all play out. Rigs was good at tactics, at strategizing. And he'd known the moment he'd received the assignment that it was going to turn ugly.

"Christ, Rigs, I swear if you tug on that tie one more time, I'm going to use it as a noose."

Rigs glared at his buddy, or should he say traitor. The next guy on his list he was going to murder then wipe up with his tiny square of cloth. Of course, Sam Montgomery, aka Midnight, didn't mind wearing a tux. The guy looked like a million bucks in his. Suave. Professional. He fit in, along with the rich businessmen and CEOs. He didn't have a hair out of place. His damn shoes reflected the overhead lights. He could have walked in straight off the pages of GQ.

Looks weren't something Rigs had really wasted much time worrying about. He'd never had any issues finding a willing bed partner. Had even dated several pretty women for a few months, once upon a time. But now...

Between the scars and the stress, Rigs looked like a thug. One that had seen hard times and come out the other end tired and beaten. Like the kind of people he and his buddies were supposed to keep *out* of the auction. Shaggy hair, stubble, and a scowl he'd perfected over the past several months, people stared at him, shuddered, then looked at Midnight, as if needing the other man to cleanse their visual palate. Rigs had lost count of the number of times women had gasped, lifted their hands to their mouths before politely trying to talk it off as seeing a spider.

Well, the entire room must be full of fucking tarantulas because that was the only explanation that fit their reactions.

He glanced across the room. Russel or Ice, as he was affectionately known, was married to one of the few woman who hadn't flinched, cringed or screamed when she'd first taken in Rigs' battle-worn face. Harlequin James, or Foster, now, had managed to look Rigs in the eyes and talk as if the scars weren't there—weren't glaring at her like a damn beacon of his greatest failure. He'd been sweet on her ever since. Not in a romantic way—she was devoted to Ice, and they'd gotten hitched in Vegas only a month after Ice had popped the question. More like a sister. One he'd already taken a few bullets for—that he'd kill to protect.

Rigs gave Midnight a shove. "I don't see why we had to get dressed up. I look out of place. Any tango with half a brain will make me with just a glance."

"What the hell are you talking about? You look fine —when you're not yanking on that tie."

"*You* look fine. I look like I killed the guy who owns this tux then took his place so I could blend in. Which I don't."

Midnight sighed. To his credit, he didn't call Rigs out—lecture him on how his scars weren't nearly as bad as Rigs made them out to be, and that most people hardly noticed them. He would have given good money to know who these "people" were Midnight seemed to think looked beyond the marks because they sure as hell weren't in this building.

Rigs fisted his hands to keep them by his side instead of around Midnight's throat, casually scanning the room. "Hell of a turnout. Bridgette's clinic is going to receive some serious funding if this crowd is half as rich as it looks. Did you see some of the items up for sale?" He whistled. "More money than I make in a year."

"You and me both, brother." Midnight turned when Bridgette walked over and pressed a kiss on his cheek. "Everything all right, darling?"

She nodded, smiling at Rigs. Bridgette was another one who hadn't been fazed by his looks. Who always made eye contact whenever they spoke—which wasn't often. Rigs went out of his way to avoid any kind of contact beyond his ex-military brothers—men who'd bled as much as he had. And, now, here he was, standing beneath the crystal chandeliers, exposed.

Bridgette rested her hand on Midnight's arm—a visual show of affection. They had finally set a date. October. When they'd attended Ice's impromptu wedding, she'd suggested following suite—finding a chapel right then and making it official. But Midnight had kissed her and calmly told her he wanted her to have the wedding of her dreams because he was going to personally see to it that it was the only one she'd ever get. She'd teared up—Rigs hadn't really understood why. She'd seemed happy, but there had been tears dotting her face. Women. Who really understood why they did anything? Not him. She'd kissed Midnight and casually said October.

Bridgette brushed back some hair that had pulled free from her complicated knot, glancing at the people seated off to their right. "There're just about to start the second half. I can't believe how much money we've raised, already. Do you know how many women I'll be able to help?"

Midnight smiled. "All of them. And you deserve it. What you've been doing these past months—couldn't be prouder. I'm just glad Jeremy called—got you to accept this offer. You tend to be a bit...stubborn when it comes to help."

She laughed. "Just because I busted your ass when you showed up to be my bodyguard doesn't mean I shun everyone."

Somehow, Midnight held back from rolling his eyes. "Right. It's just me."

Her eyes glassed over. "Yeah. Only you. Forever."

And fuck if Midnight didn't do something Rigs had never seen the hardcore Army Ranger do. Ever. Midnight's expression softened, and he kissed her. Right there. In the middle of an op. No concern for his surroundings. A group of tangos could have picked that exact moment to bust in, guns blazing, and Midnight would have been busy losing himself in his fiancée's mouth.

Rigs averted his gaze. Bad enough he seemed to be the only one not blindsided by love. Completely focused on the mission. Watching them kiss—seeing their obvious happiness—it stung. Especially, when he knew he'd never find that. Never have someone look at him with complete and utter adoration. Sure, he could probably find someone to have sex with. Not every woman cared about anything above a man's waist. But love. Actual love that involved more than just genitals grinding—that involved his fucking soul? Yeah, not in the cards.

"Kent?"

It took Rigs a moment to realize Bridgette was addressing him—no one called him Kent except her. He glanced over his shoulder. "Yeah?"

"I just wanted to thank you for coming. I know this isn't really your scene. But even though Jeremy hired security, I just feel better knowing you, Russel, and Sam are here. My own secret Black Ops force."

Rigs snorted. "A Marine, a Ranger, and a PJ. Not exactly your typical Spec Op squad. And you didn't even let me bring any explosives. I feel...naked."

This time, Midnight rolled his eyes. "There were bomb sniffing dogs at the entrances. The last thing we needed was to have one of them attack you. You're just lucky that's a rented tux, or there'd most likely be some residual powder on it." He cracked a smile. "Though, seeing you try to outrun a German shepherd might have been worth it."

"You know, you're all pretty cocky for people who have to live knowing I could wire your damn tooth-brush to explode."

"You're one of the good guys. I'll take my chances." He turned to Bridgette. "I was just going to do a round of the room. Why don't you walk with me? It'll make me look less obvious, and I get to know you're safe. A double win in my books."

Bridgette's face lit up. Just beamed with joy. She took his arm, said something that sounded like goodbye to Rigs then walked off with Midnight.

Fuck. Rigs was definitely going to kill Hank.

Rigs looked over at Ice. He swore the man sensed when someone needed him—probably a PJ thing because he hadn't met a pararescue tech, yet, who didn't have the sixth sense—because the man stopped talking to one of the guests and glanced over at him, eyebrow arched. Rigs nodded then made a twirling motion with his hand—signaling he was going to do a perimeter check. Ice gave him a thumb's up.

The announcer's voice sounded, again, as Rigs walked toward the east side of the building. He'd do a circle—check out the front entrance then go for a brief walk through the rear gardens. Though there was secu-rity at the main entrance accessible from outside the gated grounds, and another couple guys walking the perimeter, he felt better doing his own recon. Getting away from the crowds didn't hurt, either. For a huge place, he'd found it next to impossible to isolate himself where he could still be effective.

Rigs gave the area one last scan—noting both Ice and

Midnight's positions—then headed for the foyer. The Bainbridge Foundation was an impressive building with enormous, arched ceilings and large columns. It sat two stories high and covered half an acre of the beautiful estate. He'd only been upstairs a couple of times, choosing to focus on the lower levels—where he could keep a closer eye on the auction.

The main floor had multiple open areas along an interconnecting hallway, all fanning out from a central sweeping staircase. There were nooks located along every wall, some with chairs, others with plants. Hanging fixtures bathed the interior in bright light, though half had been dimmed to create a cozier atmosphere.

At least, that's what Bridgette had said. Rigs wouldn't know a cozy atmosphere if it bit him in the ass. Not after growing up bouncing from one foster home to another then spending his adult life in the Marines Corps. Stark. Depressing. Those he understood. The cabin he'd rented a few miles outside of Eagle Rock embraced those qualities. But even lighting a fire didn't make the place welcoming. Not that he cared. It had the essentials. And Rigs was all about the bare necessities.

The guards at the front entrance saluted as he walked past. They looked competent enough. Not hardened soldiers, but he'd watched the way they'd handled their weapons before holstering them. That told him they could be counted on to cover his ass if things went south.

While he hoped they wouldn't have to, Rigs never

went into an op without knowing if he had backup he could trust. They weren't Midnight or Ice, but they'd carry their own weight. That was all that mattered.

Rigs turned left at one of the marble planters then quietly slipped out the back door. The sky still held a tinge of red near the horizon, a spider web of stars starting to poke holes in the indigo sky. He took a moment to breathe in the fresh air. Hints of jasmine and cottonwood drifted on the breeze, infused with a touch of pine. He smiled—a rarity for him lately—and headed for the narrow path that wove through immaculately kept gardens and groomed patches of grass. He'd make a circuit—the same one he'd done a dozen times tonight—then return to the main foyer—steel himself against another barrage of gasps as the people left the auction.

It's for a good cause. Embrace the suck. Nothing new, there.

He repeated the mantra in his head, turning right at the corner of the building, and smacked into a woman standing with her back to the pathway. He inhaled, juggling both their weight as he took several stumbling steps forward before finally regaining his balance. Soft skin passed beneath his palms as he smoothed his hands down her arms before cupping her elbows and keeping her steady until he knew she wouldn't fall. The woman grabbed ahold of his forearm for a few more moments, digging her fingers into his muscle, before gradually letting her hand fall to her side.

Did he miss the warmth of her touch?

"Shit. Er—sorry, ma'am. I didn't see you before I was on top of you."

Damn, had it sounded sexual other than inside his head? Because for the first time since Ice had dragged his ass out of the rubble amidst a blanket of gunfire, Rigs *felt* sexual. Maybe not like his old self, but there was a definite stirring in his pants—the kind he hadn't experienced since before nearly dying. Since simply getting through each day took every ounce of effort. Yet, one touch of her silky flesh beneath his palms, and bam—his dick took notice.

Thankfully, it wasn't a full-on boner. Just a twitch. A small surge of blood. But after being basically dead meat between his legs for eighteen months, it felt like a raging hard-on.

Of course, she hadn't turned and raised her gaze to his, yet. Hadn't done much of anything other than gasp and breathe. But he knew, in about three seconds, the warm feeling building in his chest would be extinguished. Turn cold and unforgiving like her stare.

She shook her head, inhaling roughly when the motion seemed to shift her balance, again. Rigs stepped closer, holding her tight and praying his dick didn't decide to swell to full attention. Because there'd be no way to hide it from her. Not with her body hugging his, her ass rubbing against his crotch. Damn, another few passes and he wouldn't be able to will his growing erection away. Wouldn't be able to do anything besides apologize after the fact.

The woman steadied herself, her small hands covering his at her waist. "That's okay. I hadn't realized I was standing so close to the corner. Guess my count was off."

Her count was off?

"If I'd been completely focused, I would have noticed you in time to side-step around you."

She chuckled, gently untangling them then taking a step away as she half turned. "No, really…"

Her voice cut into a gasp as her head whipped around, throwing her off-balance. He caught a glimpse of wide eyes in profile before she tanked to the right. Rigs lunged for her, catching her before she'd tumbled onto the stone path, then tugged her against his chest, again. He splayed one hand across her stomach, the other up by her rib cage as he kept her balanced.

Her heart kicked against his palm, and he didn't miss the increased rhythm. The shiver that shook through her, or the sound of her frantically drawing in air.

"Are you okay? Did I hurt you?"

She shook her head, again, visibly pulling herself together. "No. I just…I thought for a moment there was a flash of…" She sighed then slowly slipped free. "It's nothing. Thank you."

Rigs stayed close, sweeping his gaze the length of her. He took the opportunity to study her before she finally turned, and it all fell apart. To take in her blonde hair swept up into some kind of clip, and the silver pair of earrings dangling from dainty lobes. Her black dress skimming her form, flaring out just below her waist. It went over one shoulder, exposing the long sleek line of her neck and the hint of her other shoulder blade. Her pale skin gleamed in the early moonlight, and he wished he could hold on to her a bit longer. Give himself time to memorize the feel of her smooth flesh against his hands. The beat of her heart against his palm.

Instead, he slowly released her then stepped back. She shifted her weight, and the gently flowing skirt swished around her knees, showing off black boots with only an inch of height.

She finally turned, but before he could see what color her eyes were—or hide the left side of his face like he normally did—he caught a scratch of claws on stone. Rigs spun just as a large dog jumped over one of the planters, landing square on his chest. They fell back together, hitting hard. A tongue swept up the side of his face—right across the raised scars—followed by a playful bark.

"No. Blade. Leave it."

Her voice barely sounded above a whisper, but the dog stilled, turned ever so slightly before retreating, circling her ankles then sitting at her left heel.

Rigs pushed onto his hands, watching her as he shook his head. Just his luck, he'd bumped into one of the dog handlers—maybe one still in training because the dog's behavior seemed…off. Though, he'd thought all the bomb-sniffing dogs had left once the auction had started.

The woman reached down and clicked a leash on the brute, her other hand rising to her mouth. "Oh my god, are you okay? First, I nearly trip you, and, now, this. I'm so sorry. I'd just let him off to have a bit of a run—he gets nervous around people sometimes, and there're so many inside. We're both doing some training—adjusting, really—and we needed some air, but I thought we were alone out here. Did he hurt you?"

Rigs laughed. Fuck, he tried not to, but her words came out as an endless stream, all pushed together as if it had been one long word. And the way she was staring at him—Christ, it knocked him off his feet in a completely different way. No horror. No revulsion. Not even idle curiosity that he got from people who wanted to know how he'd gotten the marks.

No, her face was relaxed and flushed, and so damn pretty, it made his chest hurt. Right in the center. Over his withered, shredded heart. She extended a hand—off to the right and not really close enough to help him up—but he didn't need it. He rose easily to his feet, brushing the dust off his pants.

She jerked upward once he'd risen, lips pursed, her gaze searching in front of her. "Are you okay?"

"Fine. He's a big boy. What was his name?"

She smiled as she angled to better face him, one hand gently stroking the dog's head as it sat at her feet, tail thumping, tongue lolling out one side. "Blade."

"Blade. That's…different."

"It's after the movie. The trilogy. Wesley Snipes. Vampires."

"Right. He was some kind of half-breed savior or something."

"Anyway, I'm really sorry. I don't usually let him loose away from home. He gets…excited."

"And playful. Haven't known a bomb dog to tackle someone who isn't carrying explosives." But maybe the animal just had really good instincts. Could smell that

Rigs had made a career out of blowing shit up. For all he knew, he had C4 in his blood. Sweated powder out his skin.

If anything, her smile widened, and he swore he heard her chuckling. "Actually, he's not one of the bomb dogs." She fidgeted with the end of the handle. "He used to be. Served two years in Afghanistan, but he was… injured. He recovered," she added as she scratched Blade's head, again. "But he's…got some issues. No one would take him, would even consider trying to retrain him. Except I have this friend, Carl, who's amazing. He trains animals for movies and law enforcement and for personal assistance, and he's always rescuing them off of death row—giving them a second chance. He figured we'd make a good match, since I needed…" She sighed. "I'm rambling, aren't I?"

He didn't miss the breathy quality to her voice or the hint of flush on her cheeks and neck. If he didn't know better, he'd have thought there was something sparking between them. One of those instant attractions he'd heard about but had never experienced.

"It's fine. I did nearly bowl you over. So, he's part of the security here, then? You're training?"

"Not exactly. We're just…" She swallowed. "It's a long story. Anyway, I'm really sorry he knocked you down."

Rigs narrowed his eyes. There was something different about her. The way she kept tilting her head. The tone of her voice. While he had excellent night vision—maybe not as perfect in his left eye, anymore— the way she was standing with her back to the moonlight, the deep shadows masked most of her expressions, making it hard to get a true reading on her. He kept trying to see what color her eyes were, but he couldn't make them out in the dim light.

He offered her a smile and prayed he wasn't simply baring his teeth as his scars pulled at his skin. "No harm done. I hope I didn't ruin your break."

"No. I was just about to call him and head back in. If I hide out here much longer, I might never leave."

She'd said it as a joke. He knew it, but it was painfully obvious there was a healthy dose of truth in her words.

"You're not a fan of auctions?"

"I'm not a fan of crowds." She cringed as soon as the words were free before lifting her chin and pursing her lips. "Enjoy your walk. It's a lovely night. Must be why there were others taking advantage of it earlier."

"There are others out here?"

"There were. I mean, I heard a lot of footsteps. Scuffing noises. So... But they pretty much stopped after I came out about ten minutes ago."

Rigs scanned the area. The auction was in full swing. It didn't make sense that more than one or two of the guests would be walking the grounds. The hairs on his neck prickled.

"I'll keep an eye out. Perhaps, I'll see you later. Though, I'll try not to crash into you, next time."

The muscle in her jaw clenched, and she looked away. "Right. *See* you later. Blade, up."

The dog stood, moving a few steps over with her to a bench that was hidden in the shadows. She turned away from Rigs, fusing with something before shifting back. She had a handle in her left hand, a folded cane in her right.

She seemed to orient herself. "Blade, forward."

Blade started up the path, walking diligently at her side. Rigs stared after her, unable to do anything other than watch her disappear around the building. Everything shifted into place. Her odd behavior. The dog. Her seeming indifference to his scars. If he hadn't been half-focused on the way she'd felt in his arms for those precious few moments, or how much he wished he could get her back into them, he would have realized it straight off. Wouldn't have been an utter ass and told her he'd *see* her later.

Because his mystery woman wouldn't see anything later. She was blind.

CHAPTER 2

ADDISON BAILEY HEADED for the door on the south side of the foundation, forcing herself to breathe—in then out, then in, again. It should have been easy. She'd spent her entire life breathing without ever thinking about it. But right now—making her lungs work felt like an enormous feat. One worthy of some kind of medal. Because as soon as she stopped consciously drawing oxygen in then blowing it out, her chest constricted, and her throat closed up. She just wasn't sure if it was because of the guy in the garden or the fact that for a split second, she could have sworn she'd gotten a glimpse of flowering plants, shadowed grass, and large tanned hands gripping her waist.

Which was crazy, albeit possible, considering her usual circumstances. But why her brain would pick, now, to suddenly kick back in when it had been stubbornly locked in the darkness since her injury seemed... insane. Nothing had changed—other than meeting that guy.

Which was also crazy. Surely, having some strange man hold her for all of sixty seconds wouldn't be the reason her neurons rebooted. Finally allowed her to see, again, when nothing the doctors or psychologists had done over the past year had resulted in any kind of cure.

She tripped a step, stumbling upright just as Blade stopped. She frowned, wondering if he was waiting for her when she realized they'd reached the door. She'd made a habit out of counting each step—a throwback to the months before she'd gotten Blade, where one miscalculation generally ended with something smacking her in the head or shin. But she'd apparently been too busy contemplating her mental state to back Blade up. Not that he needed it.

Despite what everyone had told her—how he'd never make the transition to guide dog, regardless of Carl's brilliance as a trainer. That she was crazy to put her safety at risk because she felt connected to a dog— one with obvious issues. She didn't care that he had visible scars. That he had probable PTSD. She had her own demons—the kind that woke her most nights. That haunted her waking hours. All she knew was that the prospect of saving him had saved her. Given her a reason to get up in the morning. Pull herself together in order to be worthy of his efforts. Hell, without him, she probably would have ended up like her sister. Broken. Unable to face the rest of her life scarred and alone.

Addy hadn't been able to help Gwen. To save her. But she'd been given another chance with Blade. And she wasn't going to fail—wouldn't change her decision even if given the chance. For better or worse, they'd learn to cope together. Besides, he'd never let her down, yet.

Addy sighed and glanced over her shoulder. More out of habit than anything else because despite whatever had just happened back in the garden, she knew she wouldn't see anything. But if she tilted her head just right, maybe she'd hear *him*.

A shiver wove down her spine, and she rubbed one arm in an attempt to warm herself. She was definitely going crazy. It was the only way to explain her reaction to the guy. She didn't do emotions—hadn't since she'd woken up blind in the hospital eighteen months ago. But there was no denying that as soon as he'd grabbed her in an attempt to keep them both upright, her skin had tingled. Actually tingled as if she'd been touched by a live wire. Having him let go so quickly had left her slightly dazed, and she'd had to maintain her grasp on his arm until the world had stopped shifting beneath her feet.

His incredibly chiseled arm. Even through his shirt, she'd felt his muscles flex. They'd been hard, like rock, and she'd had the urge to run her hand across his chest —see if the rest of him matched.

Blade whined, pulling her out of her thoughts. She reached down to scratch his head. She wasn't the only one apparently effected by the guy. Blade had never reacted like that before. If anything, he shied away from strangers, yet, he'd just pinned one to the ground— barked with the same playful tone he used when she played fetch with him—and she couldn't help but wonder if he'd sensed the same pull she had. If the dog was equally affected by the guy's charm and gravelly voice. The kind that made her wish she'd stayed a bit longer. Had properly introduced herself so she could hear him say her name instead of calling her ma'am.

She smiled. Remembering how he'd inhaled just before Blade had taken him down. There'd been a frenzied moment of licking and barking before she'd called off the dog. And the guy had laughed. Actually laughed when she'd stood over him, apologizing. He hadn't seemed at all upset that her hundred-pound mutt had knocked him onto his ass.

She'd heard that, too. A resounding thud. While she was still adjusting to her vision loss, she'd already started developing the sixth sense most blind people seemed to have. An eerie sensation when someone else was in the room, even if she hadn't heard them come in. Better hearing. It was all a bit unnerving, really.

But, now, she had Blade. And no one was getting close to her without her knowing about it. And if that meant he might knock a few strangers on their asses, well, she wasn't going to lose any sleep over it. The world was a dangerous place, and while she hated to admit it, she was vulnerable, now. There were lots of people—men—who'd enjoy taking advantage of her current limitations. If Blade made them think twice, she was grateful.

Not that every man was that way. *He* hadn't been. She could tell by the way he'd held her while she'd been letting the world stabilize—contemplating her sanity when she thought she'd caught a glimpse of her surroundings. His grip had been firm, but gentle, as if he was afraid he might hurt her. And she'd secretly wished he'd stay close. Keep holding her.

But she'd stepped away. And just as well. She wasn't fit for conversation, let alone anything more. Besides, who'd want to get involved with a woman whose future was a big empty black hole? One wrought from her own devices? She'd planned out her entire life at age six, and until eighteen months ago, she'd been right on track. But now? Now, she was living on a medical leave salary and trying to find the motivation to get through each day.

Blade whined, again, and she reached for the door, opening it wide enough they could both get through. He got them inside then obediently headed left when she called out the command. Thankfully, she'd been to the Bainbridge Foundation several times before she'd lost her sight—misplaced it. She needed to remember she wasn't truly blind. That it was all in her head. A by-product of trauma and god knew what else because the doctors didn't have any answers, other than what everyone kept saying under their breath—that she was mentally unstable. Or, as she preferred—batshit crazy.

Whatever the reason, her previous visits to the building meant she was familiar with the layout. It was the only reason she'd agreed to come tonight. To put both her and Blade through more training while Carl enjoyed the auction—her backup if things went side-ways. Not that she needed him. If Blade got spooked, she already knew how to navigate the floor plan. And she always had her foldable cane. Because she never knew when her own demons would strike—when she'd get lost in flashes of that night. The one she couldn't remember. That seemed as lost as her damn vision. No sense being unprepared if Blade suffered something similar.

God, what a pair they made. A washed-up cop, and an ex-soldier dog. Though, she liked to think that together, they were nearly whole.

Blade took her right around a large statute then angled her toward the corner. He kept his pace steady, gently pulling her along. She smiled to herself. They were definitely getting the hang of working together. She'd learned to trust that he wouldn't crack her head on an overhanging branch or sign, and he'd come to understand she wasn't going to abandon him. That they were partners.

The announcer's voice echoed through the open space as she neared the next corner. She'd cleared her mind enough to count her steps, this time, and if she'd oriented herself correctly coming in, she was only a few away from another short wall that ended at the grand staircase. She remembered being awed by the grandeur of it the first time she'd attended a police function at the foundation. It had reminded her of southern estates like in *Gone with the Wind*. Incredibly wide and curving gently off to the right, it wasn't hard to imagine elegantly dressed women making a dramatic entrance down the steps.

Of course for her, not falling when she entered a room was considered dramatic. An unnoticed threshold or change of flooring was enough to trip her up—land her face first on the ground. And in her dress, that wasn't something she wanted to experience.

"Blade, left."

The dog took one step then stopped, angling in front of her. Addy frowned. It wasn't like Blade to disobey her.

She straightened, adjusted her grip on his harness then stated the command, again. "Blade, left."

The dog refused to move, pressing against her legs when she tried to walk forward. Maybe she was still too far away from the corner—had miscounted her steps—and he'd gotten confused. Fine, she'd adjust.

"Blade. Forward."

Nothing. If anything, he pushed her back a few feet. Addison took a deep breath. This was what Carl had called intentional disobedience. Though, it was generally something guide dogs did to overcome a dangerous situation their handler had missed. Like not hearing a car at a crosswalk and telling the dog to enter it. But... She was in the middle of the building. Even if she was slightly off, there wasn't anything dangerous. A wall to her left and a large hallway with open areas like the one she'd just traversed to her right.

The main entrance was opposite the staircase with the auction room through a set of French doors at the end of the enormous foyer. Even if there were people hanging about, Blade should navigate her around them, not refuse to let her pass.

Then, he growled, low and throaty. Not happy sounds like when he'd been on top of the guy with the sexy, raspy voice in the garden. This was pure aggression. The kind a predator made just before it struck.

The hair rose along the back of her neck. After a dozen years on the force, she'd learned to trust her instincts, as well as those of her partner. And everything about Blade told her there was a threat she couldn't see, but one he'd already assessed and was actively attempting to address.

Addy stilled, quieting her breathing in the hopes of hearing...something. Anything to give her a clue as to what was going on or what direction the danger would strike. Voices from the auction still echoed in the background, but there was another sound. Hushed but familiar. Like...

Footsteps. Faster than a walk. The kind of pace police used when positioning themselves to strike.

The realization had her tightening on Blade's harness. She urged the dog back when what sounded like a can clicked across the floor way off to her left.

Grenade.

It registered inside her head before the word actually took shape. Her training kicked in. Had her crouching and curling over Blade, his head pressed against her stomach, her back to the threat. She covered her ears just as a couple of blasts rocked through the building, shouts and screams quickly following.

It took a few moments to orient herself, thankful the wall had provided decent protection. That, or she'd just gotten insanely lucky with the heart of the explosion far enough away it only had minor effects. Blade whimpered, the loud noise obviously far more damaging to him.

A series of dull pops had her moving. Even with her ears ringing slightly and her head a bit fuzzy, she recognized the sound—AK47s. Which meant things were quickly turning deadly.

Addy pushed onto trembling legs, half carrying Blade against the wall. It would take him longer to get his balance back, and they needed to not be sitting anywhere obvious while that happened.

More footsteps.

The huge area echoed the sound, making it hard to pinpoint. She flicked her cane open when someone pounded around the corner, the click of boots on the inlaid floors stopping next to her. A hand settled in her hair, shoving her to her knees then yanking back her head.

"Yeah, you're the one."

A deep voice followed by another click. Had it been a camera? The release of a safety? She grabbed the man's hand and tilted her head forward in an effort to wrench his wrist when Blade leaped out of her lap. The guy released her and took two hurried steps back. She heard the snarl, the scream. The distinct muffled growl of Blade's mouth locked around flesh.

He was in full attack mode.

She pushed to her feet, twisting to face them, when there was a single trigger pull. Blade whimpered, all other sounds cutting off. Her stomach roiled, then she was moving—narrowing in on that last tangible noise. Two steps and a swing of her cane. Upwards and away, just like a batter. She didn't have a plan. Didn't have anything other than her instincts honed from years of training. But she'd be damned if she went down without a fight—limited or not.

She connected, the firm hit reverberating down the shaft and into her hands. Good. She hoped she'd broken the fucker's arm. A quick pivot and another swing connected with what felt like the guy's chin. It was high above her, and the smack was definitely on flesh, not clothing.

The air moved and fingers settled on her shoulder, scratching at her skin. Perfect. She used his hand as a focal point, spun and grabbed his arm, using her other as a bridge across his elbow. She didn't need to see him —had practiced these moves endlessly for the past twelve years. They were ingrained. No different from brushing her teeth or washing her hair. She pulled his body on a diagonal to keep him off-balance as she rolled his entire arm forward, sweeping the pressure from his elbow up to his shoulder, getting the lock she needed.

The guy screamed as his bone rotated inside the joint, dropping him to his knees. She followed him down, increasing the pressure until it popped out.

She let go, reaching for where she thought his belt would be. No way he was only packing the assault rifle. The bastard was sure to have a pistol stashed some-where. Her fingers landed a bit high, more on his ribs. Fucker was wearing body armor. Definitely not a good sign. She smoothed her hand down, quickly finding a thigh holster. Another flick of her wrist and she had his weapon.

The guy flailed beneath her—trying to get his feet under him—muttering an endless string of curses. She raised her hand and brought the pistol's grip down across the back of his neck. Missed the first time, low, but the second one connected. So, did the third. The bastard stilled.

Her chest heaved, the gun cool against her palm. A shiver shook through her, a weak whimper grounding her. She flipped the gun around, brushing her fingers along the barrel. It was full size, the brand's letters embossed on the stock. It was hard to decipher—possibly a Sig Sauger. Safety felt wrong for a Glock, and it weighed a bit more than her Beretta had. She guessed a forty-five, especially if these guys wanted casualties that didn't get back up. Which meant more of a kick-back, and she'd have to compensate.

She searched the guy's belt, removing what felt like a radio then scooted to her right, sweeping her hand across the floor until she located Blade. He licked her wrist, followed by a single thump of his tail.

"Hold on, buddy. There's bound to be help on the way."

She'd have called, herself, but her damn cell was in her purse, which was with Carl. Shit, she knew better than to go anywhere without it. Especially, now. She wasn't the fearless cop she'd been before. Couldn't calmly assess a situation and take appropriate actions. She was lucky she'd been able to react. If Blade hadn't attacked...

Pain blossomed in her chest. He'd come to her defense without hesitation, and, now...

Fuckers would pay. She'd call in every damn marker she'd accumulated over her career if need be. But she wouldn't rest until someone had captured every one of the people involved in the robbery and tossed their asses in jail.

It had to be a robbery. Some gang after the items up for auction. Though, they were insanely well equipped. The flashbangs. The body armor. The multiple weapons. Not your usual street gang. And what had the guy meant when he'd said she was the one? Did they think she was still a cop? Posed a threat? She'd been involved in enough raids the local gangs might recognize her.

"Alpha three, update."

Addy whipped her head down. The blast of static sending a chill down her spine as the radio vibrated in her hand.

"Alpha three?"

Damn. How many more? Were they close? They'd obviously come looking for the guy she'd cracked over the head. Whose arm Blade had locked onto.

She'd have to pick Blade up—get them somewhere safe. Maybe in one of the alcoves. Cower and wait for help because she couldn't *fucking* see. Couldn't be the version of herself she'd spent thirty-two years making. The one who met danger head-on.

God, she hated this. Hated feeling powerless. Being the one waiting for help to arrive instead of riding to the rescue. All her training, and there she was, trying to figure out a place to hide until the real cavalry arrived.

Footsteps sounded high above her, moving fast, then

racing down the steps. She heard a gasp, the clatter of a magazine being changed. Addy pushed to one knee, braced herself, and prayed he'd make one more sound when a flash of light jolted her back, giving her a moment of visual clarity. A single snapshot of the room. Of the smoke curling through the air, the spent canister lying on the floor in the distance. Of the man limp at her feet, and the other guy charging toward her, one hand on the trigger guard as he cupped the new magazine beneath the stock.

Then, it was gone, nothing but the magazine slotting into place filling the void, followed by the harsh cock of the gun as he loaded a round into the chamber.

She adjusted her angle then fired three quick shots. The guy's grunt signaled she'd hit him. The thud meant he'd been knocked down. But if he had body armor like the other bastard…

She blinked, willing herself to break through the darkness, again, but it didn't work. Instead, she sat there, waiting. She couldn't charge over. Couldn't go for the head shot if he sat up—not unless he said something. Gave her a way to orient herself. Even then, it was a long shot. As it was, she had no way of knowing if she'd killed him or simply knocked the wind out of his lungs. Subdued him for a few precious minutes. Ones she could have used to secure him. Would have in her previous life.

Was that a cough?

But if she tried for a head shot without knowing for sure—without another glimpse of her surroundings— she could hit someone else. A civilian—like her. And that wasn't a risk she could take. She wouldn't know-ingly trade her life for someone else's.

Had his hand just squeaked across the floor?

She strained to hear anything concrete, when a voice called out behind her.

"Get down."

CHAPTER 3

BLIND. How the hell had he missed she was blind?

Rigs muttered to himself as he turned and continued his sweep. Of all the insensitive, asinine things to say... He'd *see* her later? God, he was as bad as the people who gawked at him or liked to joke that he had a little "something" on his face.

Those comments either ended with him giving the asshole his patented death glare, or with the person on their ass after a quick move knocked them down.

And here, Rigs had gone and done the same thing. All because he'd been too busy catching his breath. Fantasizing about holding her, again. Feeling that silky skin pressed against him. Tasting it to see if it was as creamy as it looked. He'd been so damn preoccupied, he hadn't even bothered to ask her what her name was.

He gave himself a mental shake. He really hated being the asshole.

A gust of wind twirled around him, cooling his heated skin. Maybe once he got back in, he could find her. Apologize for his behavior. See if he could buy her a coffee as compensation for his lack of tact. Anything to spend more time with her. He wasn't sure what it all meant. If he was even ready to consider something remotely personal. But just thinking about never seeing her, again, made his stomach clench. His lungs refuse to inflate as he fought to draw in a simple breath. That had to mean something, didn't it?

It meant he'd lost what was left of his mind. He didn't have much to offer. Nightmares. Paranoia. The lack of any real social graces. And what happened if she ever wanted to have sex? Hadn't he read somewhere that blind people used their hands to visualize a person's face? All those long slender fingers skimming across his jaw, tracing the ugly, raised scars. Then, moving on to his chest where they were even more pronounced.

Rigs didn't know which was worse. Seeing the disfiguring marks or actually touching them. Besides him, only doctors or nurses had ever touched them. And Ice. The man had tried really hard to stitch him up without leaving marks, but Rigs' flesh had been ragged and torn, and he'd been damn lucky Ice had done as well as he had in the midst of a gunfight. That Ice had even risked his ass to save him.

No, the more Rigs mulled it over, the worse the idea sounded. She most likely already thought he was a jerk. Best to just leave it at that. Let her find someone else, unless she was already attached but didn't wear a ring. He'd looked. Nothing but pretty bare fingers.

Yup. He'd definitely lost it because he'd never

noticed a woman's hands before. Or at least, not before getting her name. Before they were wrapped around his dick.

Rigs sighed, doing his best to shove all those thoughts—shove *her*—into a box and file it away. Mark it as dangerous goods that he'd purge, later. Any woman that messed with his head this much after a single meeting was the kind of trouble that lasted a lifetime.

Compartmentalize then forget. That was his best strategy, and he excelled at strategy. Except he doubted he *could* forget her. Not that easily. Not when his hands itched to touch her, again. Five seconds without her, and he was already jonesing for another chance.

Which wouldn't happen until he'd done his damn job. She'd mentioned hearing other people, and despite the warm air, the growing moonlight, and the pretty gardens, he just didn't believe that the guests would leave when the auction was still actively going.

He crossed over to the west side, searching what he could see of the woods beyond the groomed yard. Deep shadows pocketed the forest, but he didn't see anything that looked out of place. Still...

The hairs on his neck prickled, again. There was something about the rightness of it that was wrong. He stood staring for a few minutes, trying to sort through what was bothering him, when it clicked. No guards. There were supposed to be guards walking the back perimeter, and even if they'd stopped to chat, he should have seen some evidence of them, by now. They weren't trying to be stealthy. The entire point of having them patrol the estate was visibility. A deterrent to anyone who might think about trying to breech the security. Cameras, alarms—they weren't that difficult to bypass. But armed men... Bullets—the prospect of getting shot —a far better motivator to leave the place alone.

Rigs cursed, slipping his cell out of his pocket. He hit Midnight's number, frowning when nothing happened. The stupid phone was nearly fully charged. He'd double checked before he'd left. He tried, again, but the line wouldn't connect, despite having full reception.

Shit. Someone was jamming the signals. Preventing anyone from calling out. Calling for help. Something was going down. And it had to be soon.

He took off, winding his way back as quickly as he could while still being vigilant. Constantly scanning his surroundings. He was essentially going in blind—no intel on numbers or intent. Though, he suspected robbery was the prime incentive. Still, had they killed the guards or merely subdued them? Were they armed or planning on using stealth? Racing in with nothing but his gut feeling, a non-working cell, and the fact he couldn't see the guards could get him or others killed. He knew firsthand that even the most strategically planned ops could go sideways. His face was testimony to that. Which meant he needed to be smart.

He paused at the corner—the same one where he'd crashed into *her*. Where a piece of the old Kent had been resurrected—and stopped. Were those mumbled voices? He pressed his back against the wall then peeked around the corner. Two figures stood next to the door, dressed in black. The glow from the interior of the building gave a muted outline of their silhouettes. Black masks, ear protection, and goggles covered their heads. The raised panels on their torsos hinted at body armor, and there was no missing their weapons—AK47s held shoulder high, an extra pistol on their thighs. And Rigs knew they'd have more magazines stashed in pockets.

A faint hiss of static, then one of them was talking and nodding, too far away to hear the words.

They had a comm system? Shit. And no one came that heavily armed without intending on using deadly force. They were obviously waiting for some kind of signal, coordinating their entrance through multiple points. Take the guards by surprise.

Rigs scanned back up to their heads. Ear protection most likely meant some kind of concussive grenade. And the goggles—they didn't look like high end night vision goggles—NVGs—but he couldn't tell for sure. They were either planning on killing the lights or including a blinding flash as part of the distraction.

Fuckers probably had flashbangs. Disrupt everyone's vision and hearing long enough to seize control. They could easily take out the guards before anyone could recover. Which meant it was likely they would target the entrance and the auction room at the same time.

Rigs weighed his options. He could shoot them. Head shot from this distance was a snap. But he didn't have a suppressor. Without knowing numbers and locations, announcing his presence could get innocent people killed. Or dramatically change the nature of their infiltration—and not for the better.

He reached behind him, retrieving his Ka-bar from the scabbard between his shoulder blades. He only had the one knife—damn oversight he wouldn't make, again. He'd need to take out one and reach the other before the guy could shoot.

Or, he waited for this signal, downed the guy who went in second then caught up to the first before he got more than twenty feet inside. Unlikely the bastard would suspect anyone coming at him from behind.

Rigs readied the knife, still vigilant for other movement or noises around him, as he stood there, waiting. The men exchanged a few words, nodding at each other before the guy who'd been talking held up his hand, showing five fingers.

Rigs grinned when he went to four. How fucking nice of the asshole to count it down for him. Rigs eased out, staying low and in the shadows, constantly judging the right trajectory, when the lights winked out behind the door and explosions shook the ground.

Damn, he hated being right.

The men held steady until the emergency lights blinked on then headed inside. Rigs flicked his wrist. A glint of silver and the rear man dropped. The guy's partner must have heard him fall because he popped back out, muzzle sweeping the pathway. Rigs dove to the side, rolling across the stone walkway as bullets pelted the surface, chipping off bits of rock. He came up within arm's reach, blocking the man's hand as the guy tried to swing the gun toward him.

A quick jab to the elbow and the AK clattered to the ground. The creep pivoted, deflecting Rigs' next punch and throwing one at his head. Rigs used his palm to knock it just shy of hitting his jaw as he stepped into the attack. It only took a wrist grab and shoulder lock to have the bastard tilted forward and down, completely immobilized. Another step and a twist, and he'd slammed the jerk's head into the wall. It cracked hard, leaving behind a bloody mark on the stone before the guy collapsed on the ground.

Rigs took a moment to remove the guy's belt and bind his hands and legs. He considered simply capping the bastard, but the police would want answers, and dead men were a lot harder to get information from.

The man's earpiece buzzed. Rigs bent over him, slipping it out then holding it up to his ear.

"Alpha three."

Damn. Whether it was the bastard unconscious at his feet or the one with the knife in his throat, Rigs didn't know. But he knew what happened when the guy in question didn't answer, and none of it was good.

He grabbed their weapons, slinging the AKs over his shoulder then shoving their pistols in the back of his pants. He preferred his own weapons, but leaving the others around for someone else to pick up wasn't a good idea. Not to mention that getting shot with weapons he'd abandoned would be a stupid way to die.

The door opened silently, and he darted inside, stopping at the first wall. Smoke still curled through the dimly lit area, snaking along the floor toward the corner of the room. He scanned right then headed for the large statue obscuring his view to the left. He assumed they'd have their forces concentrated on the auction site, with a few outliers manning the exits. But he'd have a better idea once he'd reached the next corner.

He moved in behind the statue, when three shots rose above other shouts and cries. Loud. Close. These shots were different. They weren't the close pop of an AK. These were single rounds taken from a pistol—just like the ones he'd confiscated. He slipped out then froze. Actually, fucking froze. She was crouched beside her dog, one operative off to the left. Still. Maybe dead but definitely unconscious. Another was sprawled on the floor fifty feet away, feet twitching. The pistol looked oddly comfortable in her hands as she cocked her head to either side, trying to home in on the downed man.

The guy coughed, then slid his palm along the floor, pushing himself upright. He rubbed his chest, glaring at the woman. Like the others, he had on body armor. Shots to the torso wouldn't kill him—only piss him off. The bastard was going to fire, and unless he made a noise...

Rigs took off. Fuck not making a sound. Alerting them. Fuck everything but getting to her. Stopping that asshole from killing her before Rigs had even learned her name. Christ, had she walked into the middle of it? Had Blade bolted at the sound of the explosions? She'd mentioned he'd served in Afghanistan. That he had issues. Just thinking she'd had to deal with any of this alone...

But she was in Rigs' sight line. He couldn't take a shot with her so close to the crosshairs. Not until he knew she wouldn't suddenly move on him.

Two seconds, and he'd cut the distance in half. Two seconds, and the guy she'd downed had his senses back and was lifting his arm. Readying his damn AK.

"Get down."

She reacted immediately, going to her stomach as Rigs aimed, still running. He didn't need to stand still to make the shot. He'd spent years practicing real world shooting. Running. Rolling. In vehicles, popping up out of the water. Every way imaginable. Under any circumstances.

The bastard never had a chance. Hit him square between the eyes, spraying a red mist out across the floor as he fell back. His head hit hard, the sound dull. Hollow. The woman gasped then twisted, holding the gun out toward him.

Rigs stopped, taking a quick scan of the area before lowering his voice. "Easy, sweetheart. I'm one of the good guys."

Her eyes rounded, then she lowered the weapon. "The man Blade knocked over, right?"

"That's right." He closed the last of the distance, kneeling beside her. "You hurt?"

She shook her head, her pretty blonde hair swishing over her shoulders. It had pulled out of the clip, the long strands hanging in soft waves around her face. "Blade…"

He'd already noticed the patch of blood on the dog's shoulder. The smear of it across the floor. There was more on his snout, though Rigs suspected it wasn't Blade's. "Let's get you both somewhere safer. Before more of them come looking."

Out of habit, he offered her his hand then silently cursed himself. But if she'd heard him or somehow sensed what he'd done, she didn't let on, rising swiftly before turning toward him. He crouched next to the dog. The canine thumped its tail once, licking his wrist as he let the animal sniff his hand.

"Easy, Blade. I'm just gonna carry you, okay?"

"He won't bite you. He's not like that."

"You might want to tell that to the other guy. Looks like he tore the guy's arm pretty badly."

"He was going to hurt me. Blade knew that."

"Not complaining. In fact, Blade's at the top of my list of favorite dogs."

The animal whimpered as Rigs rolled him against his chest.

"I know, buddy. Hang in there. Bullet wounds are a bitch." He kept his voice low—just enough to comfort the dog—keep him from lashing out from the pain. "We'll head back to one of the alcoves. It's ninety degrees to your right. Straight forward for about forty feet."

She nodded then followed him, cane barely skimming the floor. She didn't shuffle the way he'd thought she might—the way he'd probably walk if he lost his sight—only stopping when she got to the edge of the alcove. "How much farther?"

Rigs stepped in beside her. "Take my arm. I'll guide you around the planters."

Her hand settled on his forearm, her fingers firmly gripping his arm. She didn't talk, moving quietly with him around the left side of the planters to the back. He placed Blade gently on the floor then repositioned the plants so they were closer to the entrance—provided a bit more protection.

The woman was kneeling beside the dog when he turned, running her fingers along the canine's neck. She raised her face to Rigs'. "They set off a couple of flash-bangs. One toward the main entrance. The other farther down. The auction room, I imagine. They have body armor, AK47s and pistols. Sigs, I think."

He smiled. Fuck. Who was she? "Correct on all accounts. And they're jamming cell signals. I took two down outside. Plus, the two you dealt with in here makes four. I'm guessing maybe four more in the auction room with others manning the entrance or scouting the perimeter. Could be ten, total."

She held out her hand. "They have coms. I grabbed one of their radios."

Rigs took it, turning it over in his hands. "The two outside had ear pieces. Definitely organized. I'll assume the guards are either dead or subdued. That leaves my partners in the auction room."

Her sightless gaze settled on him, and his damn heart gave a hard thud. Beautiful blue eyes gleamed in the low light. "You guys cops?"

"Ex-military."

"Encouraging. Which branch?"

"MARSOC. I've got an Army Ranger and a PJ with me."

"Special Forces? Damn." She nodded at the com. "I don't know what kind of radio that is, but if they're smart enough to block cell coverage, maybe they have police channels on there. You'll want channel nine."

Rigs focused on the unit, punching in the channel she'd asked for. "Got it, if it works."

"May I?"

He gave her back the unit, listening as she called out, keeping her voice hushed. Someone replied, asking for verification. She rattled off a badge number and a code, then outlined what she knew before handing it over to him.

Rigs took it, filling in any remaining info before placing it on the floor beside her. "Looks like SWAT's about ten minutes out."

"Shit. A lot can happen in ten minutes."

The dog whimpered, and her chin quivered.

Rigs removed his vest then folded it up and handed it to her. "Here. We can try and slow the bleeding. My buddy, Ice, always carries a medic kit. He can help once we take care of these men."

"Thanks." She pressed down after he'd placed her hand over the wound. "I'd be dead if he hadn't…"

"You said Blade's an ex-soldier. He's tough. It'll be okay. But I want you to stay here. I'll come back when it's safe. I'll call out. If you hear anyone else come this way…"

"I shoot first, worry about who I killed later. Though, with their armor, I'm lucky if I can knock them down. I can only really aim at where I hear them, and it's too risky to go for anything other than a torso shot."

"Hopefully, you won't have to shoot anyone else. Just, stay down and quiet."

Her lips quirked. "I really hate this."

"Me, too."

He didn't tell her that the part he hated was leaving her there. Alone. Vulnerable. Though, she obviously had some serious training—he'd bet his ass she'd been a detective of some sort—there was no denying she was at a substantial disadvantage. These men meant business. Not being able to fire off an effective shot—one that would keep the bastards down for good—put her at a huge risk. One that ate at Rigs' gut.

Just by looking at her, he knew she wouldn't back down. That if she thought, for even a moment, that she was all that stood between life or death for the people at the auction, she'd walk straight down the damn hallway, hoping to hit anything that made a noise.

He couldn't imagine how she felt. How he'd feel if he had to stay behind—let others deal with a threat he'd spent years training for. He only hoped she trusted him enough to follow his directions.

"All right. Hold tight." He scooted forward, glancing back at her. "About what I said before…"

She snorted. "You take care of this, and you'll be forgiven."

"Deal. By the way. The name's Kent. Kent Walker, though everyone calls me Rigs."

She wet her lips, swallowing hard. "Addison. And I'll share my last name when you come back—alive."

CHAPTER 4

"THEN, I'll definitely be coming back." The guy's voice whispered across the space, then he was gone. Just gone. Not a sound. Not a footstep. Not so much as a scuff or a breath. Nothing. As if he'd vanished.

Addison forced herself to breathe. To keep pressure on Blade's shoulder as she strained to hear something from beyond the small alcove. The one she was hiding in because she was a liability.

He hadn't phrased it that way. Kent. His name was Kent. And he'd actually been extremely diplomatic. Hadn't scolded her for firing literally blind at what she'd perceived as a threat. Despite her momentary glimpse, she knew it had been risky. But Kent had treated her— like a person. Not the way most people saw her.

He obviously hadn't realized she was blind until she'd put on Blade's harness and walked away. Which explained his slip-up. Not that it mattered when faced with the real possibility that none of them might make it out of the damn auction alive.

MARSOC. Kent was an ex-Special Ops Marine. And he had two other veterans with him. Men trained to kill. To survive. And one was a medic. Bet the bastards heading this scam hadn't counted on that. She hadn't.

Or maybe it was just Kent she hadn't counted on. Someone who looked beyond her obvious disability to the woman beneath. The cop beneath. Because, damn it, she was still a detective at heart. Still the same person who'd taken an oath to serve and protect. Who'd lived for the thrill of putting creeps like the men threatening this establishment behind bars. Losing her sight—even if it was all in her head, somehow—hadn't changed that part of her. Hadn't banished it to the darkness like everything else.

Plus, the two you dealt with in here...

That's how he'd phrased it. Even if he'd finished the last guy off. He'd accepted that she wasn't powerless.

Until, now. Though it was insane, a part of her had hoped he'd want her help. That he'd tell her to follow along behind him. Which she knew was impossible. The cold hard reality was that she wasn't a cop. Wasn't capable of covering his back. She'd gotten lucky, and she needed to remember that. Sure, having a couple of moments of sight was encouraging. Hell, it was miraculous considering she hadn't experienced so much as a flash of light since that night. But it didn't change anything. Not until she'd figured out how to make the transition permanent. Make her vision stick. Until then, she was stuck on the sidelines. This wasn't the beginning of her resurrecting her old life. And if Kent wasn't as good as she prayed he was, it might not be the beginning of anything other than a quick death.

Addy focused on what she had control over. Pressing on Blade's wound, murmuring reassuringly to him. Listening for any sound that meant trouble was coming her way. Blade had taken a bullet for her. The least she could do was protect him with the same unyielding determination.

Minutes ticked by, nothing but the same voices yelling from within the auction. The same threats mixed in with the occasional dull pop of one of their guns. God, were they killing people with every pull of the trigger? Was she sitting there, out of the line of fire, the Sig heavy and cold in her hand, while civilians died in her place?

Except that she was a civilian, now, too.

Tears pooled behind her eyes. Hot, angry tears that burned all the way down to her soul. She closed her eyes, trying to muscle back some form of composure. Was this what the rest of her life would be like? Waiting for someone else to take action? Forever hiding in the shadows because she couldn't live in the light? How was she supposed to move on, find a way to feel worthy, when she'd lost the part of her that had made her Addison Bailey? Being a cop hadn't been her career—it had been an extension of her soul. A calling she'd worked hard to make a reality. And, now?

Now, she was reduced to a fraction of the person she'd been. Someone living in the dark, fighting imaginary demons that never truly went away. How could they? The one defense against them had been taken. A reality that slammed into her with unforgiving clarity.

She was *blind*. It didn't matter if it was psychological. If technically, her eyes were fine. The reality was that, at that moment, she couldn't see. Had no way of knowing if she'd ever regain her sight. Reclaim her past. Had nothing but an endless future of darkness ahead of her.

Addy opened her eyes. Not that it helped. It didn't change *anything*. Didn't stop the images inside her head from playing out amidst the darkness. The flashback from taking hold as memories flicked across her mind in the only form of vision that worked.

Voices sounded around her. Ones she knew. Blood soaked through her shirt, pain bright and piercing through her shoulder and chest. She blinked, and Will was there—just like he had been every day for the past four years, since she'd become a detective—above her, hands pressing down.

"Damn it, Addy, stay with me. Don't you dare fucking die on me."

Her mouth opened and closed, muted groans the only sound making it past her clenched jaw. He was bleeding, too. A line across his forehead. The drops falling onto her chest—mixing with hers. Then, he arched back, a red spot blossoming between his eyes. He crumbled forward, covering her, crushing her into the floor.

"Kill her, too."

That voice, again. Deep. Dark. One she'd heard before.

"The whole place is gonna blow. We're out of time. Leave her. She won't survive."

His partner. She knew that much. They worked together. A hooded face wavered into view followed by the barrel of a gun. Something sweet wafted around her. Floral. Out of place. Then, the world exploded into a bright light. Into dust and debris and finally…nothing.

"Addison."

She raised the gun, held it firmly in her left hand. Her right wouldn't move. Wouldn't lift from the bunched material beneath her palm. But it didn't matter. She wouldn't miss.

"Addison. It's Kent."

They were out there. Waiting—waiting for her to die. To have her body carried out in a black bag, just like Will's.

"Easy, sweetheart. Give me the gun."

Why would she do that? When it was all that stood between her and death? But…there was something in his voice. It wasn't like the others. It didn't make her stomach heave or feel like ice in her veins. *His* voice was comforting. Warm, gravelly tones that soothed the pain inside her head. The one that smothered her whenever she tried to remember. Make sense of the visions that danced in the darkness.

"Addison."

She swallowed, tilting her head to the side. A whimper sounded beside her, a familiar thump jolting her back. Fingers closed around her hand. Firm. Calloused. The same ones that had held her earlier.

She tried to zero in on his breath. The heat from his body. "Kent?"

"Right here, sweetheart. You can let go of the gun, now, okay? It's over."

Gun? Over?

He pried the Sig from her hand, moving closer until his body skimmed hers. "It's going to be okay. Ice—Russel just went to get his kit. He'll be back in a few minutes. There're paramedics treating anyone who got injured. Russel said he'd get some supplies so he can help Blade until the vet gets here. He's on his way. About ten minutes out."

"Blade. Shit... What happened? The men?"

"Taken care of. There were only three in the auction room. Once I made a move, Sam and Russel had my back. It was over in seconds. The tangos never stood a chance. Then SWAT showed up before the men outside could clear off."

"Is everyone okay?"

"The guards didn't make it. But most of the people from the auction escaped with nothing more than some bad memories. A few were injured. One dead. But considering the alternatives..."

She nodded, still forcing the lingering memories aside. It was hard to distinguish between them. To sort out the present from the past when she couldn't ground herself. Couldn't open her eyes and *see* what was right in front of her. Instead, she reached for Kent. Wrapped her fingers around his arm. He was strong. A tangible link to this moment. To the chaos still unfolding around her.

She heard it, now. High-pitched chatter from people on the brink of hysteria. Groans from those who were injured. Calm, detached murmurs from the paramedics and SWAT members fanning out around her. Footsteps sounded in every direction, the hard click of boots unmistakable. It was protocol. The members would scour every inch of the estate, inside and out, before they'd start allowing people to leave—ensure none of the infiltration team were still hiding or trying to masquerade as one of the crowd. Probably have the bomb dogs brought back in, just to be thorough.

Blade could have helped if he hadn't come to her aid —wasn't bleeding out beside her while she sat there, fading in and out of memories.

Kent's hand covered hers. God, it felt good. The weight. The gentle, but firm, curl of his fingers over hers. He didn't talk. Didn't make her feel weak for wanting the reassurance. In fact, she could have sworn his hand had been shaking, too, when he'd touched her. Which was stupid. The guy was MARSOC. Marine Spec Ops soldiers didn't shake. Ever. Not in the midst of a gunfight or while sighting an enemy a thousand yards off. And certainly not when holding a woman's hand. They were all about steel determination and laser focus.

But imagining he *might* have been shaking made her less self-conscious of her own reactions. The way her hand trembled while maintaining pressure on Blade's side. How her breathing had quickened, roughened, or that her heart rate had kicked up. She kept herself fit. Always had. Even after the incident, she'd worked hard to regain balance and stamina—to remake herself as tough, if not tougher, than before. So, knowing her pulse was pushing triple figures unnerved her. Especially, when a remote part of her brain was convinced it was the man holding her hand that was the cause, not the near fatal encounter with armed men.

Which was ridiculous. He was ex-military. A warrior, and he'd acted like one. Riding in. Saving the day. Him and his partners—nothing they'd done was remotely out of character or suggestive that he felt anything other than common concern for her. Like he did for everyone else in the building. And with her being blind, it seemed natural that he might think she needed a higher level of protection.

Except, he hadn't *treated* her as if she needed more protection. Had sounded confident that she could defend herself, if needed, when he'd left. Even now, he was holding her hand, but it didn't *feel* like the action of a man whose only motivation was to calm a woman he saw as being vulnerable. It felt…comforting. More like a boyfriend holding his girlfriend's hand because he wanted to be there for her. Wanted to help shoulder some of the stress.

She groaned inwardly. She'd definitely lost it. Slid into some alternate reality where her brain turned to mush, and her hormones controlled her thoughts. That was the only explanation. She'd spent the past eighteen months alone. Barely talking to people. Fighting to get through each grueling day. She'd rarely connected with friends—hadn't been able to stand their pity. The hushed sighs they thought she couldn't hear. The tones in their voices that told her they were uncomfortable being around her. That they didn't know how to act, anymore. That their friendship had suffered irreversible damage, much like she feared her brain had.

So, sitting there, thinking of Kent in any context other than as a concerned soldier doing his job was unrealistic. Wasn't it?

Footsteps racing toward them. The rush of air as someone settled down close to her. She twisted toward the newcomer, trying to get a sense of where the person's face would be, when Kent gave her hand a squeeze.

"Addison, my buddy Ice—Russel is here."

She shifted her focus from Kent's voice back to where she *felt* the other guy. "You're the PJ, right? The pararescue tech."

"That's right." His hand covered hers—right over Kent's. "Rigs told me we had a soldier down. Can't let that go without doing all I can."

He released her hand, followed by the zip of a bag. The clatter of instruments being laid out. He lifted her hand from Blade's shoulder, gently placing it beside her other hand on Kent's arm. "Looks like a couple of gunshot wounds. I'm not an expert in dog anatomy, but I'd say they both hit high. Missed his vital organs."

Blade thumbed his tail.

Russel laughed. "Don't worry, big guy. We're gonna fix you up. Not losing a soldier on my watch."

It was hard to follow what Russel was doing. There were too many other sounds all mixing together. But she did her best to focus. To narrow her senses to the area directly in front of her, all the while willing her brain to give her another snapshot. Anything to reassure her that she wasn't on the verge of losing the only good thing to happen to her since her injury.

Kent must had realized what she was trying to do because he gently cupped her waist and twisted her slightly. "Russel's just cleaning the wounds before he puts some coagulating powder over them. He's also got a bag of saline from the paramedics. He'll hook up the IV once he has the bleeding under control."

She turned toward his voice, brushing his nose with hers. God, he was so close. Right there, his mouth an inch from hers. All she had to do was purse her lips and she'd be kissing him. "Thanks."

"No problem. I'd want to know what was happening if it was my partner."

Russel chuckled. "That, and Rigs needs an excuse to get closer to you. He has a thing for pretty ladies that can kick a bad guy's ass."

She smiled. She knew what Russel was doing. He was trying to lighten the mood. Ease her stress, because joking meant things were going to be okay. That he wasn't that concerned with Blade's injury and had time to make her feel better.

"I got lucky." She motioned to Kent with her head. "And he finished off the last guy. All I did was knock him down."

Kent scoffed. "You hit the guy square in the chest three times from nothing more than the sound he made. That's MARSOC quality shooting, right there. Not to mention knocking another unconscious. I saw the bastard's body. Did you whip him with your cane?"

"He shot my best friend. So, yeah. I took a chance that he hadn't moved and swung. Got lucky and connected. After that... It wasn't too hard to subdue him. Done it a thousand times before. Even blind, I can handcuff a guy without thinking about it." She snorted. "Or in this case, pistol whip one."

Russel whistled. "That's impressive. Which brings me to my next question. Rigs and I have a bit of a wager going. We figure with your moves, the way you were able to call in the cavalry, you're probably a detective. Mr. Explosives over there insists you're narcotics. But I say homicide. Now, you should know, there's a case of fine Irish whiskey on the line, here."

"Mr. Explosives? Is that why they call you Rigs? Because you rig shit to blow up?"

Russel laughed. "Beautiful and smart." Something clattered on the floor, and Russel grunted. "Rigs—Kent was one of the best explosives ordinance soldiers I ever worked with. He could wire your damn soap to explode if he wanted. He also took a few bullets for my wife when she was in danger, so... I owe him."

"Fuck—I mean bugger off. I'd do that for strangers. You know Red's family."

Russel chuckled. "You know Harlequin hates it when you call her that."

"Yup. Now, Addison, who's buying that case of whiskey?"

She let a smile take shape. Lift the corners of her eyes. "That would be Russel. Sorry. Kent's right. I was narcotics."

She heard Kent mutter a hushed, "Hell yeah".

Russel huffed. "Great. That's gonna go straight to his damn head. How long were you on the force?"

"Twelve years. I graduated high school early, fit a three-year-degree into two, and joined when I was nineteen. Spent eight years walking a beat then made detective. Another four in narcotics before..." She cleared her throat. "That was eighteen months, ago. I've been...adjusting since then."

Kent's fingers squeezed her leg. "It's obvious you haven't lost your edge."

She shrugged. What was she supposed to say? Sure, if someone made enough noise, or touched her, she could react accordingly. But that was about it. "Nope. Just my sight, which kind of puts a whole damper on the 'being a cop' thing."

Silence. At least, from them. Around her, noises still beat at her like a drum. Constant input she wished would stop. It was one of the reasons she avoided crowds. It made it hard to stay focused. To navigate her surroundings with all the auditory overload.

Another clatter of instruments. "Okay, Blade, I've got you ready for transport. I've stopped the bleeding, have an IV up and running and bandaged your shoulder. The vet should be here any minute. He'll have some meds to ease the pain and will undoubtedly criticize my technique."

Addy reached out one hand, smiling when Russel clasped it. She knew it was him. His hand felt different. Larger. Not quite as calloused. And his touch was more clinical than the one still holding her left. "I don't know how to thank you—"

"You took two of those assholes down by yourself. That's thanks, enough. Made it easy for us to finish the job. Besides, Blade's a veteran. And you're a cop. We take care of our own."

"Still. Thank you."

"Glad I could help. Vet's here. And the SWAT guys want to go over everything. Get statements."

Kent moved his hand off her thigh and over to her waist. "We'll both be there once the vet's done."

"I'll let them know. We'll chat later, Addison."

She nodded then twisted toward Kent. "Both?"

"Two of those men are your handiwork, sweetheart. SWAT will want to know what happened."

"I didn't really do that much—"

He silenced her with a finger over her lips. God, it was so warm. "You were incredible. But for now, let's focus on Blade. The officers can wait."

She shuffled a bit closer when he drew her against his side, telling herself it was only to orient herself. "Thank you."

"You're welcome. But you still owe me something."

She frowned. She *owed* him something? "What's that?"

"You promised you'd tell me your last name if I came back, alive, and I kept my end of the bargain."

"So you did. It's Bailey. Addison Bailey."

CHAPTER 5

ADDISON BAILEY WAS GOING to be the death of Rigs. No question. Because in less than an hour, she'd somehow wormed her way into the heart he'd left behind in the rubble—the one that was scarred and broken like the rest of him—and shoved the damn thing back into his chest. Guaranteed that she'd be the one to rip it out the next time with her small, incredibly capable fingers.

Rigs didn't like the idea. Not at all. When he'd finally gotten a look at what hid beneath the bandages the doctors had covered him in for weeks, he'd decided right then and there he'd spend the rest of his life alone. Maybe the odd hook-up. One-night stands when he got tired of his own fist. But anything more...

And he'd done his best to make peace with it. He wasn't thrilled. Seeing his buddies settle down—find partners that made them better men. Better warriors— wasn't easy to swallow. He was happy for Ice and Midnight. Adored the women they'd fallen in love with.

But it was hard watching them, knowing he'd never have anything close.

And yet, here he was, sitting with his arm around Addison's waist, her hand beneath his, and all he could do was will time to slow down. Give him another few seconds with her snuggled against him. Her soft curves hugging his side. It didn't make any sense. He didn't have any romantic notions that this was the start of something magical. Magic didn't exist, at least, not from his experiences. And definitely not directed at him. He'd only just met her, and under extremely volatile circumstances. Anything either of them felt was likely a byproduct of the adrenaline. No different than after all his missions overseas. The ones where he'd been able to fuck away the stress, either with his hand or a willing woman if one was handy.

But this felt different. He didn't want any available woman who would overlook the scars. He wanted to stay there with Addison. Just like this—holding her hand, giving her a shoulder to lean on when her world was so uncertain. She'd been every ounce the warrior he and his buddies had been. More so, because she'd done it all by sheer instinct. Sheer power of will. She'd risked her life with the odds so stacked against her, it had been a virtual wall in front of her.

Kent swallowed against the tight feeling in his chest, cursing when he felt a tremor move through him. It was the second time he'd trembled since returning to her side. The first had been when he'd arrived. A part of him had braced for the worst—her body splayed out beside her dog's, a hole between her eyes, her blood a sticky pool beneath her. Seeing her sitting there had been like a punch to his gut.

Then, she'd aimed the Sig at him. But it wasn't *him* she'd really been aiming at. He wasn't a medic like Ice. Didn't have degrees in psychology. But he knew a damn flashback when he saw it. Had suffered through too many, himself, not to recognize the symptoms—shallow, choppy breathing. Pale clammy skin. Vacant stare that had nothing not do with the fact she was blind. She'd been caught in some kind of waking nightmare, and it had taken a few minutes of talking to her in order to snap her back.

He'd reached for her, and damn if his hand hadn't been shaking. That same hand he'd used to set countless explosives. That had remained steady through years of missions. But the thought of her dead...

It had rocked him to his core. As he'd sat there— watching Russel work to save Blade—doing his best to keep the worry out of his voice as he'd relayed what was happening—Kent had realized he had two choices. Either he walked away, now, before there was even a chance of something happening. Or...

He embraced the suck. The suck being the inevitable ending—the one where *she* walked away, that heart she'd shoved back in his chest clenched between her fingers. Because her being blind didn't change the fact he was scarred. Given time, she'd feel them. Discover they weren't just on the outside, that they ran all the way to his soul. And that's when she'd realize she had far better options out there than a used-up soldier who didn't know how to fit in.

Her hand trembled in his then steadied as she drew a deep breath, leaning just a bit more against him.

Embrace the suck, it was.

Even if it only lasted tonight. If all he got was a chance to hold her hand, maybe drive her home. Oh yeah, he'd see she got home, all right. Try to weasel a cup of coffee out of her tomorrow. He'd even brave a café. Brave the gasps and stares because it meant more time with *her*. Addison Bailey. The woman who would be his undoing.

The vet finally looked up—managed to hide all but a small flinch as he met Rigs' gaze before staring over at Addison. The man reached out and lightly touched her arm. "It looks like Blade's stable enough for transport. I've given him some medication. It'll make him sleepy. Help with the pain. We're lucky there was someone trained on hand. Probably saved his life. He'll need surgery, and it'll be a while before he can come home, but I'm optimistic he'll make a full recovery."

Tears glistened in her eyes, a few slipping over her lashes before she steeled herself—buried her emotions just like Rigs had done a thousand times since the IED. "Thank you. Whatever it takes. Whatever the cost."

"I promise I'll do everything I can. Do you have a number I can call you at?"

"I just got a new one…" She paused, a frown marring her pretty face, and Rigs made a mental note to ask her why, later. "And I haven't memorized it, yet, but it's in…" Her brow furrowed as her lips pressed into a line. "I forgot. I left it in my purse with Carl… Oh my god. I don't even know if he's okay. If he was hurt. I've been so preoccupied. I..."

Rigs gave her another squeeze, nodding at the vet. "You can call me. I'll make sure Addison gets the message."

He rattled off his cell, helping Addy stand in order to give the vet room to move—position Blade on the small cart he'd brought in with him.

The man straightened. "I should have some news in a few hours."

"Doesn't matter what time it is. I'll be awake."

"Very well."

Addison bit at her bottom lip as the cart rolled away, the clatter from the wheels blanching some of the color from her face.

Rigs cupped her jaw as he thumbed her chin. "He's going to be fine. You heard the doc. A bit of R&R, and he'll be good as new. Chewing your favorite pair of shoes."

She gave a watery laugh. "He seems to prefer boots. Already lost my best pair of hikers."

"Then, you might want to hide the ones you have on. If they taste half as good as they look, he'll go after them, next."

She smiled, and damn, his stupid scarred heart gave a hard beat. One that left an ache in his chest, again. Bruised his ribs.

"Thank you. Do you think we can check up on my friend? I should have asked straight off, but..."

But she'd been worried about her partner. Her best friend, as she'd put it.

"Sure. What's his name?" Was that jealousy burning just beneath his skin?

"Carl Jones."

"All right. You stay here while I go and check. Then, we'll head on over and have a chat with the SWAT leader. Okay?"

She nodded, that beautiful blonde hair bouncing around her shoulders. Rigs took a moment to tuck some of it behind her ear. Get just a feel of how soft it was because it looked like silk. Endless strands of spun gold that gleamed, even in the muted light.

The locks spilled across his hand. Christ, it was even softer than he'd imagined. The mass brushing over his knuckles, giving his skin a pale golden hue. He stood for a moment then forced his hand back to his side. It wasn't easy. He'd once spent two hours disarming a trip mine a fellow soldier had stepped on. Had tried a dozen different techniques before finally being able to find a way to bypass it. And it hadn't been easy to bypass, either. Had taken all his training, and a healthy dose of luck, but he'd found a way to reroute the damn switch.

Pulling his hand back, turning and actually walking away to get intel on this Carl guy—the one she'd mentioned a couple of times, and who'd quickly taken first spot on Rigs' shit list on the chance he was more than just a friend—felt twice as hard. Twice as taxing. But Rigs managed it—barely.

Took him five minutes to track down the guy, have a quick conversation—confirm that he was strictly a friend, no fringe benefits—then start back, doing his best to rush without *looking* as if he was rushing. He reached the corner then tripped a step when he spotted four men caging Addy in. They had their backs to the room, their hands fisted at their sides. A flush colored their cheeks, and a light sweat beaded their foreheads.

Rigs cursed. They were either anxious or angry, neither of which sat well with him where Addison was concerned. He glanced at her. Her lips were pursed, her eyes narrowed. She had her arms crossed over her chest, her back stiff. A similar flush sat high in her cheekbones, fading down her neck and across her upper chest.

The sight flipped a switch inside his head. Had him quickening his pace. The men jumped when he appeared beside them—whether from his face or how he'd simply materialized next to them because he'd made damn sure they hadn't seen or heard him coming, he wasn't sure—all of them taking a few steps back and allowing Rigs to shift in beside her. Stare them down. He didn't try to hide the scars. Not when it was obvious the marks made the other men shift restlessly on their feet. Good. Rigs would stand there all night just to get them to back off.

Addison inhaled, her hand immediately finding his arm. "Well?"

He smiled to himself that she'd recognized him without asking. That either his scent or his energy registered on a level she identified with. He kept his gaze fixed on the newcomers. "Your friend's fine. He cut his arm when he slipped and landed on some glass. He's out in one of the ambulances getting stitched. He looked pretty wiped. I told him I'd see you home. That you'd call him tomorrow—let him know how Blade was doing." He handed her a small clutch bag. "I got your purse."

She took it. "It seems all I do is say thank you."

"My pleasure." He kept staring at the men, vowing they'd be the first to look away.

Addison sighed. No way she hadn't picked up on his tension. On the firm strain of his muscles beneath her fingers. "Kent, I'd like you to meet Detective's Paul Johnson and Trent Seymour. They're from my old unit. The other two men are Agents David Colby and Shawn Townsend. They're DEA. My old precinct runs a lot of joint ventures with the agency."

Rigs extended his hand, shaking each man's hand stiffly. "I hadn't realized narcotics had been called in. Do you think this robbery was drug motivated?"

The dark-haired one—Johnson—snorted. "No. We were in the area, coming back from a stakeout that didn't pan out, when the call went out. When we heard Addy had radioed it in, well… We couldn't just sit there and not try to help. But it looks like you and your friends took care of the problem. It's Walker, right? Kent Walker. That's what SWAT said. You're an ex-Marine. And your buddies are ex-Special Forces, too." He grinned, but it looked more like a snarl. "Pretty damn lucky for everyone that you three were here, or the night might have ended differently."

Kent smiled at Addison. "We had some help."

"Right." Johnson glanced at his partner then back to Rigs. "Anyway, it seems Addy's just fine. We…worry about her, now."

Addison huffed. "You realize that implies you didn't worry about me, before. When I was busting drug dealers and facing down meth heads."

The blonde standing next to Johnson—Seymour, she'd called him—stepped forward. "You know that's not what Paul meant. It's just, things are different, now. *You're* different. You're… vulnerable."

"Vulnerable? Just because I haven't fully recovered, yet, doesn't mean I'm helpless."

Johnson sighed. "Must you always make it sound as if we think less of you?"

"Maybe because you do. You treat me like I'll break if you breathe on me the wrong way."

"That's not true."

"Isn't it? You just spent the past couple of minutes yelling at me because I took a stand."

"You fired a gun in the middle of a fucking building! With absolutely no idea who you might hit. Do you know how insane that is? How lucky you got?"

"I knew exactly where I was aiming. *Who* I was aiming at. I heard the click of the magazine. His breath wheeze out of his lungs. His boots scuff the floor. It wasn't random. And I chose not to fire, again, when I couldn't pinpoint him after he'd been knocked down. So, don't lecture me on morality. I would have let that asshole shoot me before popping off rounds just in the hopes of saving myself."

"God, do you even hear yourself? No wonder you haven't regained your sight. You're still as delusional as you were eighteen months ago."

Rigs shifted forward, cutting Addison off before she

could reply. "I don't care who you are, you're crossing a line."

The guy laughed, and Rigs clenched his fist to keep from knocking the bastard on his ass. "I'm not saying anything that she doesn't already know. I assume she hasn't told you. That this blind act she has going on is all in her head. There's nothing wrong with her eyes. That's why they call it *hysterical* blindness."

Addison set her jaw. "It's called conversion disorder, you prick."

Johnson shrugged. "I don't care what it's called. The end result's the same. Unless this is your way of telling us you've got your sight back?" He held up one hand. "How many fingers."

Rigs grabbed the guy's hand and shoved it out of Addison's face. "This isn't a joke, and you're not funny."

"What's not funny is having a *blind* woman fire a bloody gun."

"I'm a trained cop. It's different." Addison's chin quivered as she pushed back her shoulders, doing her best to own her space. "And I've been having...flashes, okay?"

"Flashes?" Johnson arched a brow. "What kind of flashes?"

"Snapshots of the room. It's not much, but it's enough to orient myself. And what I saw in that split second assured me I wouldn't hit anyone else."

"A split second? That doesn't sound like your vision returning. More like a flashback. Probably from the raid that night. I'm sure it seemed real—"

"I know the difference between reality and a flashback, Paul. And this was real."

"There never was any reasoning with you. Looks like nothing's changed. But the reality, as you put it, is that until you get better, permanently, you'd best remember that you *are* blind and start acting that way." Johnson frowned as he nudged his partner. "I'm just glad it worked out in your favor, this time." He nodded at Rigs. "Mr. Walker."

Rigs moved in front of the men when they tried to walk past him, using his death stare to back them up a step. "I don't know that much about conversion disorder. An oversight I intend to correct. But I do know that Addison is part of the reason tonight didn't end with a hundred bodies littering the floor. If she hadn't taken those two men out... The odds would have been much graver. So, instead of talking out of your asses because you weren't here and couldn't possibly know what the situation was or what the risks were, you could try thanking her for putting her life on the line to stop what most certainly would have become a blood bath."

Seymour scowled. "Like my partner said. We're glad things didn't turn out worse. But you should think twice before encouraging her. If she'd missed on just one of those shots—"

"But she didn't. Honestly, I haven't seen shooting that accurate outside the Teams."

"If you think what she did was heroic, then, you're just as delusional as she is. We'll see you 'round, Addy."

Addison tightened her grip on her cane, tapping it

on the floor until the men's footsteps faded. "You didn't have to do that."

Rigs turned, admiring the simple beauty of her. The way her hair hung just below her shoulders. The adorable furrow in her brow as she stood there, fuming. She was pissed, and he thought she looked stunning.

He moved back beside her, positioning his arm so she could hold it, again. Not because she needed it, but because he wanted her to touch him. Any way he could get. "Just told them the facts, sweetheart."

Her lips quirked, and he wondered if she'd just, now, clued into the fact he'd been calling her sweetheart. "They have a point."

"They have an opinion. It happens to be wrong, but they're entitled. You were a cop for twelve years. As long as I was a Marine. What you did tonight was all those years of training kicking in. I guarantee that in the space of a heartbeat, you had it completely pictured inside your mind. All the sounds, the smells. They gave you a mental map, and you fired based on your best judgement. That's all any of us do at any given time. God knows, I've gone in under the cover of smoke more times than I can count. I had to rely on my instincts to decipher what was a threat and what wasn't. Not every situation can be picture perfect. I don't doubt that if you'd heard anything to suggest there were people around, you'd be lying on the floor, now, instead of him. And it'd be your body inside that black bag."

Rigs couldn't go there. Couldn't let the thought manifest because it was too easy to picture. Picture her skin an eerie gray, her blonde hair dull and tangled.

How her limbs would have been limp at her sides, maybe turned at an unnatural angle. He'd seen a lifetime's worth of soldiers killed by war. Knew exactly the kind of damage a few rounds of bullets would have done to her body. The ragged flesh. The blood. And he couldn't contemplate it because it messed with his head. Made his chest constrict, his damn hands shake, again.

He drew a calming breath. "And then, there's the part where you got a flash of the room. Sounds like you had it all under control."

He didn't quite understand how she could get flashes. What conversion disorder was or if it meant her sight loss was only temporary, even if her dick of a colleague had alluded to it. Facts he'd unearth whether through her or Ice. His buddy was bound to know something, and Rigs would make damn sure he was an expert in conversion disorder before the next sunrise.

Her mouth gaped open, and her eyes rounded. "You believe me?"

"Of course. Why wouldn't I?"

Addison's jaw clenched, and she tilted her head off to the side. She focused on his face for a while before granting him with a sweet smile. "Didn't you say something about talking to SWAT?"

"Yeah. We should probably head over. Would you like my arm or would you prefer to get there by yourself?"

God, he hoped she wanted his arm. But he'd respect her decision. Understood that, after the confrontation with her former colleagues, she might want to prove her independence, even if just to herself. She didn't have to prove how strong she was to him. Her strength showed through in the way she carried herself.

Addison hesitated, still tapping her cane against the floor before giving his arm a squeeze. "You promise not to crash me into planter or statue?"

Hell, no. She was under his protection, even if it was just for tonight. Just getting her out of there and seeing her safely home. He wouldn't say those words out loud. Wouldn't suggest she wasn't capable of doing those things for herself. But it didn't mean it was any less true. "Scouts honor."

"Then, lead on."

CHAPTER 6

THIS WAS SO MUCH MORE than Addison had bargained for. And it had nothing to do with the attempted robbery. The armed men. She'd faced twelve years of that. Had spent her entire adult life in the line of fire. First, on the beat, then, as a detective. Narcotics hadn't been an easy division to work in, but she'd held her own. Until the raid. Until her life had descended into darkness. Ground to a resounding halt. All of which had changed two hours ago. The moment she'd met Kent.

She forced herself to swallow past the dry rasp of her throat. She was seated next to him in what she assumed was some sort of truck. It sounded big. Gravelly—like his voice. And he'd had to boost her up to get into it with her dress hampering her movements a bit. It had seemed innocent enough, except where she could still feel his hands around her waist. His body pressed against her back as he levered her up. She'd felt the firm planes of his chest and abdomen, not to mention the hard ridge at his groin.

Not that it had surprised her. Cops weren't that different from soldiers, and she knew the kind of adrenaline rush that accompanied any form of take-down. The high that heightened every sense—that demanded release. And there was no better release than sex.

Not that they were going to have sex. Maybe the old Addy would have slid over—palmed his thigh. Suggested they find a mutual way to work off the pent-up tension. Ease that rock-hard bulge she'd felt between his legs. Stem the needy ache between hers. The one she hadn't experienced since losing her sight. That was part of the reason she felt off-kilter.

She barely knew Kent. And, yet... She'd felt an instant connection to him in the garden. One that had grown exponentially since then. But it was more than just physical attraction. Unspoken sexual chemistry. The entire time they'd spent talking to the SWAT leader, Kent had treated her as an equal. Like a regular member of his team. Not that she deserved anything less. But after being shunned by her friends and colleagues, it had come as a nice surprise.

He was a nice surprise and completely out of her league.

"You okay?"

She jumped at the sound of his voice, turning her head in his direction. Other than those two words, he hadn't made a sound since leaving the foundation fifteen minutes ago. If it weren't for the steady slap of the wipers across the windshield, the cabin would have been dead silent on his side of the truck.

Not on hers. Even she heard the rough sound of her breathing. The loud pounding of her heart. Was it echoing through the cab as much as it was inside her head? Fast, hard beats that made her ribs shake. And all because of the man sitting beside her.

She worked up a smile. "Fine. Why?"

"You look exhausted. I thought if I was quiet, you might doze off, but you seem...edgy, now. Which is understandable after the night we just had. Not your typical fundraiser."

Of course, he'd picked up on her anxiousness. Just not the reason behind it. "It's not the shooting. I realize I'm not the same person I used to be, but that wasn't anything I haven't faced before. I'm just..."

Unnerved by you. By this unspoken spark between us that has me tied in knots. That I want to ask you to stay the night but have no idea how or if you'd even be interested.

"...worried. About Blade. I've only really had him a few months but sitting here, without him, feels... wrong."

"Why don't we call the vet? See if we can get an update?"

Damn. In all the commotion, she hadn't even gotten the vet's number. So much for still being a cop. Still having her edge. She'd barely held it together tonight. Nothing like the hard-assed detective she'd once been.

"I...I forgot to ask for his number, which is so not like me. I'm usually very good at the details."

"Your partner was shot. Your best friend, I believe you phrased it. Cut yourself some slack. I'd be distracted, too, in your shoes."

Except where he'd been nothing but calm, cool grace under pressure. Not once had she heard his voice waver. His breathing speed up. Sure, she'd *imagined* his hands shaking, but that had been in her head. Like all her problems. A way of making herself feel better. Trying to fool herself into thinking she was more than just idle concern to him.

His hand settled over both of hers. Warm. Strong. "I got his number. We'll see if we—"

A loud blast of music cut him off.

"Seems the man beat us to it. Walker."

"Mr. Walker, this is Dr. Conrad."

"Doc. I was just about to call you. I have Addison with me, and we were hoping you could give us an update on Blade?"

"He'll be sore for a while. And might walk with a bit of a limp until his shoulder fully heals, but he came through surgery just fine. I'll be keeping him sedated for a while." The vet chuckled. "From what I've heard, he's like his owner. Only rests if forced. Why don't you drop by tomorrow, Addison? He should be strong enough for a short visit. Say, early afternoon?"

Addison opened her mouth to answer, but all that made if past her lips was a strangled squeak. She hadn't realized how scared she was Blade wasn't going to make it—that she'd cost him his life—until the vet had started talking. And her damn throat had closed up.

Kent squeezed her hands. "I'll see she gets there. Thanks, Doc."

The line disconnected.

"Breathe, sweetheart. It's all gonna be okay."

That word, again. Breathe. Hadn't she been trying to do just that when the world had erupted into smoke and gunfire? When she'd nearly lost Blade because she hadn't been able to avoid danger?

Addy forced in a few quick gulps of air, praying it would be enough to keep her lungs working.

Another squeeze of her hands. "Better?"

She nodded, aware her voice would belay the lie. Better implied that she had herself under control, a feat she feared wouldn't happen as long as Kent was beside her. Sitting there, his hand on top of hers. She opened her fingers just enough his slotted between them. But if he minded the way she clung to him, he didn't say anything. Didn't sigh or huff. In fact, the air around them settled. The energy she sensed, calming.

They sat in silence for a few more minutes before the truck slowed to a halt. She waited for him to continue, but he turned off the engine.

Addy frowned. "Is there a problem?"

A deep chuckle. "No problem. We're here."

"Here?"

"Your place." He squeezed her hand one more time then it was gone. Nothing but the ghosted feel of his fingers twined through hers lingering behind.

They were home already? She was sure it had taken Carl twice as long to drive her to the foundation, and it hadn't been dark or raining. "That was…fast."

He snorted. "Driving slow's for puss—er, wimps. And after the kind of crap you drive in while on deployment, a rainy summer night is pretty tame."

Of course, he'd driven in worse conditions. He'd

spent twelve years in the Marines. God knew how many of those in the MARSOC unit. She just wasn't used to always being a passenger. To having to rely on someone else to get anywhere she couldn't walk to. It was one of the things that frustrated her the most.

Her door opened, and she jerked back. She hadn't even heard him get out of the truck. But in the space of a couple of heartbeats, he'd rounded the vehicle and reached her side. Then, he unclipped her seatbelt and offered her his arm.

She used it to steady herself as she swung her legs to the open door, hoping she could judge the distance without tripping. He snaked one hand around her waist and tugged her against his chest, holding her tight as he stepped back and shut the door, keeping her suspended.

She inhaled, and his spicy scent filled her senses. The one she knew she'd be able to pinpoint any time. Any where. It held hints of leather and gun oil, and something earthy that she suspected was just him. He exhaled, fluttering the strands of hair around her face as he slowly lowered her to the ground. She got a hint of that hard ridge beneath his pants, again, before he eased back, placing one of her hands on his forearm. His muscles flexed beneath her fingers as she tightened her grip just enough to ground herself.

The air around her shifted, then he was at her side, his other hand cupping her waist, his body pressed lightly against hers. He stood motionless, obviously waiting for her to set the pace.

She focused on where she thought his face was—by the sound of his voice, he was a good six or seven inches taller than her. "You don't have to be my guide. I know it's late. You must be tired, too. And you already took the time to drive me home. I'd understand if you'd rather just drop me off."

Not that she wanted him to leave. She didn't. In fact, she'd already planned on asking him in for coffee. Surely, that was innocent enough. A thank you for saving her from riding in a taxi. From facing the endless miles alone, still wondering if Blade would make it. It wasn't synonymous with sex, was it? And did she care if it was? If he interpreted it that way? Made a pass? Would she accept?

He stiffened, a rough breath whispering around them. "I said I'd see you safely home. Abandoning you on your driveway doesn't fit that description. Besides, it's been my pleasure, and I'm not much of a sleeper, to be honest."

His voice sounded different. Strained, and his body seemed harder. As if he was bracing himself for battle. And she suspected there was a deeper meaning behind his statement. A darker reason he didn't sleep.

"But it'd be wise to get in out of the rain. Your dress doesn't look like it mixes well with showers."

How had she missed it was still raining? Now that he'd mentioned it, she felt the cool drops dot her arms and face. But until that moment, all she'd felt was his skin beneath her palm, his body pressed against hers.

She nodded then sighed. "My key's in my purse, which I left on the seat."

"I grabbed it when I helped you out." He placed it in her other hand. "Can I get the key for you?"

"Okay. It's on a silver keychain."

The zipper opened then closed. "Got it. Ready? From where I parked in your driveway, your porch is about thirty feet from us on a path just off to our left. There are three steps up then another couple straight to your door."

She smiled. "Are you always this considerate? No one else I've been around ever describes my surroundings for me. Gives me a visual inside my head. Thank you."

He swallowed, the sound thick. As if he'd had to force it down his throat. "Just holding true to my promise not to smash you into anything. Whenever you're ready."

She got the feeling he would have stood there all night, waiting for her to move. The rain slowly drenching them. And never once complained. Never asked her to hurry inside. But he'd been right. Her dress didn't mix well with rain showers, not to mention the sudden chill as the wind gusted across her damp flesh.

A shiver lit up her skin with goosebumps as she started off, Kent keeping pace at her side. She kept track of her steps, smiling when he counted down the ones just before her stairs. It was the first time she'd walked up to her steps without Blade and didn't worry about tripping. About kicking the bottom step or ending up too far back.

They stopped at the door, and she heard the telltale click of the lock turning over before a swirl of warm air curled around her shoulders. She took two steps in then instinctively reached down to unleash Blade before she remembered he wasn't there. Wouldn't be until he'd recovered from saving her life.

Addy pressed her eyes closed, doing her best to will away the building tears, when Kent sighed. His arm moved out from beneath her fingers only to brush across her back a second later. Then, he was lifting her —hugging her against his chest as he shut the door, locked it, then started walking. He stopped a few moments later then turned and lowered them onto one of her wing-backed chairs.

He positioned her in his lap, his arms looped around her shoulders and back, her head tucked into his chest. His breath sounded above her as he rested his chin beside her head. "It's okay to be upset. To be worried about Blade. He's more than just a service dog. He's family. And I know how I'd feel if someone I loved took a bullet for me."

Her chin quivered, a few tears spilling over her lashes to land hot and wet against his shirt. "You wouldn't cry."

"We all release stress differently. Personally, I prefer to blow shit up. And I have a feeling this is about more than just Blade." His grip tightened. "I promise I won't think you're any less of a badass if you let go."

She shook her head, all the while more tears leaked out. This wasn't like her. Being weepy. Showing her emotions. She'd spent a lifetime bottling them up. Pushing them down whenever they threatened to unhinge her. Eighteen months, and she hadn't cried, yet, over everything that had happened—losing her sight. Losing her partner. Letting go, now, while wrapped in

Kent's arms, seemed dangerously intimate. More so than if she'd pounced on him in his truck, and they'd had sex in her driveway.

He sighed. "At least, close your eyes for a bit. Rest."

She cursed the flutter of heat that flared to life in her chest. "Like this?"

He chuckled. "Got nowhere to go. And I can't think of a better way to spend the next little while. So, rest. I'll make you some tea or coffee when you wake up."

She burrowed against his chest, telling herself it was only for a minute. Just long enough to push everything down, again. To find her strength. And not the kind she got from him. From just sitting there in his arms. That kind of strength was a mirage. Destined to fade as soon as he walked out her door. And he'd be doing that shortly. Because once the adrenaline wore off, he'd see she wasn't worth his effort. Was as crazy as Johnson had claimed. It was only a matter of time.

CHAPTER 7

He had nowhere to go? He'd make tea for her once she woke up? He wasn't sure he even knew how to make tea.

Rigs shook his head as he shifted a bit lower on the chair, keeping Addy tucked against him. She'd fallen asleep in the space of a heartbeat. Awake one second. Limp against him the next, her warm, steady breath caressing his neck. And he knew, he'd sit there all night —fuck, all weekend, if it meant having her in his arms. He could do it. Had once spent three days in the same four-foot hole, waiting for a chance to blow a bridge. So, sitting on her chair, her gentle weight nestled in his lap...piece of cake.

Except that his damn dick didn't want to listen to him—stay politely tucked away like it should. He'd been fighting for control ever since he'd met her, and the adrenaline rush from the takedown at the foundation hadn't helped him will it away. He'd had to strategically shuffle sideways after helping her out of his Chevy.

Afraid she'd rub against his damn boner on the way down. If he hadn't actually witnessed the way she'd instinctively reached for Blade, only to remember a moment too late that her companion wasn't there—hadn't felt her pain, her fear as she'd fought back tears—he wouldn't have been able to place her on his lap without jabbing her in the hip.

But her distress had tempered his desire, and he'd managed to hold her without making a complete ass of himself. Having to explain why he was sporting an erection when she was worried about her best friend.

Rigs closed his eyes, thinking through a few complicated training scenarios until his muscles eased, and he felt marginally back in control. All he needed were a few deep breaths and...

Shit. He shouldn't have inhaled because now all he could smell was the floral scent of her perfume mixed with the touch of citrus from her hair. And beneath that —hints of sulphur and smoke.

He cinched his arms a bit tighter, listening to her heartbeat echo inside his chest until the sound eased the tumbling feeling in his gut. The one that couldn't stop picturing all the ways she'd put herself at risk, now that she didn't have Blade for a couple of weeks. How easy it would be for someone to take advantage of her, cop training or not. She couldn't see a threat coming until it was on her—either touching her or sounding off a warning. Without Blade to come to her defense...

Not going to happen. Rigs would see to it personally. Find a way to convince her she needed him close. He'd have to tread lightly. Word it in a way she wouldn't think he was protecting her. If he'd learned anything about Addison Bailey, it's that she didn't want to be perceived as weak. And she wasn't. But she was at risk.

Her colleague's words looped through his head as he removed his cell then hit Ice's number. No way the man was sleeping, yet. Harlequin had been photographing the scene—making a documentary of sorts of what had happened. Maybe getting evidence for insurance. Whatever the reason, Rigs knew Ice wouldn't leave Harlequin's side for a second. And that was before armed men had burst into the auction.

"What's wrong, buddy? That pretty detective mess with your head so much you can't remember the code to Quinn's loft?"

"I'm not at the loft. And I remember the code just fine."

"Your truck break down?"

"Like I can't fix it if it did. I have a question."

"The answer's a resounding yes. You should absolutely get Addison Bailey's number. And you should ask her out for coffee. Tomorrow, if not sooner. There's got to be a twenty-four-hour café somewhere near you."

"Can't. She's sleeping."

"Wow. That was fast."

"Not *with* me, jackass." He didn't add that she was *on* him. Bad enough Ice knew Rigs was seeing double because of her. No need to give the man more ammunition. "She's exhausted. Between the armed men and Blade getting shot…"

"Of course. I didn't mean to sound like an ass. Just… with all that sexual tension between you two, I thought maybe..." Ice sighed. "How's my star patient? Any news?"

"The big guy's gonna be just fine, though he'll be out of commission for a bit. I told the vet I'd bring Addison by tomorrow. Might make her feel better. She feels responsible, knowing he took a couple of bullets trying to keep her safe."

"Just like any good soldier would. So, what's the question, then?"

"Conversion disorder. You heard of it?"

Ice blew out a rough breath. "Sure. Not that I'm an expert or anything. But I rescued a few guys who suffered from it for a while, afterward. Read up on it just for my own curiosity. Why?"

"After you left, some of Addy's colleagues showed up. Guess they heard the call go out over the police radio. Two of them were real douchebags. Anyway, one of them said she had hysterical blindness, and she corrected them by saying it was conversion disorder. I was hoping you'd fill me in. Explain how that translates into her being blind."

"That's what she's got? Shit. Do you know what preceded it? Generally, it stems from some kind of trauma, either physical or emotional, though usually both. And I'm not talking about a simple gunshot wound or a broken heart. Near death stuff."

"The assholes mentioned something about a raid, but... I haven't had a chance to ask. It didn't seem like the right time."

"Thinking there really isn't a right time, Rigs."

"I'll figure it out. But you haven't told me what it is, and how she can be blind if her eyes are fine."

"Conversion order isn't really understood that well. Basically, it's a psychological condition where a person has blindness, paralysis, or other neurologic symptoms that can't be explained medically."

"How long does it last?"

"Your guess is as good as anyone else's. Often a few days or weeks, but it can be permanent if the patient can't find a way to break through—overcome whatever psychological conditions are preventing them from getting better."

"Which means—"

"She must have experienced something pretty fucking horrible. Maybe witnessed something her brain isn't quite ready for her to process. Either way, there's really nothing anyone else can do. It just takes time."

"So, there's a chance she could see, again? Permanently?"

"Sure. She could wake up in the morning and be just fine. Or…"

"Or she could be blind for the rest of her life."

"It all depends on her. Has she had any kind of indicators that she might be recovering?"

"She mentioned she's been having flashes. She described them as snapshots of the room. It's how she knew there wasn't anyone else around when she fired at that tango. No idea when else she had them or for how long."

Christ, had she had one while they were in the garden? Had she seen his face? The scars?

"That's...encouraging. Not quite a benchmark, but the fact she's gotten even a glimpse of sight back means she has a chance to beat it. You might want to see if she'll talk about it. Maybe figure out if there's a common element that triggers the flash, and try to recreate it. Unless it's armed men about to shoot her. Pretty sure you wouldn't survive another round of bullets aimed at your girl."

"She's not *my* girl." But damn if the thought didn't flood his body with heat. Didn't jerk his dick inside his pants—make his heart do a little dance inside his chest.

"Right. Just like Quinn wasn't mine after I'd driven her home from that bar."

"This isn't the same. *I'm* not the same."

"Rigs—Kent. Do me a favor? Don't screw this up because of what you've worked up inside your head. Addison seems like a pretty amazing woman. One who knows firsthand about demons and scars, even if hers are on the inside. If anyone's going to remotely understand how you feel and what you've been through—are still going through—it'll be her. Give her chance."

"You say that like I have a choice."

Ice chuckled. "Got you by the balls, huh?"

"Something worse. My damn heart."

"Guess you didn't leave it behind, after all." Voices sounded in the distance. "Gotta go. But...check in tomorrow. And call if you're worried about her. I'll do what I can."

The line went silent.

Rigs tucked the phone back in his pocket, staring down at the woman in his arms. He couldn't imagine what she'd gone through to lose her sight. She'd been incredibly brave. Not the kind of person to let an injury get the better of her. Still...

He wasn't exactly the poster-guy for mental wellness. Had spent the better part of two years hiding—telling himself he was healing when he knew damn well that he was avoiding people. Avoiding life. Pretending that he didn't lose a bit more of himself every time someone reacted to his scars. That it didn't hurt. But he'd been lucky. Midnight, Ice, Montana—they'd all reached out. Gone out of their way to make sure he didn't spiral so deep he wouldn't ever climb out. Who had Addison had in her corner?

From the sounds of it, no one, other than Carl and Blade. He couldn't imagine how hard it was to get through each day knowing she was responsible for her own symptoms. That it was all inside her head.

He'd have to find a way to broach the subject without sounding judgmental, like Johnson and Seymour had. The last thing she needed was more pressure.

Addison moaned, twitching in his arms. He shushed her, dropping a kiss on her head as he gathered her closer. She snuggled against him, inflaming his dick, again, then settled. He shifted just enough to relieve the throbbing ache—ensure she wouldn't suddenly wake up with him poking her because he doubted his erection was going down anytime soon. Not with her scent filling the air, her skin touching his where one of her hands rested on his neck. Best he get comfortable, because he wasn't moving until she'd slept. Until he'd gotten the feel of her out of his system.

Of course, that would likely take more than a few hours. Days. Maybe weeks. Fifty years seemed like a reasonable amount of time.

He snagged an ottoman with his foot, dragging it close enough he could brace his feet on it. Angle Addison so she leaned more fully against him. Ensure she wouldn't roll off his lap if she woke suddenly from a nightmare.

No doubts she had them. If her injuries were bad enough to mess with her head to the point she couldn't see, she'd definitely have nightmares. Images. Voices. Memories she might not remember but played in her head whenever her defenses were lowered. That's part of the reason he didn't sleep much. Despite all his training, all his skills, he couldn't control what looped inside his brain once he closed his eyes. And knowing he was vulnerable…

Easier to avoid it, like he had everything else. Pretend he was fine when he knew he wasn't. Even now, a part of him felt edgy. Restless because he hadn't scouted the perimeter. Noted all the exit points and sight lines. Hadn't laid a few well-placed trip lines. Not actual explosives, but a small charge that would light up the darkness—alert him if anyone tried to infiltrate her home.

Which he knew was crazy in its own right. Like Ice had told him months ago—civilians didn't wire their damn homes. Didn't have armories with enough weapons to take on a few dozen tangos. But…he wasn't the average civilian. And he'd vowed he'd never get caught on the wrong side of a surprise, again.

Christ, it was a wonder he hadn't gone blind. Hadn't suffered the same fate as Addison. She seemed far more stable than he was. Didn't seem fair that she was stuck in darkness when he spent all his time trying to hide in it.

Though, if his damn heart had its way, he wouldn't be hiding much longer. Not if he wanted to spend more time with her. And he *definitely* wanted to spend more time with her. All his time. He wanted to make her breakfast in the morning, spend the day talking. Maybe go for a walk. Get a coffee. Take her to dinner, then hold her in his arms all night. They didn't even have to have sex. Not that he didn't want her, but, sitting there, her whispered breath sounding around him, her silky hair curled around his neck, was better than most of his sexual encounters over the past decade. Which might have scared other guys, but not him.

If Rigs had learned anything about himself, it was that he was a switch kind of guy. Things were either on or off. He was either happy or sad. He either committed to a mission or he didn't. There wasn't anything in between. No half-assed decisions.

Most spec ops soldiers were switch men. They had to be. Had to make split decisions in the space of a heartbeat without agonizing over the choices. They needed to know their limitations, their strengths. There wasn't time to be almost ready. Almost certain. Once the choice was made to go, he was all in. Two hundred percent. And he'd make damn sure he reached his objective.

Which was currently curled up in his lap, lightly snoring. It didn't matter that they'd just met. That he didn't know if this was a fleeting moment or the start of the rest of his life. He'd already decided he'd embrace the suck—risk her leaving with his heart clenched in her hands. No going back, now. All he could do was steer into the hard.

Rigs chuckled. He didn't have a clue how to proceed. He'd never been involved in a serious relationship—couldn't bring himself to do that to someone when he'd planned on spending his life in the Teams. He'd witnessed too many families torn apart by death or injury. His face case and point. So, sitting there, holding Addison, wondering if she felt even a fraction of the connection he did—it was alien. Uncharted waters. All he could do was dive in and hope he didn't drown.

She smiled in her sleep, and fuck if his heart didn't skip a beat. His hands suddenly clammy. Now, he understood what Ice had been talking about. Why the man had been so singleminded. Who knew one tiny firecracker of a woman could bring Rigs to his knees? Make him rethink his future—willingly put himself out in the open. Until a few hours ago, it hadn't seemed possible.

Rigs sighed. No sense worrying over how he'd gotten here, now. Better to put his energy into moving forward—with Addison.

He relaxed, watching her sleep as the rain continued

pelting the window, the occasional flash of lightning illuminating her face. How her long, dark lashes contrasted against her creamy skin. Or the cute way she furrowed her brow, mumbling a few times before easing. He didn't know how long he'd sat there, mesmerized by every tiny nuance of her face, when the front doorknob jiggled.

He sat up, every nerve instantly primed, every muscle tensed. It could have been the wind. Or his head playing tricks on him. But after the attack on the foundation, he wasn't making any assumptions. Instead, he stood, twisted to place Addison on the chair, then knelt, quietly removing his Beretta from his ankle holster. All the while watching the door—straining to hear someone try to turn it, again.

Thunder boomed overhead, but it didn't quite crush the pad of footsteps past the picture window in front of him. Didn't obscure the slightly darker shadow from moving across the floor.

He leaned over Addison, giving her shoulder a firm shake. She blinked as she bolted upright, her sightless gaze searching the room as she obviously tried to orient herself.

"Easy, sweetheart, it's just me. I wouldn't wake you, but there's someone outside."

Her focus settled on his face. "Kent? And did you just say there's someone outside?"

"Pretty damn sure. Heard the door jiggle then footsteps, followed by a shadow past your window. I'm gonna check it out. I want you to stay here until I get back."

"Screw that. If there's someone out there, I'm better off shadowing you." She held up her hand. "I know. Blind as a bat. But I've done this a thousand times. Could do it in my sleep. And if you go out there alone, you'll be putting yourself at risk because half your focus will be back here, with me. Wondering if I'm okay. If someone snuck in the back door. If you made a mistake by leaving. Or, have I read you wrong, and you're not the protective type."

Fuck.

She pressed her lips together. "I won't slow you down or trip you up. You have my word."

Despite getting booted from the Marines, Rigs was still a soldier. Once a Marine, always a Marine, wasn't just a catch phrase. It ran soul deep. He'd trained, fought, bled, and damn near died for his country. For the sake of the mission. He'd learned to make hard decisions based on facts. Emotions didn't win wars, and they sure as hell didn't factor into strategy. It didn't matter if he hurt someone's feelings. Winning—living was the endgame. And he was all about the endgame.

At least, the old Rigs was. The new one—the one that was willing to brave cafés and restaurants. That would gladly sit for days in the same chair just to hold Addison in his arms… *That* Rigs—Kent… He heard the desperate plea in her voice. Saw the raw emotions cross her face. Felt her fear of rejection. And damn if it didn't mess with his head. Make him see the situation from a different point of view. Namely, hers.

He opened his mouth to say, no. Not going to happen. Cold day in hell before he'd willingly put her in the line of fire, ex-cop or not. He'd vowed to keep her safe, even if he'd only thought it inside his head. So, until she told him to fuck off, he'd hold true to that promise. Put himself between her and danger without hesitation.

But damned if the words wouldn't form on his tongue. Wouldn't make it past the hard thump of his heart as he watched her worry her bottom lip between her teeth.

"I don't need your word, Addison. You've already proven how tough you are. Besides, it's hard to argue with you when you're right." He moved closer, stopping just shy of touching her, knowing she could sense him. Feel his body heat. "Okay. Keep one hand by my shoulder, the other on my waist. I'll tap your knuckles once for left, twice for right. And stay low."

"Got it."

She rose gracefully, any hint of sleep gone, then placed her hands as he'd instructed. He turned toward the door, making his way across the room. Addison followed. No hesitation. No missed steps. And the way she matched his movements… It was as if they'd trained together for years. Knew exactly how the other would react.

She stopped when he reached the door, waiting for him to continue. He counted down in a low voice, silently opening the door when he reached one. Rain fell in steady sheets, reducing the visibility to only a few feet. A light fog curled across the ground, obscuring the grass and pavement.

Rigs waited until she was clear then quietly closed the door, wedging a small scrap of paper near the bottom. He scanned the area before shifting left and following the house around to the front window. He stopped at the corner, indicating his intentions with a quick tap to her hand at his waist. She moved seamlessly with him when he stepped out, keeping in the shadows lining the wall. He searched the ground, but he couldn't see any footprints in the grass, not with the fog rolling in and the rain washing any kind of evidence away.

Addison pressed against him, her lips grazing his ear. "I just heard the gate creak. It's off to the left around the side."

She'd heard the gate creak? Christ, he hadn't heard anything, and he'd been vigilant. Which meant the chance it had been the wind rattling the doorknob was pretty fucking low. Shit. He should have said no. Locked her in the damn bathroom with his Beretta. Told her to shoot at anything that came through the door. He had a Sig in his truck. Chances were, he could have gotten to it before anyone had landed a fatal shot on him—that's what it would take to stop him. Prevent him from staying at her side. Him dead—and she would have been safe. Mostly.

Damn, there wasn't a concrete solution. She'd been right. His focus would have been divided, like now. Only, it would have been worse. Worrying someone would get the jump on her. That she wouldn't have a way to pinpoint where to shoot. That she'd miss. It had been hard enough at the foundation. Knowing he didn't have a choice. Here. Now... At least with him, he could put his body between her and a bullet if necessary.

He clenched his jaw. "Glue yourself to my ass and don't fucking sway from it."

CHAPTER 8

WHAT THE HELL had she been thinking? She should have stayed in the damn house. Had him lock her up and give her a weapon. She still had her Beretta in a lockbox, hidden in her closet. It would have taken two minutes to retrieve it and crouch behind the bed or her dresser —let Kent patrol the perimeter on his own. What if she screwed up? Put him at risk? God…got him killed? And all because the thought of him being alone…facing someone, again, without backup…scared her. Made her stomach clench and her chest tighten.

Addison gave her head a shake. He hadn't been alone, before. He'd had his buddies to back him up. Other Special Forces soldiers. And having to babysit a blind ex-cop wasn't really the kind of help Kent needed. Addison knew by the flex of his muscles beneath her palms, the edgy tone to his voice, he was nervous. But not about the possible target. It was her. He didn't want *her* to get hurt.

She'd just have to see to it she didn't screw up or put him at further risk. That she used the few advantages she had, like hearing the gate creak when she suspected he hadn't. She kept insisting she wasn't helpless. About damn time she believed it and acted accordingly.

Addison shuffled closer as Kent moved forward. Like at the foundation, he didn't make a sound. No whisper of breath, no footsteps. It was as if he'd vanished. Except for the two places she touched him— and the familiar energy she'd come to recognize as his.

He murmured for her to stay put for a second then truly vanished. It was eerie the way he disappeared. There one second then gone. If someone had told her he'd been abducted by aliens, she would have believed it because she'd never met anyone who just vanished like he did. Hadn't met anyone that skilled before. Sure, she'd been good at being stealthy. Had executed a lot of sting operations without ever blowing her cover. But Kent took it to a whole other level. And she couldn't help but wonder why he'd left the Marine Corps. Especially, when he still seemed so capable.

Questions for later—after they'd secured her home. After she'd proven that it hadn't been a mistake to let her shadow him. She'd sensed his reservations. Though, she wasn't sure if it was because she was blind or if it was just his nature. If he'd have had the same hesitations if she could see. He definitely radiated old-fashioned chivalry, and she'd bet her ass that he saw himself as a protector. That the moment she'd agreed to let him drive her home, he'd made some kind of pact with himself to keep her safe. And

Marines never backed down once they'd accepted a mission.

Kent stopped. "The gate's ajar. I suppose there's a chance it's all been the wind, but…"

But those kinds of coincidences rarely happened. Required biblical intervention.

"It's always latched, on the off-chance Blade gets spooked and bolts."

He grunted a reply, tapping her hand then heading down the narrow path. She pictured it all in her mind—the fencing. The stone pavers. How the yard continued on past the end of the house. She had no idea how it looked, now. Originally, she'd kept it neat and tidy. A few flowers and bushes but nothing too ornate. For all she knew, the company she'd hired to tend to the grounds only pretended to do it.

Kent stopped, again, and she suspected they'd reached the rear corner of the small house. His lips suddenly caressed her ear as he tugged her flush against him. "We'll do a full circuit of the perimeter, unless there's obvious evidence someone went inside. If it's all good, we'll go clear the house, room by room."

She nodded, and he gave her a squeeze then eased away, picking his way toward the back door. She followed, shivering at the drench of cold rain against her skin. So much for her dress not mixing well with showers. She should have changed the moment she'd gotten home, instead of falling asleep in Kent's arms.

Another shiver that had nothing to do with the weather.

Kent continued along the rear of the house, pausing

occasionally whenever thunder rattled overhead. She kept pace, straining to hear any noise above the storm, when something scuffed behind her. She cocked her head, trying to hone in on the sound when light flashed across her vision—illuminating the yard as it blinked into view. The white glow of the fog as it curled along the ground. The overgrown bushes near the fence. The silhouette of a man emerging around the corner—dark-colored hood obscuring his head, the big black barrel of his gun outlined in harsh relief.

Time slowed—freezing into another snapshot. The gun half raised. A hint of white where the guy's mouth would be.

"Shooter! Six o'clock."

It all happened at once. Kent's arm wrapped around her waist as he plastered his body against hers then spun, shoving her behind him and somehow pressing her to the ground. She caught a glimpse of brown hair and stubbled skin in the next flash—what looked like long scars slashing up his cheek toward his hairline before the world went black, nothing but his ghosted image lingering in the darkness.

She braced herself for the inevitable report of a gun —she assumed Kent was armed. God, she hoped he was armed. Why hadn't she told him about her personal weapon? Offered for him to use it if necessary? Surely he didn't go anywhere without a weapon tucked some-where, did he? And why the hell hadn't she asked?

The next roll of thunder made her jump—had her reaching out for him. She hadn't heard anything. No shots. No grunts or scuffs. Nothing but her own blood pounding through her ears, her breath rasping through her chest. The patter of rain on the small paved deck. Had he left? Was he bleeding to death, right now, just a few feet away? Just enough she couldn't sense him? Help him?

A hand clasped hers, and she recoiled.

"Easy, Addy. Still me."

"Christ, you scared me. When I didn't hear... Where is he?"

Silence.

"Kent?"

"There's no one there. At least, not anymore."

"What do you mean, there's no one there? He was at the corner of the house. He had a gun with a suppressor. I *saw* him!"

His hands engulfed hers. "Another snapshot?"

"I know what you're thinking, but I didn't imagine it, and it wasn't a flashback. It was real. *He* was real."

"I didn't say it wasn't real. It's just... I didn't see anyone."

"How could you miss him? He was standing right there! Hoodie. A hint of a smile. His shadow moving along the wall."

His grip tightened. "There's no wall, sweetheart."

"What are you talking about?"

"You said his shadow moved along the wall. The lightning would have cast it against the bushes, not the house." Air moving. He'd knelt in front of her. "Come on. I took a quick scout around. There's no one out here. Let's check the house. Get you warmed up."

She shook her head, stumbling to her feet then tripping backwards against the house. She pulled her hands away when he tried to take them in his, again. "I *saw* him. He was wearing a dark-colored hoodie. He had a gun with a suppressor. He was coming around the corner—"

"I believe you. But he's obviously gone. Must have bolted when you shouted out that he was there. Regardless, you're soaked, and you're shivering. Let's get inside, clear the house, then we'll talk. Okay?"

He hadn't raised his voice. Hadn't injected any kind of judgmental tone into it that suggested he was lying or trying to placate her. But she'd caught the hint of worry. The slightly higher pitch. He wasn't saying she'd imagined it, but he was obviously concerned for her well being.

Good. So was she. After not having any indication her condition was getting better, to have all these flashes in the span of a few hours unnerved her. It didn't make sense. Why this was happening, now? Why she couldn't seem to make it stay? And she knew she'd lose her sanity if it continued. Being blind was one thing. Seeing the world in a series of occasional snapshots no one truly believed she'd experienced was crippling.

"Addison."

"Fine."

He took her hand then quietly led her back toward the gate. It creaked as it slid closed, the telltale click of the latch engaging echoing around them. They rounded the house then headed for the front porch, stopping beneath the overhang. The wind gusted, and she wrapped her free hand around her torso in an attempt to combat the chill.

Addy waited for Kent to open the door, but instead, he backed her up, positioning her beside one of the posts then told her to wait. She tried to follow his movements, but all that registered was the rain against the roof. The splash of drops in the puddles on her driveway.

"Kent? I thought we were going to clear the house?"

She'd kept her voice low. Barely an exchange of air because despite what he'd said, she couldn't shake the feeling someone was watching them. Waiting to strike. And the fact he'd half hidden her behind the post only amplified her stress.

A rush of air and he was at her side—pulling her firmly against him. "Someone's been through the front door."

"What... How do you know that?"

"I left a small piece of paper wedged in the frame. So, I'd know if it was opened. It's lying on the porch. There aren't any wet footprints, but a pro wouldn't leave any. I sure as hell wouldn't. Which leaves us with three possibilities. One—the asshole's still inside, waiting for us to come through the door. Two, he's come and gone, and the threat's over."

When he didn't continue, she nudged him. "And three?"

"Bastard's gone because he left us a surprise."

"A surprise? You mean like a bomb or something?"

She felt his shoulders lift. A shrug.

"That's what I'd do."

"You were an ordinance soldier. I doubt many people think along those lines."

"Only takes one to kill us, sweetheart."

Obviously, this wasn't an argument she'd win. Not that she was going to argue. "Okay, so, what do you want to do?"

"Option four. My truck. We'll go someplace safe for the night, then I'll come back and check it out in the morning."

Without her.

He didn't say it, but it hung between them. He wanted to come back when he didn't have to watch out for her. When she wasn't liable to get him killed because, no matter how much she wanted it, how much she willed it to be true, she couldn't back him up.

The truth settled hard in her stomach. Not that she blamed him. She *was* a liability, and she *couldn't* watch his back. Not unless her brain decided to give her more than a five-second glimpse of her surroundings.

Kent's hand gripped her elbow, then they were walking. Her driveway tapping beneath her boots before she heard the truck locks disengage. He opened her door and lifted her up before she could do more than gasp—reach out for something solid to grasp. She was still searching for the seatbelt buckle when his door opened, allowing a gust of rain to sweep through the cab.

She tried to focus on where she thought he was, still fiddling with the belt. "If you're worried about someone rigging the house, aren't you concerned—"

"Truck's clear. Already checked." His hand settled over hers and clipped the seatbelt in place. "Hold on."

He'd already checked? And why did she need to...

Kent hit the gas, knocking her back in the seat. She reached for the frame as the vehicle spun beneath her, executing what felt like a full three-sixty and pinning her against the seat cushion. She braced one hand against the window, inhaling as the truck fishtailed a few times before finally straightening. She gripped the handle near her head, wishing like hell she could see—anticipate any other maneuvers he might spring on her in the hopes of keeping her stomach below her throat.

Kent didn't seem to have any issues with his stomach. He wasn't breathing hard like she was. Probably didn't have a death grip on the steering wheel. She knew her knuckles were most likely white, much like she suspected her face was. It wasn't that she had a weak stomach, but not being able to see what would happen next definitely messed with her equilibrium.

They traveled in silence for several minutes—Kent putting his truck through a couple more of those hard, full spins, before the rumble of the road slowed a bit. The energy around her calming ever so slightly.

She forced herself to swallow without gagging. "Anyone following us?"

Not that she thought anyone *could* follow them. Not with the way he'd been driving. The endless stunts he'd executed.

"Nothing so far. But..."

But he wasn't taking any chances. Wasn't letting up his vigilance.

She nodded, wondering if he even noticed. "So, where are we headed? Do you live nearby?"

A sigh, higher than she'd thought. Damn, the guy was big. "No. But even if I did, I wouldn't risk taking you there. Not when there's a chance they've made a connection between us. That they know my name. That I drove you home. Ice—Russel's wife, Harlequin. She has a loft not too far from here. She keeps it for when she has to come back to do assignments. She's a photographer. Russel tries to coordinate it with jobs so she isn't alone. I usually stay with them if I'm working out this way."

"You never told me what you do. I assumed it was some kind of…security."

God, she'd almost said mercenary. Because that's what immediately sprang to mind. All those strong, firm muscles she'd felt, and his obvious skill with a gun —being a hired soldier seemed like the logical conclusion. He'd killed the guy threatening her at the auction without pausing—still running toward her at a sprint. She'd heard his footsteps. He hadn't missed one.

"Pretty much. I work for a company called Brotherhood Protectors. We provide personal security for anyone who needs it."

She laughed. "You're a bodyguard?"

"You say that like it's a bad thing."

"Not bad, just…unexpected." Hell, if he'd said assassin or CIA, she would have been less surprised.

Kent chuckled. "What were you thinking? Spy?"

"Or a contract killer."

"Not sure how either of those would make me one of the good guys like I'd claimed, but… I hope the truth doesn't disappoint you."

"It's a nice surprise. And trust me, surprises rarely turn out that way for me."

"Ain't that the truth."

She paused. He'd had that tone, again. The same one she'd heard when he'd talked about not sleeping. The one that sounded as if it was torn out of him—had to scratch its way to the surface.

"So, are all of the people who work for this company ex-military?"

"Mostly Special Forces, to be honest. SEALs. Rangers."

"Christ. I bet you're busy. Who wouldn't want a MARSOC as their own personal security guard? So, Russel and your other buddy—"

"Sam, though folks call him Midnight."

She smiled. "They all work for the same place?"

"Helps if you have people you trust watching your back. I'm sure you know all about that. Had a partner you trusted."

A stab of pain through her head made her wince as she nodded, absently rubbing her temple.

"Hey? You okay?"

"Fine."

"You don't sound fine. And you winced."

He'd noticed her wince?

"It's nothing, just a pain in my head. I get them, sometimes." *As in every day since the raid.* She could practically hear him frowning.

"Anything in particular set them off?"

Breathing. "Mostly when I think about the raid that left me…" She waved her hand in front of her face. "The doctors call it retrograde amnesia. Like being blind isn't enough. I don't remember anything about that night, either. Only what I've been told. But yeah, I had a partner. His name was Will. Will O'Toole. He had my back from the first day I joined narcotics. Never once let me down. He...he died that night."

A swirl of air, then his hand landed on hers. Engulfing it. "I'm sorry."

"Me, too. Guess that means I was lucky."

"Funny how living doesn't always feel that way." More of the same, rough tone.

"Sounds like you have some experience."

"Some." He gave her fingers a squeeze. "Why don't you rest? We'll be there in about twenty."

"You want to focus on the road. On checking if we're being followed instead of making idle conversation."

"That obvious, huh? But you really should rest. You barely got any before I woke you up."

What she wouldn't give to be back in her house, snuggled in his lap. While she wasn't sure how long he'd held her, it was still the most relaxing rest she'd gotten since coming home from the hospital.

"Not tired." How could she be? Her heart was still pounding in her chest, her muscles still braced for any sudden shifting of the truck. "But it's okay. I'm fine just sitting here. I mostly talk to Blade, and he hasn't answered me, yet, so..."

She tried to chuckle, but it fell flat. Nothing like having her lonely, pathetic life put in the spotlight. Laid bare for all to see.

A sigh, then his fingers opened, slotted through hers and closed, again. "Addison."

"You're right. I should try to sleep."

She closed her eyes to give the pretense of resting. Anything to avoid the awkward atmosphere growing between them. She hadn't meant to sound as if she couldn't sit there without him carrying on a conversation. But her social skills had deteriorated since the raid, and it seemed everything she said, lately, just came out wrong.

That, or simply being near him short circuited her brain. Made it hard to focus on anything other than the warmth of his hand. The solid feel of it.

The miles droned on, marked by the steady hum of his truck. The slap of the wipers. She was just on the verge of actually dozing off when the truck rocked to a halt. He released her hand and touched her shoulder, jerking her back from the haze. She looked around for a moment, before remembering it wouldn't help, then focused on his side of the truck.

"We're here. I'm sure Harlequin has some clothes you could borrow. Get you out of that dress, not that you don't look stunning in it, but you'd probably prefer something that isn't soaked through. I'm sorry I didn't think to tell you to change, first, before you fell asleep."

She pushed her hand through her hair, wondering if she was sticking it up in every direction. "It's fine. Are you sure your friends won't mind us showing up in the middle of the night?"

"Nah. They probably just got home."

His door opened then closed, followed by hers. Like

before, he lifted her down, waiting until she was stable then leading her to some kind of elevator. She grabbed Kent's arm when it shuddered into motion, using his strength to keep from toppling over.

Kent muttered something then wrapped his arm around her waist, holding her close until the machine rumbled to a halt, and she heard the doors whoosh open. Another few steps, Kent punching in a code, and they were through a door and into his friend's apartment. She sensed a change in Kent the moment the door closed behind them. His muscles eased, and his grip on her waist loosened. He obviously felt safer here.

He stopped and shifted in front of her, one hand cupping her chin. "I'll go see if I can get some clothes, then we'll change, and I'll make you that tea I promised."

She smiled. "Do you even know how to make tea? You don't strike me as a tea type of guy."

"I could rig a bomb from what's under Harlequin's kitchen sink. Pretty sure I can figure out how to make a cup of tea."

She heard the smile in his voice. The lighter tone, and damn if the thought of him happy didn't make her smile, too. "Or you could let me…"

Another flash of light. Of the room just appearing out of the darkness. They were in a large, open area, a kitchen off to one side, living space to the other. Kent had his back to a hallway, his broad shoulders blocking most of her view—except for the silhouette poised behind him—arm extended. Ready to pounce.

She reacted on instinct. On years of facing shadowed threats. One step, and she had Kent shoved to the side. Had her hands up in front of her.

Another, and she'd grabbed the guy's wrist. Stepped into his attack. Had him off-balance and off to her right. A spin, a shift in her arm, and his elbow was locked beneath hers, his body bent forward. He grunted, but Kent was already at her side, gripping her shoulders.

"Easy, sweetheart. It's just Russel."

He was chuckling, just like the guy she had in the arm lock. She looked up, saw the way his eyes crinkled in humor—his incredibly blue eyes. Even with the lights out, there was enough of a glow coming from outside— street lamps or maybe the moon. Had it still been raining—there was no mistaking the stunning color. As if everything else was bleached into grays except his eyes. Even the scars running down his face didn't draw her attention. Didn't detract from the sheer beauty of him or the brilliant blue staring back at her.

She could *see* him.

She released her hold. Barely noticed the guy turning—standing beside Kent because she couldn't stare at anything other than *his* eyes.

Both men frowned, then those beautiful blue eyes narrowed. "Addison? Can you...see us?"

She tried to answer. Tried to make her lips move the way his had. Luscious full lips she wanted to taste. Feel slanted over hers because, in that instant, she realized *he* was the reason she was having flashes. Whatever was happening between them—some miraculous twist of fate. The kind she'd stopped believing in—it had jump-started her brain. Given her a reason to *want* to see, again, when she hadn't even known she'd been searching for one. Needing the promise of a future, of something bigger to push her past the never-ending darkness. Vanquish the demons lurking beneath her skin.

Then, it was gone. Nothing but unforgiving blackness. All that color extinguished with a blink of her eyes. Leaving her unbalanced. The world tilted beneath her feet, and she fell.

CHAPTER 9

Rigs lunged at Addison, catching her before she'd wobbled and crashed into a piece of furniture. He tugged her against him, one hand cupping her neck, the other around her waist. Her frantic breath washed over his chest, cooling his damp skin, not that he cared. He could be naked in a snow storm, and he'd still hold her. Cradle her in his arms if it meant calming her down. Helping ground her when she was obviously unstable.

She'd caught him off-guard—a rarity. One minute, they were talking, the next, she'd shoved him sideways and had Russel in some kind of arm lock. Rigs wasn't sure who was more surprised—him or Ice, because the other man's eyes widened. Then, he was laughing.

The tension had eased until Rigs had glanced at Addy. That's when he'd noticed the odd expression on her face. The way she was staring directly at him. A focused stare. Not like the searching gazes she'd had before. This one was narrowed in on his eyes, and he got the unnerving sensation of being watched.

She was looking at him. Actually *seeing* him. He knew it. He had the gut-wrenching realization that she could see his scars. That he hadn't covered them up, even told her about them, and now they were visible. On display just like they'd been back at the auction.

But she'd stumbled back and fallen off to one side before he could think of a way to explain. Not that he would have let her fall. Hit her head or worse. Didn't matter if he had to throw himself across the room. Leap over couches or walls—he'd always catch her.

Of course, all he'd had to do was reach out—pull her against him. Even Russel had made a move for her, the PJ in him kicking in. But Rigs had gotten to her, first. Grabbed her elbows and rested her head against his chest. Her hands instinctively splayed across his ribs, one landing right on top of some of his scars. Christ, could she feel them? Was the sensation as unnerving and new to her as it was to him?

He waited for her to recoil. Demand to know what was wrong with him. What he was hiding beneath his shirt. But she didn't move, other than to lean more fully against him. Press herself harder against the marks he'd feared she'd noticed.

One hand lifted to rest on the back of his neck, her nails scratching lightly against his skin. And bam, his dick was back to being a pipe between his legs. Hard. Demanding. No indication it was going down anytime soon. She had to feel it. She was completely flush against him, her groin lined up with his. Even with clothes on, his erection was notched against her mound.

Seeking the soft, warm flesh he knew hid beneath the dress.

Addison smiled against his chest then slowly eased free. He waited to see if she'd smirk or glance at his groin, even if she couldn't see it. Maybe comment on his condition.

Instead, she wrapped her arms around her ribs and turned toward Russel. "I'm sorry about the arm bar. I should have realized it was you. I mean, of course it was you. Who else would it be in the middle of the night? But... I got this sudden flash, saw your silhouette and reacted."

Ice smiled. "No harm done. In fact, I'm impressed. Few people get the jump on me, honey. Though, I was looking forward to knocking Rigs on his ass before he realized I was there."

Rigs snorted. "Not a chance, buddy. I heard you coming. I just wasn't concerned since I knew it was you."

"Fuck that. I didn't make a sound."

"Right. You keep telling yourself that, PJ."

"Marines." Russel exaggerated his sigh—probably for Addison's benefit—then gently brushed her hand, allowing her to orient herself to where he was standing. "You said you got a flash. Does that mean it's gone, again?"

She nodded, her shoulders drooping. "At least, this one lasted a few more seconds, but... I don't get it. Why it won't stay. I try to will it back, but..."

She bowed her head, and Rigs closed the step between them—took her in his arms, again. "We'll figure it out. But first, let's get you into some dry clothes, while I fill Ice in on what's happening. Why we crashed his house at four am."

"Thinking you could both use some dry clothes." Russel smiled. "Maybe ones that aren't black tie appropriate."

Rigs grunted. "We didn't get a chance to change out of them. Trust me, I didn't want to get dressed up in the first place."

"That's only because you spent most of your time with Midnight. No guy should look that good in a tux. Why don't you two head to the bathroom, and I'll bring you both some clothes? There are towels in the cabinet if you'd like to have a shower. Warm up a little."

Addison accepted Rigs' arm, smiling in Russel's direction. "Thanks. And sorry you're getting dragged into this."

"No apologies needed. Like I said at the auction, we take care of our own."

Addy nodded then followed Rigs to the main bathroom. He grabbed a couple of towels then helped dry her off, averting his gaze while he held the towel up for her as she undressed. He did his best to ignore the thud as the wet material hit the floor. The soft pad of her feet when she stepped out of it, then took the towel and wrapped it around her. Now, wasn't the time to think about how soft her skin felt as it brushed against his, or to admire the creamy tones highlighted by the gray cotton of the towel. How her blonde hair spilled across her shoulders, curling around her neck. Christ, she was beautiful.

Addy scrunched her nose up, tilting her head off to one side. "Do I want to know what you're thinking? Because I can sense the tension."

Of course, she could. She could probably tell he still had a boner, too. It felt so heavy, so fucking hard, that it most likely weighed the air down around it. Put out some kind of gravitational field.

"Honestly, I was thinking how beautiful you are, and that it took a year's worth of control not to sneak a peak at you while you were undressing."

She laughed, and his dick throbbed. God, the sound. All breathy and light, and it didn't take much to picture her in his bed, laughing and smiling in his arms after a few rounds of hot sex. Not that he was sure it'd be just sex because she made him want things he'd locked away. Given up on.

"Not like I would have known if you had."

Rigs took her hand. Held it gently in his. "No way. If I ever get the pleasure of seeing you like that, it'll be because you want me to. Because you want my hands on you as much as I do. Not because I'm a giant douchebag."

He cleared his throat, happy when Russel interrupted them as he gave Rigs some clothes. Because the way Addison was looking at him, now—all soft, sexy smile with her lips slightly parted. A tinge of blush on her cheeks. The kind she'd get after he'd claimed her mouth and kissed her. Tasted every inch of the skin along her neck and shoulders. It made his chest hurt. His heart pound painfully against his ribs.

"Would you like to have a shower? Warm up? I can

leave these clothes on the counter for you and wait outside."

That smile faded, and it was as if someone had flicked a switch. Drained all the light and happiness out of her. She ran a hand through her hair, tugging on the strands as if the action soothed the tension straining her muscles. "Thanks, but...we didn't get a chance to grab my cane. And without Blade..." Her lips pursed, and the skin over her nose bunched. "I *hate* this part. I can't even take a shower in a strange bathroom because I'm paranoid I might trip on something. Slip and fall getting in or out, or hit my head on a shelf I can't see. And all because my brain's fucked up. *I'm* fucked up."

Shit. How had he forgotten about her cane? Forgotten that she might not want to have to rely on him to simply move around. Walk from one room to another without ending up covered in bruises. While he didn't regret the decision to bug out in his truck—avoid what could have been a deadly situation—he could have been better prepared. Kept her cane on him—just in case. He was the one who'd fucked up.

She was right. One wrong turn and she'd smack her head on the shelf off to her left. Or slip trying to step over the tub, and he'd come back in to find her on the floor, her blood pooling beneath her. Not a chance. Not on his watch.

He closed the distance, took her hands and placed them on his chest. Right over his heart. Praying she didn't feel the edges of his scars. "Addison..."

"No, it's true. What Johnson said about it being all in my head." She tried to tug her hands free but gave up when he wouldn't release his hold. "There's nothing wrong with my eyes. No medical reason why I can't see. But no matter what I do, how much I try to force myself, I just can't..." She blew out a thick breath. "I'm crazy. It's that simple. And if you were smart, you'd think twice before jumping down this rabbit hole, because it's just like Wonderland in here. Nothing's the way it should be."

"Sweetheart, that doesn't make you crazy. It makes you human. No..." He stopped her from interrupting with a press of his finger across her soft lips—the ones he wanted to claim. Taste until his damn lungs gave out. "You're not the only one with demons. Or who's been hiding."

He sighed. He wasn't sure he was ready to tell her everything, but she deserved to know he wasn't all that sane, either. "I didn't leave the Marines because I wanted to. My last mission..." He choked back a curse. "I was part of a recon team. We'd been sent in early to scout the area—rig protection for the infiltration guys coming in behind us. But somehow, the insurgent cell knew we were coming. I saw the IED just soon enough to avoid being killed, outright. Got trapped under a collapsed wall in the midst of this huge firefight. Russel..."

He swallowed against the rush of emotion. Fuck, Ice had done more than just save Rigs' life. He'd given Rigs a second chance. Given him this night with Addison, and he'd brave a thousand IEDs to have this time with her. Stolen moments apart from the rest of the world.

"Kent, if this is too hard..."

"No. I just haven't told anyone, before. Never had anyone I wanted to tell. The few friends I have already know the story. Most of them were there. Anyway, Russel risked his life—his career—disobeyed orders and hauled my ass out of there. Took us two days to walk to a viable extraction point, with Russel pretty much carrying me the entire way. Bastard saved my life, and I'm not sure I've ever really thanked him for it. Been too angry to be thankful. Spent the past two years hiding, too. Trying hard to make peace with the fact I'll never be the man I was."

Rigs opened his mouth to include the part where he'd been hurt—had huge, disfiguring marks running up and down his face, his chest. But even as he willed the words to form, they got stuck in his throat. Lodged around the fear of her rejection. Of losing the precious few moments he might still have with her.

Instead, he watched as her head tilted back, those beautiful blue eyes searching his, even though he knew she couldn't see him.

She waited until he'd moved his finger. "Maybe not. But I can assure you that the man you are now…"

She smiled, and his damn heart did that jumping thing inside his chest. Leaving an ache he wasn't sure would ever go away. Not without her firmly rooted in his future.

She tapped him on the chest—over where it hurt to breathe. "I'd trust this man to have my back. And I haven't trusted anyone in a long time."

He swallowed. Fuck, the way she was looking at him. Maybe not *looking* looking, but that smile. Those eyes. The trust and joy, and damn, it sure as hell looked like more than just lust on her face. Which was ridiculous. They were still strangers, weren't they?

Russel's words from earlier looped in Rigs' head. His buddy had said he'd felt the same way about Harlequin. Hadn't been able to think clearly after one drink and a drive home. And damn if it wasn't the same for Rigs. Standing there, holding Addy in his arms, the terry rubbing on his forearms, her soft hair curling around his arms. She belonged there. Her hand on his arm. Whether she ever regained her sight, she belonged with him.

"Then, you'll believe me when I say that I'm not about to jump off this ride just because it gets a bit bumpy. So, you'd best get comfortable with me hanging around. I'm not going anywhere. Now, about a shower... If you'd like one, I can help you out with that. I promise to be a complete gentleman."

As much as he could while still sporting an erection. He'd managed to get it under control, but if she accepted—dropped the towel. Maybe let him soap her back—no doubt he'd be rock hard, again.

Who was he kidding? She could be dressed in a brown paper bag, and he'd still think she was the most desirable woman he'd ever held in his arms. Still want her with a need that should have scared him. Should have had him heading for his truck, and a one-way drive back to Montana.

Instead, he waited. Let her decide if she was ready to make herself vulnerable in front of him. Seducing her. Taking her to bed. That didn't compare to the intimacy of letting him care for her. Of holding her hand as she stepped naked into the shower. Trusting him to keep her safe when she had nothing to defend herself with. Despite her training, he had several inches and a good eighty pounds on her. And he wasn't too shabby in hand to hand, either.

Not that he'd ever hurt her. Hurt any woman.

Addison tilted her head, blind gaze still focused on him before she smiled. "Are you sure? You won't be able to avert your gaze *and* keep me safe. Might make your pants a bit...uncomfortable."

As if he wasn't already uncomfortable. Hadn't spent most of the night with his dick heavy and hard between his legs. Pressing against his fly until he thought the zipper would just bust apart.

"I said I'd be a gentleman. Not that I'd be unaffected, as you've already noticed. I'd apologize but..."

But he wasn't sorry. Wasn't going to hide the fact that she excited him on a physical level. Belay that...an atomic level because he was pretty damn sure it went beyond the usual five senses. That their attraction—the spark he'd felt back in the garden—was etched into their DNA. That it had been lying dormant, just waiting for him to bump into her. To start a chain reaction that he feared wouldn't end until his heart stopped beating. Though, even death didn't seem like an adequate barrier, right now.

Addison's smile widened. "Then, I'd love a hot shower. All I really need is a hand getting in and out—a breakdown of the layout so I don't give myself a concussion."

"You're not getting hurt on my watch. I thought I told you that already? As for the layout...there are some shelves on your left just past the tub, which is directly behind you, but as long as you just get in and out, you won't hit anything. And I sure as hell won't let you fall."

Did he imagine her inhaling? The increased flutter of her pulse near the base of her neck? Or the flush of pink that wove all the way to the top swell of her breasts?

But she broke eye contact before he could be sure. "Is there soap?"

Did her voice sound strained? The same, rough tone that was in his? He peeked inside the shower. "Soap. Shampoo. The works. I'll turn on the taps. Do you like it warm, hot or worthy of third-degree burns?"

"Slightly hot is fine."

He started the water, metering the temperature until he was sure it wouldn't scald her skin. Leave her anything but relaxed. Then, he arranged the bottles and soap so they'd be easier for her to reach without knocking over. All he had to do was help her over the ledge, then he could stand on the other side of the curtain—give her some privacy. Try to hold true to his promise of being a gentleman.

Then, he turned, and the gentleman in him vanished. Or maybe he exploded. Either way, nothing of that honorable guy remained. Not with Addison standing beside him—naked. No towel. Nothing but smooth, creamy skin. A light blush laced along her cheeks, with her golden hair cascading around her shoulders. Though, he had imagined how she'd look without that sexy black dress hugging her curves, his imagination hadn't done her justice.

The toned muscles complemented by soft curves. The way her nipples tightened against her breasts, sitting high on her chest. The light dusting of trimmed hair between her thighs, which didn't even hide the slightly swollen folds. Folds that gleamed in the light.

Christ, knowing she was wet. Wet for him…

Her brow furrowed, and some of the lightness in her expression dimmed. "Kent?"

Fuck. Here, she'd taken a risk. Stripped down, and all he'd done was stare at her. Tried to swallow past the huge lump in his throat. The one that was making it hard to breathe. To think. He didn't know if he wanted to shove her against the wall, sink into that tight heat, or run. Because this—*this* was real. Like one of her flashes, only it was a snapshot of the future. Of where they'd been heading to from the moment they'd met.

He had to say something. Anything.

"Fuck, you're stunning."

Shit…anything but that! He'd promised not to stare. At least, that had been the assumption when he'd said he'd be a gentleman, hadn't it?

She laughed, and just like that, the tension eased. The tight feeling in his throat loosened, finally allowing him to take a breath. Maybe get the right words out, this time.

"Come on. Your shower's waiting."

She held out her hand, and he took it. Twelve years in the Marines. Twelve years of dodging bullets. Of bleeding for the mission. Of the kind of training that would have killed a lesser man—had cast endless recruits out on their asses. And *not* tugging her against his chest—claiming that sexy mouth with the full pink lips. Lifting her up and sliding inside all that soft, warm woman… Hardest damn thing he'd ever done, short of walking away from her at the auction.

Christ, had that really just been a few hours ago? It felt like a different era. His life before Addison. The dark ages.

Addison moved with him. If being on display unnerved her, she hid it well. Other than the light blush, she seemed completely at ease. He, on the other hand, was sweating. He never sweated, unless he was working out. Wiring a bomb? Cool and collected. Getting shot at? Blown up? Still never felt this out of control. This unhinged. And all because of the tiny hand clasped in his. The one that held more power over him than he cared to admit.

She stopped with him at the edge, turning her head. "All clear?"

"Nothing but empty tub."

"Thanks. I won't be long."

"Take all the time you want." Besides, he needed time to get some oxygen back in his lungs. Some blood back in his other head. Not that he was sure waiting outside the curtain would allow either of those things to happen. But it beat standing there, faced with nothing but endless soft skin and luscious curves.

She lifted one leg, stepped inside, then placed the other. He released her hand just as she pivoted, and her foot slid out. Rigs wasn't sure how he ended up in the shower with her—her body cradled against his. Her frantic breath washing over his neck. If he'd jumped over the side or just willed himself there because all he remembered was seeing her start to slip. Hearing the squeak of her foot across the tub floor. Seeing the wide-eyed expression on her face as she'd teetered to one side. Then, he was there. Holding her. Thanking all those years of training. The reflexes he'd honed on the battlefield that had simply kicked in. Had him reaching for her before he'd even registered he needed to move.

Addison gasped, her hands splaying out across his chest. Damn, those scars. Right beneath her palm. She had to feel them. Raised. Unusually smooth. Tougher than his regular skin. The cotton did nothing to mask the marks.

Rigs sighed, tamping down the urge to let go—hide —because he wasn't putting her at risk. "Are you okay? Did you hurt yourself?"

She shook her head, wet strands of golden hair slapping against his shirt. "Mostly my pride. I'm not usually this clumsy. I don't even know how you moved that fast. I..."

He smiled against her head. "What good is having your own personal MARSOC bodyguard if I can't hold true to my promise and keep you safe?"

"I didn't realize I'd hired you as my personal bodyguard."

"Didn't have to. It's part of the package deal that came with driving you home."

"That doesn't sound like a viable business plan. But I'll accept." Her hands swept down his torso as she eased back, and he had to fight not to jerk away when her fingers followed the ridge of one of the scars. "Damn. Your clothes are soaked. I hope they're not ruined."

"Doesn't matter if they are. Never liked them."

Addy snagged her bottom lip, looked away, then sighed. "Well, since you're in here, and wet..." She reached for him, fingering the top button on his shirt.

Rigs reacted before he'd even thought it through—grabbing her wrists. Holding them firmly. "If I get naked, you're going to spend the rest of the shower with a part of my anatomy jabbing you in the hip. My pants are the only barrier keeping it tamed."

She smiled, and fuck if his dick didn't jerk against the fly, again. Threaten to do the job for her. But...if he got naked, she'd feel the scars. And not just through his shirt. It would be skin on skin. Completely bare. And what if she had one of her flashes while they were standing there? All of his demons exposed? There was no doubt he wanted her. Had already made peace with the fact she was his. Whether just in his mind, as friends or something more. Whether for only tonight or the next fifty years.

But taking the next step. Allowing her to see the real him—and she didn't need her eyes for that. He had no doubts she'd accomplish it with nothing more than a brush of her fingers and a tilt of her head—it scared him to the bone. The thought of her rejection. Of finally seeing the disgust he'd been anticipating since their first meeting shape her features. Rigs knew the only reason he'd had this time with her was because she couldn't see the ugly parts of him.

She tugged on her hands, and he forced himself to let go. Let her pop the first button free then move on to the next. Continuing down until the sides hung open. She only paused long enough to lift her hands back to his shoulders—shove the cotton over them. The shirt smacked against the tub, the wet sound straining every muscle.

"God, you're tense." She palmed his shoulders. Gave them a squeeze before her smile faded. Her head did that funny tilt thing as she stared up at his face. "If I read this wrong. If you'd rather just get out—"

"No." Fuck. He was screwing it up. Giving her the impression he wasn't interested, when all he wanted to do was shove his fingers into her hair and taste her mouth. Push her against the wall and thrust inside. Lose himself in her warmth. In her velvety skin. In the sweet scent of her arousal mixing with the humid air of the shower.

She raised her arms, and he knew she was going to touch his face. Cup each side with her thumbs stroking the corners of his mouth. Her right palm over the lines —the ones that stood out above his skin. The ones he couldn't hide.

He grabbed that wrist, again. Holding it just shy of touching his skin. "Addison, I…"

How did he explain without letting her in?

She drew her hands back, tugging on the one he held until he let go—let his damn arm fall to his side. "It's fine. You should probably get out before you completely ruin those pants. I should be okay, now. Thank you."

Fuck. Fuck. Fuck.

"I'll be just outside. Call me when you're finished."

She turned as he pushed the curtain aside, distancing herself as much as she could while essentially being trapped. It occurred to him, then, how brave she'd been. Unlike him, she couldn't simply retreat if the situation didn't go her way. She was bound to the small space. As much a prisoner of it as he was of his damn scars.

He didn't waste any time changing into the sweats Ice had left for him, gathering their wet clothes then heading for the door. She was washing her hair or something. He heard the heavy splashes of water. Smelled the rich coconut scent of the suds. If he wasn't such a colossal idiot, he could in there, right now. Her skin beneath his hands, her mouth pressed to his. She was offering him that. Everything he wanted.

And still, he'd managed to fuck it up.

Ice was in the hallway when Rigs popped out with the wet items bundled in his arms. The other man walked over, gesturing for Rigs to give him the clothes. "I'll hang these up to dry. You focus on Addison."

Rigs glanced into the small sliver of space still visible between the door and the frame. "She's...washing her hair."

Ice narrowed his eyes. "Are you okay?"

"Sure. Why wouldn't I be?"

"You seem...off. And trust me, that's saying a lot with respect to you. You're always off, but this is... different." He glanced at the slightly open door then groaned. "Shit. What did you do?"

"Excuse me?"

"Please. I'd thought the sexual tension was strong at

the auction, but the aura around you two standing in the living room was off the charts. Then, you slip into the bathroom. It's all easy banter echoing through the door, then the water's on. Sounds like you're both okay, then bam. You're out here, obviously wet from the shower, yet, she's still in there. And you've got that depressing funk around you, again. You'd lost that, by the way. When I last saw you at the foundation, it was gone. All thanks to Addison Bailey. But that funk is back. So, I'll ask you, again. What did you do to screw things up?"

"I didn't do anything, jackass. She slipped getting into the shower, so I lunged in after her. Got my clothes wet. That's all."

"If that was all, then you'd still be in there, holding her hand or her elbow. Fuck, washing her hair for her because the Rigs I know wouldn't leave her for a second. Not after she'd already tripped. Which means, you're running scared."

Shit. He hated that Ice saw through him. "Maybe I'm just not *that* guy."

"*That* guy?"

"The one you all seem to think is still alive inside me just waiting to burst free. The old Kent." Rigs shoved a hand through his hair, stilling the urge to punch it through the wall. Inflict the kind of pain that might make him forget about the woman in the shower. The one that was slowly stealing his sanity. The one he'd just alienated.

He raised his gaze to Ice's. "That guy's dead. Died in that rubble two years ago."

Ice stared at him, unblinking. No emotions on his face until even Rigs wanted to break eye contact. Then, his buddy nodded and turned, covering half of the hallway before glancing back at him. "You're right. The old Kent is gone. But, so what? I'm not the same guy, either. Harlequin's made me a far better man than I ever was in the service. And not because she changed me. More because I stopped pretending I was happy being alone. That there wasn't a hole inside me I couldn't fill. The Air Force couldn't fill. But she did. Without even trying. And all I had to do was let her."

He turned, again, started walking.

"She tried to touch my face."

Russel stopped, dropped the bundle on the floor then spun, slowly making his way back. "Talk to me."

Rigs sucked in a quick breath. God, why was it so fucking hot in the loft? Made it hard to breathe. To think. To calm the sudden pounding of his heart.

Russel grabbed his head then shoved it down. "Easy, buddy. Breathe. Brace your hands on your knees so you don't pass out on me."

He palmed his legs, closing his eyes against the rush of vertigo. "I never pass out."

"Right. And my hands don't shake when I picture Harlequin in danger. Remind myself there could still be a bounty on her head."

"No way anyone's getting past you."

"Doesn't mean the thought doesn't chill me to the bone, brother. Haunt my dreams because there isn't life without her. Period. So, explain what happened. Addison nearly falls, you lunge in and…"

"And I'm holding her. She suggests that since I'm already in the shower and wet…"

Russel chuckled. "Girl's got some moves. I knew I was going to like her straight off. So…"

"She manages to get my shirt off—without touching the scars—but she can sense I'm tense. Thinks I'm not interested. I try to correct her, but then she reached for me and… Fuck, I couldn't stop myself. Had her wrist in my hand, just hovering above that side of my face. I tried to let go. Explain but…" He blew out a rough breath. "She distanced herself after that. Told me she could finish on her own."

"Does she know?"

"Know what? That I have horrible disfiguring marks crisscrossing my face and chest? Hasn't come up in conversation, yet."

"Rigs—"

"Don't. Don't lie to me like Midnight does. Like everyone does and tell me they aren't that bad. That people don't see them because I just spent an entire night listening to people *not* react to my face."

"Okay. Let's be honest, then. You're right. You have scars, and yeah, they're noticeable. But we're not lying when we say *we* don't see them because we don't. Never have. I see the man who saved the unit I was scouting with when we damn near walked into an ambush. The guy who took three bullets for the woman I love. Who would have gotten on her damn bike and bled out trying to follow her. *That's* the guy I see. And I'm pretty damn sure that's what Addison would see if you gave her the chance. The man who saved her life. Who didn't treat her like she was less of a teammate. Who's kept her safe all night. It's all perspective. But only you can give her that chance."

"I want to. God, the whole time I was standing there, all I wanted was to kiss her. Feel those small hands on me. But… What if I don't know how?"

"Letting go's tough. Living a lonely, bitter life is tougher. Choose your hard, bro. Then embrace it. You were always good at that."

"I knew I wasn't going to like your answer."

"Never said you would."

CHAPTER 10

ADDISON STOOD BENEATH THE SPRAY, listening to Kent's footsteps pad across the room—something he'd done on purpose, she suspected. Letting her hear him. She waited until they were gone, then braced one hand against the side of the shower. Dread threatened to empty her stomach right there on the shower floor. The one she wished would open up and swallow her, because there was no way she could face Kent or his friends, again. Not after throwing herself at him, only to end up on the awkward side of rejection.

God, how had she read the situation so wrong? Sure, she couldn't *see* his reactions. Hadn't been able to judge his desire by his eyes. But she'd felt it. More than once. He'd been hard. And she was sure she'd heard his breathing speed up. Felt his heart kick against her palms when she'd touched his chest. Every other sense suggested that he wanted to touch her as much as she wanted to be touched. He'd basically said as much.

Except that he'd grabbed her hands—prevented her

from palming his face with every intention of tiptoeing up and finally tasting his mouth. The glimpse she'd gotten of full lips and stubbled jaw had only heightened her desire to kiss him.

A shiver ran down her spine, and she turned off the water. No sense wasting it when it wouldn't do any good. Wouldn't truly warm her up or ease the stress bunching her muscles. That was the worst part. She couldn't even leave. Without her cane or Blade, there was no way to discretely go. Maybe if she was familiar with the layout of the loft, she could chance groping her way to the door, but as it was, she was completely dependent on *him*.

Pain flared in her chest. This was why she kept to herself. Only put her trust in Blade. The reality was— people viewed her as a burden. A lifelong contract that required 'round-the-clock care. And no man in his right mind would willingly sign up for that. Kent had been better than most, but he wasn't stupid.

She had to end this. Get him to call her a cab and go…somewhere. Carl would let her stay the night— cover the taxi ride for her. She'd have to wake him up, but that was better than staying here. With Kent.

Another shiver, and she slowly shifted sideways, sweeping her hand out in front of her as she went. It only took a few steps to find the counter—the pile of clothes Russel had given Kent. What felt like yoga pants, a long-sleeved shirt, and a sport's bra and panties. Despite being summer, the air was cool, and she couldn't quite stop the shivers from trembling through her.

A knock, then a slight creak of the door.

"Addison?"

She smoothed her hands down the front of her clothes, hoping she hadn't put anything on backwards or inside out. Her hands shook a bit, and she made a conscious effort of gathering the emotions still churning inside her and shoving them down. It should have been easy. She'd been doing it all her life. Growing up in a family of police legacies, it had been bred into her. Not to mention all the upheaval she'd been through over the past few years. Then, she felt the air move, his body shuffle in beside her, and just like that, everything welled up, again.

The realization hit her hard, as it always did. She was *blind*. Until these flashes became permanent. Until they lasted more than a fraction of a second, she was still lost in the darkness, relying on others to help her simply exist. To get from one place to another. Everything she'd done without thinking—going from room to room. Driving to the store. Having a fucking life—required preparation and conscious effort. Having Blade had helped. Had lessened the overwhelming sense of loss she'd felt every moment of every day since the raid.

Except for the past several hours with Kent. He hadn't made her feel as if she was less. He'd been nothing but supportive. Had made her feel a bit like her old self. Independent. Strong. Maybe that's why his rejection hurt so much. She'd been starting to visualize a future with more than just empty days strung together. One with *him* in it, only to realize it was like the flashes she was having—lies her brain was telling her.

Addison cleared her throat. She needed to hold it together long enough to get out of there. "Is there anything I might trip over on the floor?"

"All clear." God, even his voice sounded awkward.

"And the hallway back to the living room? How far?"

"Addison, I can—"

"How far?"

Was it possible to feel someone else's displeasure? Their frustration? Because she was certain it changed the air around her. Weighed it down.

"Ten feet to the door. Another ten to the corner. Turn left and the living room is on your right. The kitchen off to your left."

She nodded then struck off, hands braced to either side. It sounded so simple. All she had to do was walk and count her steps. Easy. Except where she never knew if she was going in a straight line. All it took was a slight angle, and she'd walk into the door. Or the wall. Maybe clip her hip on the corner. And she'd fall, like she'd done a thousand times since waking up into the darkness.

Another shift of air, and a creak. He'd opened the door more for her before she smacked into it and looked like a fool.

She stopped, feeling completely disoriented. Somehow, she'd lost count when he'd rushed past her. And now, all she could do was stand there—try not to panic. She hadn't felt this way since before she'd gotten Blade. God, how had she not realized how much she'd come to depend on him? And he'd nearly died because of her.

"I'm sorry, I forgot your cane. You're two feet away from the door, now, if that helps."

She nodded but couldn't move. Couldn't seem to get her feet to start walking. Despite his directions, she couldn't picture it. Couldn't do anything other than stand there and breathe.

He was beside her, again. "Addison. About the shower…"

She shook her head. She couldn't go there. Couldn't hear him apologize for not wanting her when she still had to face his friends. Find a way to convince them to call her a cab. "It's fine. *Fine.*"

"It's not what you think. I—"

"Addison?" A woman's voice. "We haven't met, yet. I'm Harlequin."

Addy drew a deep breath, tried to focus on where she thought Harlequin was standing. "You're married to Russel."

Harlequin laughed, and there was a shift in the air that settled next to her. "Yeah."

Addison arched a brow. "Doesn't he ever leave your side?"

"Not often."

"Whoa." Russel's deep voice next to Harlequin. "How the hell did you know I was here? I didn't make a sound, this time. I'm sure of it."

"I didn't hear you. The air…changes the more people there are. It gets heavier, for lack of a better description." She sighed. "I know. It sounds crazy. Seems to be the norm for me, lately."

A hand cupped hers. It was Russel's. Too large to be

Kent's, not to mention the way he held her fingers in his
—it *felt* wrong. "No one thinks you're crazy. Actually,
that's very impressive."

"There's got to be the odd perk for being like…" She
waved her other hand in front of her eyes. "…this."

A sigh. Heavy. But she couldn't tell if it came from
Russel or Kent. Maybe both of them.

Russel placed the end of a rod in her hand. "This
isn't a cane, but Harlequin thought it might help. We
shortened one of our tent poles. It'll even fold if you
want it to. Thought it might make you feel less dependent on everyone here."

They'd made her a cane?

She squeezed her fingers around the smooth surface,
swallowing against the thick feeling in her throat. She
didn't even know Russel or Harlequin. Had shown up in
the middle of the night. Maybe even inadvertently
involved them in something dangerous. Yet, they were
treating her like family. And all because of Kent. An
extension of brotherhood.

Addy gripped the makeshift cane. "That was
extremely considerate. Thank you. How far to the
corner, again?"

"Twelve feet. Turn left. Once you're in the living
room, it's seven feet to a chair that's off to your right on
a forty-five. Or you can go left and sit at the kitchen
counter, if you'd prefer. Same distance and angle."

Must be a military thing. Being able to describe the
surroundings so accurately. Seeing as both Russel and
Kent didn't have any problems giving her directions.
Helping her visualize the space. Though, she hadn't

missed that Kent had remained quiet. While she knew he was still next to her, he'd vanished, again.

She swept the cane in front of her then stepped forward. The pole wasn't quite the same feel, but it did the job, and she made it to the corner without banging into anything.

"Kitchen or living room, honey?"

She stopped and drew herself up. She suspected they wouldn't like her request, but it beat spending the rest of the night wondering what Kent was thinking. If he'd told his buddy about her awkward play for him in the shower.

"Actually, I was thinking… It's the middle of the night, and after everything that happened, the last thing any of you need is more drama. If one of you could just call me a cab, I'll go to Carl's place. I should have just asked Kent to drop me off there instead of coming here in the first place, but I wasn't thinking clearly. And don't worry. I'll call my captain in the morning. I'm sure he'll send a couple of officers over to check out my place—secure it. There's no need for all of you to get involved. Especially if this turns out to be anything other than a simple burglary."

Had Kent just growled? She wasn't sure, but he'd made a noise that had sounded like his truck's throaty engine revs. And had the room gotten colder? Which seemed strange because she'd always equated anger to heat, yet, it definitely felt colder, and there was no doubt Kent was angry. The energy around him had changed the moment she'd mentioned leaving—as if the molecules of air were moving faster. Banging into her at an increased rate. Which should have made her warmer instead of the shiver that raced down her spine.

Then, Kent's hand clutched hers. "We're not calling you a cab, and you're not going to Carl's. The guy was barely holding it together, earlier. No way he's equipped to deal with any kind of threat against you. I promised I'd keep you safe, and letting you wander off, alone, after just fleeing your house because someone infiltrated it, isn't a viable plan."

He shuffled forward, the warmth of his body heating hers, and she suspected he was only a few inches away. "Besides, we both know this isn't because you don't want us to get involved. It's because I acted like an utter ass in the bathroom. Please, sit down. We'll talk. Figure out what's going on because I find it hard to believe it's a simple coincidence that someone showed up at your house only hours after you were nearly killed at the auction."

She frowned. "I never asked you to protect me, and I don't see how the two incidents could be connected."

"I told you—it was a package deal. And I don't go back on my promises. As for the two threats on your life... I don't believe in coincidences. Not when they carry AKs and sneak into your house. This whole situation makes my skin tingle, and not in a good way." He squeezed her hand. "Please, Addison. Stay. Maybe Russel can help shed some light into why you're having flashes, now."

She tugged on her hand, crossing her arms when he finally released her. "Don't you mean flashbacks? That's what you think they are. What my colleagues think. Memories of that night."

"I never said they were flashbacks."

"You didn't have to. I'm blind, not deaf. I heard it in your voice. The concern. The hint of disbelief. I get it. I wouldn't believe me, either. Not after spending eighteen months without any kind of sign that I was getting my sight back. All of this happening, now... Seems too much of a stretch to think you bumping into me would trigger it."

Silence. Complete silence. None of them were breathing. Were moving. It was like another snapshot, only this one of an empty dark room. She hadn't meant to reveal that last part. And now, all she could do was stand there and wait for the fallout.

A small swirl of air on her other side. Russel. "Your first flash was tonight when Rigs bumped into you? No wonder you're so off-kilter. It's obvious that after all that time, you've started adjusting. Honing your other senses. Having your body make those compensations then suddenly throwing sight back into the mix..." Russel whistled. "Talk about sensory overload. I'm impressed you haven't been knocked on your ass by it. You've described them as snapshots. How long do they usually last?"

"It varies anywhere from a couple of seconds to maybe ten. Just long enough to freak me out. Make me dizzy." She let her head bow forward as she toed at the floor. "That's if they're even real."

"You saw me. Were able to put me in an arm lock."

"Did I? Was it really you or did I just get lucky, and it

was nothing more than a replay of some takedown I did years ago? Do you know how many guys I've had jump out of the shadows at me? And I've faced my share of gangs like at the auction. It's part of working in narcotics. Raids are a norm. So, maybe everyone's right. Maybe this is nothing more than my brain playing tricks on me. My own personal movie of my life's work. Maybe I'm not regaining my sight. I thought it was real, but now…"

Russel squeezed her hand. "It's real, Addison. The men I've rescued who've experienced these symptoms all feared the same thing. Not that I'm discounting the possibility that you're also experiencing flashbacks. That's a common symptom of PTSD. But these visual snapshots are definitely a good sign."

"But…why now? And why is it so transient?"

"I'm not a doctor, but it sounds like it might be a survival mechanism. When you're in danger, your self-preservation kicks in and overrides the hold your brain has. Allows the signals to get through—be interpreted."

She snorted. "I hardly think Kent bumping into me put me in mortal danger. I've bumped into lots of things since I woke up."

"I'm sure you have, but this was a person grabbing you from behind. Even though Rigs wasn't going to hurt you, your cop instincts might have primed you to fight, and bam, you see. Then, you realize you're okay, and it's gone, again."

Addison shifted on her feet, the weight of everyone watching her making her restless. "If that's the case, then why the hell didn't it kick in before Blade got shot?

143

When that asshole grabbed me by the hair and said I was the one? When I heard the click of the bastard's AK? Why didn't my stupid survival instincts allow me to see when it would have actually done me some good?"

Movement. Kent closing any distance between them. "That guy grabbed you? Told you he was targeting you?"

A twinge of pain flared in her head. Stealing her breath for a second, before she narrowed in on Kent's voice. He'd asked her a question, but it was suddenly hard to focus. "What?"

"You just said that the man Blade attacked grabbed you. That he said you were the one."

Kill her, too...

She jerked her head to the side, searching for the echoed voice. "Who said that?"

Kent's grip tightened. "Are you okay?"

She focused in his direction. "I...I'm sure I mentioned it before. When we were talking to the SWAT leader."

"You never said anything about that creep grabbing you, first. Talking to you. I thought Blade went after him when he came around the corner at you."

"You must have missed it. I've been giving reports for years. I don't forget those kinds of details. I..."

The whole place is gonna blow. She won't survive.

She twisted, again. Who the hell was talking? She didn't sense anyone else there, but she'd definitely heard voices.

"Addison? Sweetheart, is something wrong?"

"No, I... It doesn't matter. It doesn't change

anything. Doesn't explain why I can't *fucking* see. Why I saw a man with a gun when you said no one was there."

"Easy. We'll figure it out. It's all going to be okay."

"No, it's not." She tugged free of his hand. "I can't do anything. I can't take a shower without nearly falling. I can't walk down a hallway without a damn makeshift cane. I can't even remember important details. If I were half as strong as I think I am, I would have kicked this long ago."

She took a few stumbling steps back, another stab of pain pounding through her temples. "Instead, I let my partner get shot. Put him at risk. If he hadn't been focused on me, on my safety, on stopping the bleeding, he would have seen that bastard draw. And he'd still be alive."

Hurried footsteps, then Kent gripped her arms, steadied her. "Blade is still alive. He was shot, not you." He gave her a gentle tug. "Come on. I think you should sit down."

"No." She shook her head, pulled free, more images playing across her mind. "He never should have tried to save me. Turned his back on them. He didn't have to die."

A pulse of light and the room exploded into view. The glare from the iron wrought lamps on the brick walls. The two men standing in front of her, brows furrowed. Mouths pinched tight. Harlequin stood behind them, a curtain of auburn hair surrounding a pretty face. Both she and Russel had stunning green eyes, a noticeable contrast to Kent's blue.

Then, the room switched. The brick turned to old

slatted boards as the floor faded into worn linoleum. Smoke curled through the air, the ghostly echo of gunfire popping in the distance. A sweet fragrance surrounded her as a shadow moved into view, a dark hoodie obscuring the person's face. Nothing visible but a flash of white teeth and the glint of a gun.

Another blur and she was on her knees, pain throbbing through her head. Making the room spin. She couldn't talk. Could barely breathe. Voices sounded in the background. Men shouting. Shots ricocheting. Will pleading with her to hold on. Not to die. She saw his blood mix with hers. Felt the weight of his body crush her into the floor. Then darkness.

CHAPTER 11

"ADDISON!"

Kent went to his knees, resisting the urge to pull her into his arms as Ice followed him down. His buddy reached for her neck—checking her vitals, though all Kent saw was the pale hue of her skin. The painful grimace on her face as she faded into unconsciousness.

Ice sighed. "She's okay. But let's move her into the spare room, and I'll do a quick evaluation, just to be sure."

Kent bent over her, scooping her up then curling her into his chest. Her head fell against his shoulder, a soft groan nearly taking him back to his knees. Just thinking about her in pain constricted his chest. Made his vision dim at the edges.

He shuffled her closer, hoping his body heat would soothe any lingering images that might still be playing inside her head as he made his way down the hall, nudging open the door then marching over to the bed. He waited while Harlequin pulled back the sheets, then gently placed Addy on the mattress. He brushed her hair away from her face, stilling the need to cup her jaw. Draw his fingers along her skin and smooth out the crease between her brows.

Instead, he stepped back—let Russel take his place. His buddy placed a bag on the floor next to him, then took out some instruments, running through a variety of checks. Russel mentioned what each one was, but all Kent heard was the ghostly echo of Addy's anguished cry as she fell to her knees, palming her head as if it might fly apart.

How many times had that been him? On his knees, memories looping through his mind. Sweat beading his body as he fought to find his way back—separate the past from the present. He didn't know what demons haunted her, but after what she'd told him in the truck —the words she'd mumbled before passing out—he'd bet his ass she'd witnessed her partner die. That there was much more to that raid than a simple takedown gone wrong.

"Rigs."

He blinked then focused on Ice. "Yeah."

"You okay?"

"Fine."

"You sure? I called your name a few times."

He pursed his lips. "How's Addison?"

Ice watched him for a few more seconds then motioned to Addy. "Her vitals are stable. Pupils equal and responsive. No obvious external wounds, and no evidence she sustained internal injuries tonight. Looks like she just passed out."

"People don't just pass out, Ice. We both know that. And it doesn't' take your level of training to recognize a damn flashback. Had enough of my own to know she wasn't here with us when she went to her knees. Not to mention that she was obviously hearing voices."

Ice sighed, checking Addy's forehead one more time before rising. "Did you get a chance to ask her about this raid she keeps mentioning? The one that put her in the hospital. Blinded her."

"Not yet. But she told me her partner died that night."

"Shit. Which probably means she witnessed it."

"I'm thinking there might be more to that night than a botched mission. The kind of memories that would put her on someone's shit list should she ever recover them."

"You still think these two incidents are connected, don't you?"

"It was just a feeling before. But now? What better way to hide a murder than during a high-scale robbery? No one would have thought twice if she'd been killed."

"But when she fights back...we step in, whoever's behind this has to change tactics. Sends someone to her place to make it look like another burglary gone wrong. Only, you're there..."

"Whatever it is, I can't shake the feeling that this is just the beginning. That she's being hunted."

"That's good enough for me. I'd bet my life on your intuition any day." Russel gathered his supplies, picked up his bag then stepped back. "Any chance you were followed here?"

"Seriously? You're asking *me* that?"

Russel chuckled. "Just being vigilant. Why don't you get some rest? Addison needs to sleep, and there isn't much we can do until morning. I'll call Sam. And Hank. Thinking we could use some additional support."

"You expect me to sleep? In a place I haven't secured with probable tangos on my ass and Addison's life on the line?"

"Kent. The loft *is* secure." Russel held up his hand, cutting off Rigs. "I know you don't see any building that isn't wired to explode if someone breathes on the perimeter as being safe, but Harlequin had measures in place long before I came along. And I've added to them. We're safe enough you can rest."

Kent focused on Addison. At how still she looked lying beneath the sheets, her skin too close to the white hue of the linen. It didn't take much to picture her dead, just like he'd done at the auction.

Russel's hand landed on his shoulder. "I'll personally stand watch."

Kent snapped his attention to Ice's. "You're tired, too."

"I didn't have to fend off another attack. Worry about the woman I love more than once tonight."

"I just met Addison. I don't—"

"You *do* know it's not polite to lie to my face, right? Because I've been where you are. And I'm man enough to admit Harlequin had me the moment she smiled. Just took my head a while to catch up with what my heart knew. Regardless, you watched over us when I needed a break. Now, it's time to let me watch over you."

Russel nudged him when he simply stood there, alternating his gaze between the two of them. "I bet Addy would appreciate the support. Even passed out, she'll know you're there. Will probably sleep better."

Rigs chuckled. "I don't recall you being this good at negotiating."

"Have you met my wife? I have to use every skill at my disposal to win an argument."

"It's not that I don't want to. It's just…" He sighed. "You'll keep watch?"

"Promise."

"I guess a few hours wouldn't hurt."

Russel smiled then slapped him on the shoulder. "I'll check in later."

Rigs waited until Ice had shut off lights and closed the door before stripping down to a tee and boxers. He considered losing the shirt, as well, but couldn't get his hands to fist the hem—pull it over his head. Then, Addison groaned, and he rounded the bed. The covers billowed up as he slipped beneath them, spooning into her back. She sighed then burrowed against him, shifting his hand off her hip and onto her rib cage before her fingers settled on top. Her heart kicked against his palm, the steady beat easing the tension in his muscles.

He closed his eyes, listening to the soft whisper of breath. The rustle of cloth as she moved beneath the blankets, rubbing against him, again, then drifting off. Her hair fell across his arm, the soft strands tickling his flesh. If he hadn't freaked out in the shower, he'd know how the silky mass felt bunched in his hands. Wrapped around his fingers as he claimed her mouth. Tasted her skin. She'd offered him everything he'd been hoping for, only to have him bolt. Have his demons ruin the best thing to walk into his life since Ice had given it back to him.

Then, she'd wanted to leave. It had taken every ounce of Rigs' training not to barricade the door. Hell, blow up the damn elevator shaft so she couldn't put herself at risk. And all because he'd been an ass. Not that Rigs blamed her. He'd have done the same thing in her place. Gotten out of Ice's loft as quickly as possible. Never looked back. But just the thought of her out there —alone—made him see red. He didn't know what kind of danger she was in, but he was damn sure the attempts on her life wouldn't stop until they'd either unearthed who wanted her dead, or the bastard had succeeded.

The thought had him pulling her tighter against his chest. Wrapping his arms more fully around her. Ice would guarantee no one snuck in while Rigs was sleeping. He had to trust in that. Get some rest while he had the chance because he wasn't leaving her side until he could guarantee her safety.

A part of him suspected that day would never come. That the only way she'd remain safe was with him at her side. That he'd do everything in his power to stay right where he was—Addison nestled in his arms. And all he had to do was let her in. Let her see the real him, scars and all.

He groaned inwardly. He didn't have a clue how to do that. How to push aside two years' worth of conditioning. To quiet the voices in his head. Russel was right. Addy had obviously been through a lot. Had suffered similar trauma. Surely, she'd understand if Rigs just grew a set and explained. Allowed her to touch him...

He closed his eyes. Nothing was going to happen, now. She needed to sleep, not have him waking her up because he couldn't stay still. Because his brain couldn't accept the fact she might not see him the way he feared everyone did. That the only thing keeping them apart was his own fear.

The room slowly faded, the warmth of her body pulling him under until she twitched, a muted groan rousing him. He snapped awake, cursing silently when he jostled her, taking her halfway up with him before realizing and gently lowering her back to the mattress. Light streamed in through the windows, the shadows stretching across the floor suggesting it was well past sunrise.

He scrubbed a hand down his face. He couldn't remember the last time he'd slept more than a few hours in a row without waking up in a cold sweat, ghosted gunfire echoing inside his head. Yet, here he was, more rested than he'd been in years, and all because of the woman still sleeping beside him. The one with the adorable pout as she turned toward his side of the bed, looking as if she was searching for him.

Rigs reclaimed his spot, gathering her in his arms, again. She huffed then switched positions, placing her head in the crook of his shoulder as her hand palmed his chest—right over one of the large raised welts running down his torso. He fought the urge to grab her wrist—shift it over to his sternum. If he had any hope of bridging the gap he'd caused, he needed to stop sabotaging her every attempt to touch him. Because... Damn.

Feeling her fingers flex against his body made his pulse race as if he'd just run a fifteen-mile course with his unit. Blood pounded in his ears, and the air heated around him, making him pant. All that from nothing more than her hand on his chest. How the hell would he cope with actually kissing her? Tasting her then sliding inside all that warm wet arousal he'd scented in the shower?

And he wanted to. Wanted to roll her over, kiss her awake. Beg her to give him another chance then lose himself in her curves. It the smooth press of her skin against his. He'd bedded his share of women, but he'd never experienced this level of burning need. As if he was suddenly aware of a hole deep inside him only she could fill.

Her hand shifted slightly, and it was as if he'd been prodded by an electrical shock. Tingling awareness shot down his spine, once again, spiking his dick against his boxers. Damn, would there ever be a time when he wasn't in a constant state of arousal around her? When he could temper the heat searing his skin with every tiny brush of her fingers? When he could think beyond the color of her skin, and how it would look pressed against his?

He'd trained hard to learn how to focus. How to shut out anything not involved with the mission to some hidden part of his brain. Locked away until he had time to re-examine it. But there was something about Addison Bailey that by-passed his regular responses. That cut through to the man beneath the soldier. To Kent.

And damn if he didn't want to be Kent for her. Rigs was hardened. Battle worn. Any hope of love or happiness long trained out of him. But Kent—the small part of him that she'd awakened—clung to the notion he might have stumbled upon the one person who could offer him a new future. One in which he didn't have to hide. Where the man he was, now, was enough.

"No."

Rigs snapped his gaze down to her, frowning at the grimace shaping her lips. Her voice had sounded strained—the same pleading tone she'd had when she'd insisted she'd seen an armed man behind them. The one he hadn't found. That had nearly killed him to admit to her.

He tightened his hold, running one hand up and down her arm. She quieted for a moment, then gasped and bolted upright—blankets flying. Her arms shooting out to the sides. He rose with her, cupping her elbows as he tried to steady her. She cried out, elbowing him in the ribs before scrambling for the edge of the bed.

He jumped off his side, catching her before she'd tripped trying to shift to her feet. "Easy, Addison. It's me."

Her heavy breathing filled the air as she tugged against his hold before stilling. Strands of hair angled across her face, the golden color shining in the sunlight. "Kent?"

"That's right, sweetheart." He shifted closer, letting her feel his body heat. "You passed out last night. Do you remember?"

She shook her head, blonde hair bouncing about her shoulders.

He took a moment to tuck the soft tresses behind her ear. "We're in Russel and Harlequin's spare room. You're safe."

Her head swiveled, her sightless gaze scanning the room before she sighed, no longer fighting against his hold. "It's morning?"

"Closer to noon, I think. Seems we both needed some sleep."

Her eyebrow arched as she focused on him. "We... we slept together?"

"We shared the same bed. But I didn't... I mean, you were unconscious, and I..."

"Understood. And I didn't mean to imply you were the kind of guy to..." She waved her hand at the bed. "I was just...surprised you'd relaxed your guard enough to actually sleep. You seemed...agitated last night."

"Armed men are actively trying to kill you. I'm more than agitated. But Ice said he'd stand watch, so..."

She nodded, slowly sinking back onto the bed. Rigs settled in beside her, still holding one elbow. Not because she needed his support, but because he couldn't get his damn fingers to loosen. Couldn't make himself let go of her soft smooth skin. Not with the scent of warm woman surrounding him. With her hair perfectly tousled after spending the night in his arms.

Addison glanced on where he held her then raised her gaze to his, her head tilting slightly to one side. "You said I passed out?"

He forced his hand back to his side. Fuck, focusing on anything other than how badly he needed to touch her shouldn't be this hard. Shouldn't mess with his head to the point he had to remind himself she'd asked him a question. "When we were talking. You...got upset then passed out. But Ice made sure you were okay. Seems you just needed some rest after everything that had happened."

She snorted. "You don't have to try and spare my feelings, Kent. I had a flashback, didn't I?" She waved her hand at him. "It's okay. I never said I *didn't* have them. It's just..." She blew out an exasperated breath, looking down at her hands clasped in her lap. "Maybe that *is* what's happening. Maybe I really am crazy and none of this is real."

"Addison."

She tugged free then stood, taking a couple of steps away. Rigs darted over, shoving a chair out of the way before she bumped into it and gave herself a concussion. Addison stopped, frowning at the scrape of furniture across the floor.

"See!" She wrapped her arms around her waist. "Living in the dark is one thing. Having these flashes— wondering if I'm losing my mind..."

He stepped into her, palming her back and tugging her close when her hands rose to his chest. He fought the instinctual response that had him tensing his muscles. Preparing to retreat. "We'll figure this out. Promise."

She tilted her head back, brushing her lips across his chin in the process. He clenched his jaw, forcing his lungs to keep drawing in air as she stared at him—her sightless eyes searching his. Fuck, she was so damn beautiful. So close. All he had to do was dip his head— slide his mouth over hers.

She'd welcome his touch. It was there in the way her breath caught. In how she dampened her lips, leaving them slightly parted. Inviting him to kiss her. One move, and he'd be right where he wanted to be.

Then, she raised her hand—smoothed her fingertips across his scars—and he couldn't stop the involuntary flinch. The sharp intake of his breath.

Addison froze. Hand barely touching his cheek, her weight shifted onto her toes as her mouth hovered next to his. The muscle in her jaw flexed, then she retreated. Taking a healthy step back. Isolating herself as much as she could.

Shit.

Rigs stared at her, his body primed, the voices in his head hammering at him, when she cleared her throat.

She made a point of looking past him as she wrapped her arms around herself, again. "I appreciate all you and your friends have done, but I really think I should go."

He opened his mouth to protest—to fucking explain —when a sigh sounded off to his left. He turned to find

Ice leaning against the doorway, his gaze skipping between them.

Russel stared at Rigs for a moment then focused on Addison. "It's not you, Addy."

She startled, twisting until she was facing both of them. "Russel?"

"Kent isn't uninterested. He's afraid to tell you the truth. That you won't understand."

"Understand what?"

Rigs grabbed his clothes and shoes off the floor, yanking them on as he stared at Russel. "For fuck's sake, Ice, shut up."

Ice glared at Rigs, pushing off the frame then stepping into the room. "Not this time. You want to hate me for dragging your ass out of that rubble? Fine. You want to alienate yourself—take only the jobs that keep you isolated? I won't interfere. But I'll be damned if I stand here and let you ruin the best thing to ever happen to you. Marines included, because I've never seen you this invested. This fucking happy, since Addison walked into your life. And yeah, I know it's only technically been a day. But we both know that doesn't matter. We're soldiers. We either jump or we don't. Simple as that. And you've jumped. You just won't let yourself land because you have this fucked-up notion you don't deserve to be happy. That you have to pay for not seeing that IED sooner." He took a step closer. "For living."

"I swear, buddy, you either shut up or—"

"Or what? You're already living like you're dead. Pretending you're fine when we both know you're barely holding it together. We've been patient. Given you time and space to work through this. Then, finally, someone comes along that makes you step back into the light. Leave those damn demons behind. And you're going to let her walk away because you've already convinced yourself she couldn't possibly ever love you back."

He faced Addison. "Rigs was injured when an IED exploded next to him. While he's made an amazing recovery, he was left with scars across his face and chest. The kind some people have trouble accepting. That's why he grabbed your wrist. Why he seems indifferent. I promise you, it has nothing to do with how he really feels."

A dull roar sounded inside Rigs' head, spinning the room a few times before he managed to shift his feet— brace one leg against the bed. Prevent his ass from hitting the floor. Heat burned along his face and neck, a tight feeling in his chest making it hard to breathe. He stared at his boots, willing them to move. To push past Ice and head for his truck. Get as far away as he could before pulling over and emptying his stomach across the side of the road.

Because despite everything he'd told himself earlier —about coming clean. Giving Addison a chance to see the real him—now that his flaws had been exposed. Had been put in the spotlight. All he could do was focus on pulling air in then pushing it out. He felt her staring at him. The weight of her sightless gaze pushing down on him like that fucking wall had. Trapping him in a way he wasn't sure he could escape.

A hand landed on his back, shoving him farther down. "Breathe for me, Rigs."

Anger had him moving. Had him knocking off Russel's hand then grabbing him by the shirt and dragging him across the room—slamming him against the wall. He leaned in close, looking Ice in the eyes. "You dick."

Ice didn't resist. Didn't raise his hands as he stood there, staring Rigs down. "You want to kick my ass? Go ahead. I won't even fight back. But don't ask me to stand here and watch you sabotage anything remotely good in your life. Kill what remains of the brother I saved until there's nothing left but a hollow shell. Until you find a way to end it for real. Even I'm not that strong."

Rigs breathed heavily in Ice's face. "I was going to tell her."

"When? Because she was about a second away from walking out the door. And we both know she wasn't coming back. Not, this time."

"It's not that simple."

"Actually, it is."

"Kent."

Rigs stilled at the soft whisper of Addison's voice. It was close, and he knew if he turned, she'd be standing right there. Waiting. Blind gaze pinned on him. A tremor shook through him. If he thought he'd felt exposed at the auction, it didn't compare to the raw feeling coursing through him. To the way his skin felt too tight. His tongue too large to form the right words.

He released Ice's shirt then took a quick step to the

side. "I'm going to do a sweep of Addison's house. I'll be back in a few hours." He angled his head just enough to address Addy without looking at her. Seeing the disgust he'd been fearing since they'd first met mirrored in her eyes. "I'll grab your cane and a few supplies."

Russel snagged his arm. "I called Sam and Hank last night. They're meeting us there in an hour."

"Fine. Then, I'll see you both there."

He left, using all his strength to get his feet to move. To walk down the hall, across the living room and out the door. Harlequin called his name, but Rigs just kept moving. A few more seconds, and he'd be clear.

He hit the garage running, jumping in his truck then peeling out. He couldn't think about what had happened. What he'd have to face in an hour. All he could do was drive.

CHAPTER 12

ADDISON LEANED against the wall in her kitchen, listening to the strained silence around her. If it weren't for the fact she knew there were a group of men gathered at the table, to the eerie sense of multiple bodies in the same space, she would have sworn the room was empty. They didn't make a sound. Not a scuff, a raspy breath. Nothing but deathly quiet.

Apparently, it wasn't only Marines who were stealthy. Russel, Sam, and a guy called Hank all shared Kent's ability to disappear without ever leaving the room. A feat that creeped her out. Knowing there were people who could infiltrate her home, maybe even watch her, all without her sensing it—hearing them— made her acutely aware of her current situation and how vulnerable she truly was. How much she'd relied on Blade to be her first line of defense.

She clenched her jaw to keep her emotions in check. Russel had stopped by the vet's on the way to her house, and she'd spent fifteen minutes stroking Blade's coat.

Listening to his soft snuffles as his heartbeat thumped against her palm. He'd been sedated, but simply holding him, knowing she hadn't lost him, had been enough to ease the tight feeling in her throat. Leaving him had been harder than she'd expected, and she'd had to fight to keep the tears at bay.

Tears that still threatened as she stood there, feeling more alone than she had the past eighteen months. Kent hadn't spoken a word to her since running out of Russel's loft. Since she'd learned the truth behind his odd behavior.

Scars.

Why hadn't she figured that out? She'd gotten glimpses of them. Had felt the raised lines on his chest, but… She'd been too preoccupied by the blue of his eyes, the strong line of his jaw. The hard planes flexing beneath her fingers to care about some scars. And after all she'd gone through in the past—with her sister, her own trauma—scars were a sign he'd won. That he'd fought against impossible odds and somehow made it out the other side intact. Alive.

You're barely holding it together.

That's what Russel had said. And just thinking that Kent could end up the way Gwen had made her stomach roil. Her chest constrict. Because it wasn't just Kent who Russel claimed had jumped. Addison had, too.

It was crazy. As unlikely as her flashes. But denying there was something special between her and Kent was like denying her blindness was all in her mind. And she couldn't help but wonder if he felt a fraction of the need she did. Or if Russel had been wrong, and Kent's reactions were based on the fact he just didn't feel anything for her except obligation.

The floor scuffed next to her. On the other side of the doorway. And she knew it was Kent. The hint of gun oil and spicy man. The way the air heated around her. The familiar energy that washed over her. All the clues she'd come to associate with him.

She hadn't been wrong about him being a protector. Even with the awkward distance between them, she'd felt his presence since she'd arrived, despite the fact he hadn't made a sound. Close enough to jump to her defense or maybe catch her if she tripped. And she wasn't sure if she was touched or angry.

A footstep in front of her followed by a brush of fingers along her arm. Russel.

She tilted her head toward him. "Yes, Russel?"

He chuckled. "How the hell did you know it was me?"

"Your hand. And the way the air changes when you're around."

"You are something else, honey. Okay, we're ready. Would you like to join us at the table?"

"If it's all the same, I think I'd rather just stand here." Where she felt as if she had some semblance of control.

"All right. I'll make introductions." Chairs scraped followed by the pad of feet toward her. "This is Sam Montgomery. Folks call him Midnight. He was at the auction with us last night."

Had it really just been last night?

She extended her hand, shaking the large, warm

hand that engulfed hers. "You're the Army Ranger who was with Bridgette Hayward."

A snort. "That's right. Conned the lady into agreeing to marry me."

"I was collecting evidence for the Stevens' case when... Anyway, I had the pleasure of working with her on several cases while in narcotics. She's scary good."

"I'll pass the compliment along."

Russel tapped her arm as Sam's hand left hers. "And this is Hank Patterson, or Montana to his men. Ex-Navy SEAL, and our boss."

Addison smiled. "A Navy SEAL? Impressive. And you're the one who created Brotherhood Protectors."

"Yes, ma'am. And I'm lucky enough to have snagged these guys before someone else got them. I've got a hell of a crew. Now, I understand someone tried to kill you. Twice."

She crossed her arms over her chest. "Kent seems to think so, but... It was likely just an attempted burglary, and lots of people were threatened at the auction."

A disgruntled huff sounded beside her. "I found three well-placed charges of C4 inside your house. The kind that would have made it look like your gas line exploded if you'd set them off. How many thieves do that? And let's not forget that bastard at the auction said you were the one. Those aren't random acts of violence, sweetheart."

She shivered at the endearment. God, the way it flowed off his tongue. The gravelly tones and deep, raspy voice. She had to work to appear unaffected. Not to turn and step against him. Finally take his mouth in hers. A few words, and she wanted him more than she had before.

She twisted to face him. "I get that it's odd, really odd, but... Why would someone be targeting me? I've pretty much been a recluse since the raid. I'm not involved in any new cases. And it's not like I *saw* anything I shouldn't have at the auction."

Russel cupped her elbow. "I've come to trust Rigs' intuition. It's saved my ass more than once. So, based on that, I called around. Thought it might help to get more information on the men behind the attack at the foundation. Turns out they were all members of the same gang. They call themselves the Raptors. Have you heard of them?"

Pain shot through her head, making her stumble sideways. Strong hands grabbed her waist, tugging her against a wall of muscle.

Kent's scent surrounded her, his lips gently caressing her ear. "Easy, Addy. I've got you."

She nodded, massaging her forehead as she leaned against Kent's torso. Awkward or not, she needed the support. "Sorry. I guess I lost my balance for a moment. What was the question?"

Russel sighed. "Thinking it'd be best if you sat down, first."

Kent maneuvered her over to the table, pulling out a chair then easing her into it. She heard him settle in beside her, one large hand resting on her thigh.

The table rocked as the men took their places, then

silence until Russel cleared his throat. "I asked if you'd heard of the Raptors?"

Another pulse of pain followed by echoed pops of gunfire that slowly faded into the sound of her pulse strumming through her veins. She winced but managed to stay upright, this time. "They were the gang we raided on my last night with the unit. We suspected Stevens was using them to move his drugs across state lines, but we needed more evidence if we wanted to get a conviction. That's why we were there. We'd gotten a tip that a large shipment of cocaine was being delivered. It was the kind of bust that would have taken Stevens' empire down."

"But something went wrong?"

She palmed her head at the flash of white light. "They knew we were coming. They were waiting, and by the time we realized it was an ambush, it was too late... Damn."

"Addison? Are you okay?"

She pinched the bridge of her nose. "Fine. It's nothing."

Kent shifted closer. "Let's go back to the auction. Did you recognize the guy's voice?"

She shook her head, waiting until the pain faded. "I don't think so. Nothing sprang to mind. But he only said those few words."

"That's okay. You're doing great." Russel, again. "Does the name Joseph Wilson mean anything?"

She turned toward Russel's voice. "Joe? Sure. He was part of the DEA crew assigned to the case. Along with the two I introduced to Kent, and his partner, Grace Sanchez. She was killed that night, too. Which was ironic since she and Will had been dating. It hadn't been that long, but they seemed to be wildly in love with each other. I guess in some sad way it was a blessing—that neither of them had to grieve the loss. But Joe made it out. From what I heard, he'd opted for early retirement. Why?"

"He was the only person killed at the auction."

"What?" She pushed to her feet, tripping against Kent when her balance shifted.

Kent moved in closer. "Easy."

"What do you mean he's dead? And why was he at the charity auction? He'd moved to Portland."

Russel took her hand. "His wife said he'd gotten a personal invitation. Something about repaying a debt. She wasn't exactly sure. But I find it odd that the only other person targeted during the robbery at the foundation was another member of your squad. One of the other survivors."

Addison tried to back up, grunting when Kent simply held her tight. "This doesn't make any sense. I don't even remember what happened that night. Only what I've been told. My last tangible memory is hours before the raid when we met to discuss the logistics one last time. After that, it's nothing but darkness."

"But that's changing, isn't it?"

More pain. More lights. More ghosted images and echoed sounds, until she found herself in Kent's lap, her side braced against his chest.

"Breathe, Addison."

She rested her head on his shoulder, suddenly tired. "I'm not sure what you mean."

She felt the air swirl and suspected Russel had knelt in front of her.

He took one of her hands in his. "The flashes. The flashbacks. Not only are you slowly regaining your sight, you're remembering what happened. How your partner died. Maybe how that other agent died."

Stay with me... Kill her, too... The whole place is gonna blow...

She palmed her ears, trying to shut out the sounds. Stop the flow of images into her head. Will above her, his head jerking back. Dark eyes with a hint of a smile. The glint of a gun.

"Addison."

She curled into Kent, using the steady rise and fall of his chest to calm her frantic breath. To pull her back from the edge. She blinked, and the room burst into view. Russel kneeling in front of her, one hand on her wrist. Taking her pulse. Two men standing behind him, mouths drawn into a thin line. A half empty coffee pot gleamed on the counter, the clock above the oven slowly ticking over.

Then, it was gone.

She closed her eyes, took a few deep breaths, then opened them.

Nothing.

Russel palmed her forehead. "Addison? Are you still with us, honey?"

She nodded, leaning against Kent. "I…"

Russel patted her hand. "It's okay. We'll talk more later. But I think Rigs is right. Someone doesn't want you to remember that raid, and they're willing to go to some pretty extreme lengths to silence you. Permanently."

"I'll talk to Bridgette." It was Sam. "She still has connections at the US Attorney's office. Maybe she can dig up more on what happened that night. Get some names for us to check out."

"And I'll call my contact at the DEA." Hank, this time. "Get more information on Joe Wilson and these other agents. See if we can narrow down the list."

She sighed. "This is crazy. No one knew about these flashes until after the attack. Why would they target me when I'm not a threat?"

"Maybe they were hedging their bet. Tying up loose ends before your memory returned, and you could implicate them in some form of criminal activity. Or maybe something else has changed—new evidence that could trigger your memory. Either way, we're on it. Ice?"

"Yeah, Montana?"

"You ever work with a guy called Cannon?"

"Rick Sloan? Hell yeah. Guy's Delta Force. Hard core infiltration. Been deep underground for some time. He was recruited from your Ranger squad, wasn't he Sam?"

Sam snorted. "We worked a few joint ops both before and after he transferred. The guy's about as extreme as they come. Definitely someone you want on your side. But I haven't seen or heard from him in a couple of years. Why?"

"Rumor has it he's in town on mandated rest. I realize he's still enlisted, but… The C4 element has me concerned. We could definitely use his resources. *If* he's willing to help us out."

Russel laughed. "Bastard's in town and didn't call one of us? That's grounds for an ass kicking. And he'll be willing. He owes me a few. Sounds like the perfect time to collect."

"Excellent. Why don't we meet back here tonight? Rigs? You secure this place to your satisfaction?"

Kent huffed. "That's the second time someone's questioned my skill set. Are you all trying to tell me something?"

Hank chuckled. "God, you're an ornery son of a bitch. Fine. You've got the place wired. I just wanted to make sure you were okay on your own for a while."

"Anyone so much as thinks too hard next to the property line, and I'll know about it."

Addison tensed. God, what had he done? And did she really want to know?

Kent gave her a light squeeze. "Don't worry, sweetheart. I mostly wired the place for light and sound. Even though you're bordered by larger estates, and the chance of anyone undeserving getting injured by some small charges is remote, I'm not completely crazy. No one's going to get hurt if they trip one of my precautions."

She gave him a guarded smile. "I have an alarm system. Wasn't that good enough?"

"Please. Took me all of thirty seconds to bypass that pile of junk. No one's getting past it, now, though." He grunted, lifting her up then easing her back on the chair. "I'll go double check. Make a few rounds of the area. We're not getting surprised, again."

She opened her mouth to protest, but she sensed he'd already left the room.

Hank cleared his throat. "I see Rigs' social graces haven't improved any. Damn lucky the man's brilliant when it comes to security. That, and I don't ever want to get on his bad side." He gave Addy's shoulder a squeeze. "Don't worry. We'll figure this out. Catch whoever's behind it. You're part of the family, and we're not letting a fellow warrior down."

Family. Except for the part where Kent couldn't stand to let her touch him. Where he'd bolted at the suggestion of something more between them. Something physical. Scars or not, she still wasn't convinced he had feelings for her.

But she nodded her thanks, shaking Sam's hand, again, before the two men left, leaving another void in the room. Only Russel remained behind, the telltale creak of the chair suggesting he'd taken a seat next to her.

She nudged him with her knee. "You don't have to babysit me. I know I haven't exactly been a star client, but I'm fine, now."

"Good, because I hadn't planned on babysitting anyone. Least of all a kickass detective."

"So you're a buffer, then. Between me and Kent." She waved her hand at his rough exhalation. "It's okay. I just think you haven't considered the possibility that he isn't interested. That I'm the one with too many issues."

The air swirled, then he was taking her hand. Giving it a squeeze. "Let me tell you something about Rigs. In the ten years I've known him, he's never once given a woman a second look. Long before the scars were even an issue. Sex, sure. But it never went further than that. After the incident..." He sighed. "He only went to the auction because of Bridgette. Because she's Sam's fiancée. Brotherhood and all that. Yet, he told me he was planning on asking you out. Braving a café just to spend more time with you. It might not seem like much, but for him... He's right. Telling you *was* a dick move, but I love the man like a brother. And if there's even a fraction of a chance you have feelings for him..."

She smiled then stood, motioning toward the doorway. "I think I'll go outside. Get some fresh air."

"I was just about to head out for a bit. Grab some food for everyone. If you'll be okay here with just Rigs?"

"I think I can manage." She took a few steps then stopped and glanced back at where she hoped Russel was still standing. "And thanks."

"He's worth the risk. In case you were wondering."

"I'll keep that in mind."

She headed for the patio door, vaguely aware of her front door closing. Of Russel's truck turning over then the growl of the engine fading. All her senses were focused on Kent. On feeling his presence. Finding him amidst the darkness.

The back door creaked as she shoved it open, stepping out onto the deck. She felt the sunshine on her face, the light breeze lift her hair. A soft inhale pinpointed his location, and she slowly made her way over, stopping a few feet away. She didn't face him, electing to stare blankly forward as she leaned against the railing. This wasn't going to be easy for her, and she needed the slight disconnect to get through it. Bare a part of her she'd locked away.

Kent didn't speak, but she sensed him moving closer. Within reach should she need him. And just like that, her doubts faded. Vanished like her memories of the raid had.

"Growing up, I always knew I wanted to be a detective. My grandfather was a cop. My dad. I guess it was in my blood. I still remember the day I joined the academy. Having two girls, I don't think my father really believed I'd continue the legacy. My graduation ceremony was one of only two times I ever saw him cry.

"But my sister Gwen…" She smiled at the memory. "She never followed convention. I swear she did everything she could to get a rise out of my father. You can imagine his reaction when she signed up for the fire academy. I assure you…the rivalry between cops and fire fighters is very much alive."

She paused to swallow, to tilt her head when Kent stepped closer, his arm brushing hers. "Four years ago, her crew responded to an apartment fire. I've never seen flames that intense. You could feel the heat two blocks away. Yet, she and her teammates never stopped going inside. Bringing people out. I'd rather face a gang of armed drug dealers than a wall of flames. But she never blinked. Never stopped to consider her own safety.

"On their last run, part of the ceiling collapsed.

Trapped Gwen and three other men. I've never witnessed a group of warriors try harder to rescue their own. They worked for hours to dig them out. But, by then…"

She sighed, sniffing back the thick feeling in her throat. "All of them sustained burns. Gwen had them on her face, chest, shoulders and back. She received excellent care. But even after multiple surgeries, the doctors couldn't get rid of all the scars. Couldn't erase what that night had done to her."

Addison glanced toward Kent, wishing she could see his face. Judge his reaction. "I tried to help, but… How do you build someone back up, again, when they can't stand to look at their own reflection? When they can't walk into a room without being reminded of everything they lost? On the one-year anniversary of the fire, she took her own life. Left a note saying she couldn't live with the stares. The comments. The isolation she felt. And while a part of me understood, another was angry. Is still angry that she couldn't see herself the way I did. Because beneath the marks, she was still my little sister. Still the woman I would have died to protect. For me, nothing had changed."

She took a few steps back. "I won't say I understand how you feel. What you must face on a daily basis. But I'm sincere when I say that I'd give anything to see my sister's scars just one more time."

She turned then headed for the door, stopping at the entrance. She tilted her head back toward him, offering him a guarded smile. "And for the record… I've already seen yours. Well, glimpses, anyway. But I was too busy losing myself in the blue of your eyes to notice. Because scars or not, you're breathtaking."

A grunt sounded off to her right, then he was there, fingers sliding through her hair, his body pressing against hers. He backed her against the wall, his mouth crushing down on hers. He didn't wait for her to open her lips, just gave them a twist then delved inside. His tongue tangled with hers, his lips lifting—repositioning —then returning. She wasn't sure how long they stood there, Kent eating at her mouth, giving her just enough time to gulp in air, before he finally eased back. One hand speared through her hair, the other wrapped around the small of her back.

His forehead rested on hers, his breath loud and raspy against her cheek. "I've wanted to do that since I bumped into you in the garden. I just didn't know how."

"I'm glad you figured it out. Your technique is flawless."

"About the scars…"

"I don't have to touch you there if it bothers you. But for what it's worth, it's the man beneath that has my attention. And I don't see that changing."

"God, Addison." He kissed her, again. Slowly, as if she would break if he moved too fast. Pressed too hard. "If you don't want this to go any further…"

"How many times do I have to throw myself at you before you finally get the hint?"

"I just want you to be sure, because once I start…"

She nipped at his lip, thankful when she didn't miss. "Then, why are we still standing here?"

"Just trying to gather enough control to make it all the way to your bed."

She brushed her mouth along his jaw as she made her way to his ear, licking the shell then smiling at his harsh inhalation. "Screw your control. Beds are overrated."

CHAPTER 13

KENT FISTED his hand against the brick, hoping the scratch of pain would temper his need enough to pick up Addison and carry her inside. Because the way he felt, stripping them both enough to lift her and thrust inside seemed like the only feasible scenario. The only way he could move without exploding.

Addison moaned, nipping her way along his jaw, licking at his lips. "Kent."

He pressed her against the wall, trapping her. "I'm trying very hard not to take you against the side of the house. Saying my name like that…"

She laughed, and his fucking dick surged forward, taking him within a breath of his release. If he hadn't been able to squeeze every muscle—clamp down on the blast of fire through his shaft—he'd have come in his pants.

Addison kissed his jaw—right over the scar as if it wasn't there. As if she couldn't feel it. "Then, I'll say it, again. Kent."

"Our first time is not going to be me rutting with you in your backyard."

"Then get us inside, soldier."

Hell yeah. He could do that. While he wasn't sure how far they'd get—if he'd make it all the way down the hall to her bedroom—surely, he had the discipline to open the door and get inside.

He lifted her against his chest, moaning when she wrapped her legs around his hips, her arms around his neck. He slid one hand under her ass as he groped for the door, half falling through the doorway then against the far wall. He kicked the door closed, turning and leaning against it for balance when Addison palmed his face and claimed his mouth.

Fuck, nothing tasted better than her mouth. Sweet. Hot. Her tongue battling with his as she clung to him, trusting he wouldn't let them fall.

Hell no.

Rigs twisted, bumping his way down the hall before making it into her room. The door bounced on the hinges as he carried her inside. He continued across the floor until he reached the foot of the bed. He thought about just launching them both onto the mattress. Stripping her bare then climbing on top—finally sinking into all that soft, warm heat. The heat he'd felt through his damn sweats when she'd ground against him.

But the soldier in him—the part still firing messages to his brain—managed to set her down. Release the death grip he had on her. Addison reached for his shirt, pulling it up until it caught on his holster.

"One second, sweetheart."

He removed his collection of weapons, then leaned forward, helping her tug his shirt over his head before stilling. She stood inches away, her hands raised but not quite touching him. Her head tilted to the side, then she reached one hand out—placed it on his chest.

And fuck if he didn't tense. Didn't clench his damn muscles despite the heat that burned from her touch. The need hammering inside his head.

Addy paused, her fingers curled over one of his scars. "Do you want me to stop?"

"No." He cupped her waist, brushing his forehead against hers, again. "It's just... No one's touched them. Touched *me*, since..."

Her smile made his damn chest constrict. God, it was all ruby-red lips and joy and something more that made his hands shake. Had a light sheen of sweat beading his flesh.

She drew a small circle with one finger on his chest. "I haven't been with anyone since the raid, either. I don't even know what I look like. If I've changed. What you'll see under these clothes."

"You're beautiful. No two ways about it."

"So are you. In a manly, rugged sort of way. Look..." She stepped back then grabbed her shirt, lifting it over her head then letting it drop to the floor. The soft rustle of cloth was followed by her bra, and then she was bare. From the waist up, nothing but smooth, creamy skin and pink-tipped breasts.

Addison held out her hand, taking his and placing it on her upper chest. "You're not the only one with scars."

Puckered skin moved beneath his fingertips, the obvious bullet injury breaking through his lust-dazed haze. He closed the scant distance between them, tracing the edges of another identical wound on her shoulder. A third on her ribs.

"Fuck. You were shot? Did they get the fucker who hurt you?" Because if they hadn't, Rigs had a new name on the top of his shit list. One he wouldn't think twice about seeking out. Eliminating.

Her lips quirked. "Kent."

"I'm not going to let anyone hurt you."

"You're missing the point."

Like hell, he was. She'd been injured. Taken to the brink of death judging by the wounds, and he'd be damned if anyone threatened her like that, again. Cop or not, he'd stand up for her. Put himself between her and any threat that came along. It was the only way he could picture it. Because he wasn't letting her go. Not, now, that he'd found her. Let her see behind the curtain.

Addison placed her hand over his. "I meant that you don't seem fazed by my scars. By the invisible ones inside my head. The ones making me blind. So, why is it so hard to believe I don't see yours?" She placed her hands back on his chest. "That all I feel are strong powerful muscles. Dips and curves I want to trace with my tongue."

She dropped her hand lower, squeezing his dick through his pants. "This long hard ridge I want to take in my mouth. Bet I could suck you dry."

"I don't have any condoms."

Fuck. That's not what he'd planned on saying. But it

was true. After he'd been released from Walter Reed, he'd abandoned that side of him. Had forfeited any hope of finding someone like her. So carrying around condoms had felt like a wasted effort. A constant reminder of what he couldn't have. Would never have—until Addison.

She smiled. "Something tells me you're a pretty healthy guy."

"Minus the disfiguring marks—hell yeah. Clean bill of health, and as strong as I ever was. Ice and Midnight saw to that, the sadistic bastards."

"And neither of us have been with anyone in a while. I'm on birth control, and I know I was tested for everything under the sun, so…"

Rigs froze. Fucking froze because she was telling him he could go bareback. Bare-fucking-back inside the most beautiful woman he'd ever seen. Ever had the pleasure to touch. That after two years of abstinence, his first time would be inside Addison, with all her warm, wet flesh surrounding his. No barriers. Nothing but her arousal and his. Skin on skin.

He growled. At least, it sounded like a growl. Deep. Throaty. A declaration of his intent to claim her. That's how he felt. Raw. Primal. She was far from helpless. Had dedicated her life to serve and protect. But right now, right there—she was his. His to love. To sacrifice for. To risk his life for. He'd do it for strangers. For her…

He'd do the impossible for her. And he'd do whatever it took to make this a permanent arrangement—her in his life.

Kent slid his hand up her torso, cupping her breast.

It was so soft, so smooth, her pink nipple beaded into a hard little point. He leaned forward, nuzzling the tip as he inhaled. God, she smelled good. Sweet. Warm. And he knew when he took her pants off, she'd be wet.

Wet for him.

Christ, it still amazed him. That she wanted him. Scars and all. And not in a casual sort of way. Everything about her screamed that she felt the same fire. The same unrelenting need he did. How her body flushed whenever he touched her. The dreamy look in her eyes, even if she wasn't actually seeing him. How she clung to him, right now, trusting him to take her where they both wanted to go.

God, if he was an asshole, she'd be at his mercy. She wouldn't be able to fight him off. Even with her training, she didn't compare to him. He could snap her in two without breaking a sweat.

That was something she wouldn't have to worry about, again. He wasn't going anywhere. Wasn't going to let another man touch her the way he was. She'd always be safe with him. He'd guarantee it, or die trying.

"Kent?"

Shit. Here he was, in her room, her body trembling with need in his arms, and he was obsessing over her safety. On all the ways she could get hurt. Instead of focusing on her. On seeing that blush deepen. Her nipples harden even more. He wanted her chest heaving, her voice harsh from screaming his name. From coming over and over until she could barely open her eyes.

He hummed against her skin, smiling at her sharp

inhalation. Was she anticipating the first brush of his lips on her breast? Of him taking her nipple inside his mouth?

He was.

Rigs licked the tip, and she gasped, sliding her hands off his shoulders and into his hair, anchoring him in place. She tugged, and his damn dick jerked. Christ, another couple reactions like that, and he'd lose it.

He made a second pass, licking. Sucking. Tasting her until she squirmed—begged him for more. Oh yeah, there was more.

He switched sides, loving every throaty moan, every flex of her fingers against his scalp. While he'd been in a rush before, hearing her obvious pleasure made him want to draw it out. Make it last all day. Hell, the next week. Endless days and nights of her writhing in his arms, coming apart.

"God, Kent. I need you."

He eased back, lifting his face level with hers. "Right here, sweetheart. Not going anywhere."

She tugged on his head, drawing him to her for a long, slow kiss, holding him close when they finally came up for air. "Now. It needs to be now."

He smiled at the strained tone. How her voice was deeper than usual. He dropped another kiss on her nose then reached for her pants. A few swipes of his hands and she was naked. Gloriously bare and trembling in his arms. Her scent surrounded him, her skin beading with goosebumps as he trailed a finger down her hip then between her legs, stopping on the soft vee of her mound.

"Fuck, you're soaking." The words were out before he could think. Consider that she might not like rough talk.

She moaned, wiggling in an attempt to move his finger lower. "Do you honestly think I've been dry since you drove me home? You're a hard man to forget."

"Shit."

Just thinking she'd been fantasizing about him touching her. Sliding inside. Loving her. It broke the fragile control he'd clawed back. The part of him that thought he'd be able to wait. To touch, and lick, and kiss without needing more. Without following her down on the bed and sinking inside her.

She seemed to grasp the change in him. The way his muscles tensed. His dick swelling against her stomach before he backed away—removed his clothes. Had he ripped a seam? Then, he lifted her and placed her on the bed, crawling over top as her hair settled in a curtain of gold across the pillow.

He paused. She was so damn beautiful. Her skin gleaming in the sunlight. The pale, creamy tones contrasting nicely against his tanned flesh. How her soft curves complemented his hard planes, their bodies molding together perfectly.

He wedged his hips between her thighs, his cock nudging her opening, his weight pressing her into the mattress. He went to his elbows, holding her close as he claimed her mouth, sinking the first inch of his shaft inside her.

Damn, if he'd thought her mouth was hot, he hadn't anticipated how mind-blowing her sheath would be.

Nothing but warm wet walls surrounding his flesh, squeezing along his length as he slowly inched his way inside.

Fuck, how was he supposed to do this and not come on the first stroke? Once he was finally fully seated inside her? Because it was already the best damn sex he'd ever had—the slide of his shaft. The press of her skin against his. She was making those throaty noises, again, her fingers digging into his back as she tilted her pelvis, sinking him even deeper. She had her eyes closed, her bottom lip snagged between her teeth.

Rigs kissed her mouth, smiling when she released her lip in order to open from him—tangling her tongue with his. He hissed out a breath just as he bottomed out, his balls slapping against her ass.

"Damn, so tight. Am I hurting you?"

She nipped at his chin, moaning when he drew back then gave a sharp little thrust. "God, no. More."

Her legs crossed behind his back, her body arching into him. He shifted onto his right elbow, using his left hand to palm her thigh—trace the silky skin to the back of her knee then up, again. She was wrapped around him, yet, it didn't feel like enough.

Would he ever have enough of her?

He lowered, giving a few experimental strokes. His chest rubbed against hers, his light dusting of hair likely abrading her nipples. But if the sensation was too much, she didn't show it. Didn't ask him to stop. In fact, she clawed at him, dragging him closer—lifting her hips to meet each thrust.

He started off slow—a long glide out, then a slow

push in. Each time a bit harder than the last. Slightly deeper. Arousal soaked his flesh, the wet sound of each stroke only making him harder. More desperate.

He increased his pace, the slap of his body against hers echoing around them. She called his name then lifted her hands off his back, wedging them between them until she cupped his face.

Her fingers danced over his features, and he realized she was trying to see him. Map out his face. Visualize his reactions. Was she worried he wasn't into it? That this was a one-off for him?

He pressed into her touch, still sliding in and out of her sex. "Still right here, sweetheart. Lost in you. God, what you do to me."

Her fingers stilled, one hand poised right over that fucking scar. "You're shaking."

He smiled. Did she know what that meant? For an ordinance soldier to shake? Because she was right. His hands and arms trembled—whether from holding himself up or just the fact he was finally where he wanted to be. That he'd realized he'd come home without knowing he'd been searching for one—he wasn't sure. All he knew was that she held more power over him than the Marines ever had. That he was more devoted to her than he'd been to his brothers. Because she was his. Archaic or not, it was true.

He'd killed to protect her.

Still would.

"That's how far you push me. And you don't have to see me to *see* me. Feel what you do to me. How you've got me strung tight. That it's taking all my strength not to pound you into the bed. That I'm harder than I've ever been. You don't need your vision for that."

Tears welled in her eyes, then she was arching back, contracting around him. Her walls clamping down on his dick, her heels pressing hard against the small of his back.

"Fuck, yeah, sweetheart. Come for me."

He let loose. There was no other way to describe it. One moment, he was in control. Thrusting in perfect sync with her racing heartbeat. The next, he was claiming her. Pumping so hard, so fast, her bed shimmied against the wall, tapping out a rhythm he knew he couldn't maintain.

Addison was chanting his name, still coming around him, as fire scorched his nerves, shooting forward and taking him with it. He came. Dick pulsing, balls pulled tight. Stars danced in front of his eyes, dimming his vision until the sensations ebbed, and he collapsed on top of her.

Their ragged breathing filled the room, eventually evening out as his heart rate returned to normal. Part of his brain told him to move. That he was most likely squishing her into the bed. But damn if he could get his muscles to listen. To support him.

Addison kissed his mouth, sighing into it. "Kent."

His name. That's all. As if just saying that one word had drained her. Though, maybe it had. It drained him. Drew him under. Threatened to push him into a coma-like sleep.

He had enough sense to shift over—take her with him. Spoon into her back—one of his thighs over hers, his arms looped around her, wrapping her in his embrace. He'd clean them off—once he'd caught his breath. Had the energy to move. She burrowed against him, slipping into sleep a moment later.

Rigs listened to her soft breaths. The way her chest pressed against his hand with every inhalation, her heart thumping against his palm. She was safe. At this moment, nothing could touch her, but him. And he'd see it stayed that way. Whatever the personal cost.

Addison Bailey was his. And he'd use every trick he'd learned in MARSOC, every skill he possessed to protect her—or he'd die in the process. Simple as that.

CHAPTER 14

ADDISON WOKE to the hard press of muscled man against her back, steel-like arms wrapped around her. It took her a full minute to realize she still couldn't see, instead of the instant jolt she normally had when she opened her eyes. When the darkness wouldn't go away.

Not that being blind didn't still sting. Still send a shiver down her spine despite the heat radiating off Kent's body. But being snugged against him took the edge off. Made it less frightening. He was solid. An imposing force when she'd felt as if she'd been swept away. And he was hers.

The thought should have scared her. Kent wasn't the only one who hadn't been in a serious relationship. Addy had thrown all her energy into her career. Making detective before thirty had required laser focus. Occasional trysts or short-term affairs had been the norm—until Kent had bumped into her, and everything had changed. *She'd* changed.

Now—now, she couldn't imagine going back to that

lifestyle. To pretending she was happy alone. That even being a cop had never made her feel this…complete.

Kent hummed against her neck. "Something tells me you're thinking far too hard for waking up in my arms. Makes me wonder if my technique isn't quite as flawless as you claimed. Do I want to know what you're thinking?"

She inhaled as his fingers made slow circles down her torso then along her hip. "There's nothing wrong with your technique. And I was thinking…umm, god, I love the way you touch me. But won't Russel be back soon?"

He smiled against her neck, inching his hand lower. "I called him while you were sleeping. Told him to hold off—rendezvous with everyone else tonight. Now, back to you. Your body begs to be touched. Your skin is so soft. But you didn't answer my question. What were you thinking?"

Thinking? How could she think when every neuron was focused on the slow progression of his fingers across her thigh then up the inside of her leg, pausing just shy of touching her folds—the ones she knew were drenched with arousal. Had she been like this all afternoon? Spent the hours longing for him without knowing it? She vaguely recalled Kent getting up—the sound of water splashing before he'd returned and cleaned up their combined releases. She'd been about to tell him she could do it herself, when he'd made a contented humming noise—as if caring for her brought him a sense of peace.

She'd decided to stay quiet—enjoy being cherished.

Because that's how he made her feel. Cherished and special, and anything but a burden.

His finger dipped down—circled her clit. "Sweetheart."

It was her turn to hum. "Yes. Right there."

He chuckled. "Are you sure that's where you want me to touch you?" He made another pass.

"Please. Kent. I…"

Her voice trailed into a moan as he focused on the spot she wanted, billowing heat across her body. One touch, and she was on the edge. Desperate to come.

Kent mouthed her shoulder, sucking her skin. "Fuck. So wet. I love the way you react to me." He nipped at the muscle threading into her neck. "Are you sore? Do you want me to stop?"

"No. More."

He made a sound. Part purr, part growl. Then, he was lifting her leg, tilting her hips and plunging inside. No slow build up. No letting her adjust to his width. Just his cock deep, thrusting in and out. He was thick and long. Bordering on the edge of pain without ever pushing her over. And when he changed the angle just a bit like he was doing, now…

Heat burned a path up her groin then into her stomach, clenching hard as her release coiled inside her. Like a branch bending, bending, bending—snap.

He hit somewhere deep inside—some place she hadn't known existed—and she broke. Ass grinding back against his hips, her hands clenched around the sheets as she spasmed in his arms, his name a hoarse whisper on her lips.

Kent grunted, his thrusts losing any semblance of rhythm. Hard, fast, long, short—each stroke was different from the last until he stiffened, his cock deep within her.

He reached one hand up, tunneling it through her hair and turning her face enough to capture her mouth. She cried out, licking and biting at his lips when his face appeared amidst a flash of light.

She inhaled, staring into his eyes—those incredible blue eyes that she'd almost convinced herself she'd imagined. That none of the previous snapshots had been real. But this was real. Color flushed high on his cheekbones, the skin unnaturally taut. The blue tinted irises were more of a steel gray around his fully dilated pupils. His brown hair hung in a tousled mess around his face, longer than she'd pictured with him being ex-military. But the longer length was rugged and sexy, and she couldn't look away. Couldn't do anything but stare up at him, drinking in every detail. The light pink hue of his lips. The fine lines around his eyes.

Kent met her gaze, glanced at her mouth, then snapped his attention back to her eyes. He must have recognized the way she was staring at him—focused. Attentive. He held himself still, his cock near bursting inside her before dipping down, hovering a breath away.

"Addison? Sweetheart, can you see me?"

She palmed his face over the scars. Marks she barely noticed because he was beautiful. Handsome beyond words as he held her gaze, blue eyes searching hers. She thumbed the corner of his mouth, enjoying the brush of soft skin across her finger. "I was right. It wasn't a dream before. You're...breathtaking."

His eyes widened, his chest heaving against her ribs.

She forced herself not to blink. Not to give her body a chance to steal his image away. "I thought you said you had scars?"

Something flashed in his eyes—stronger than lust. That made her feel utterly possessed. A sign that he didn't plan on this ending—then he was kissing her. Crushing their lips together. Eating at her mouth.

She closed her eyes out of habit. Narrowing her senses to his lips on hers, his shaft exploding inside her. She felt each pulse, each fierce shot of semen, as his release sparked another climax. She arched back, heat burning across her skin, her breath caught in her chest, until the sensations finally ebbed.

She wasn't sure if it had been a minute, five or all evening. If the darkness when she opened her eyes was simply the lack of sunlight because they'd been lying there for hours. Well past when the rest of Kent's friends said they'd reconvene. It wasn't until she realized she couldn't see *anything*—not a silhouette. Not a hint of moonlight or street lamps beyond the window— that she knew the blindness was back.

"No. No, don't go. Kent—"

His arms tightened around her, his body hugging hers. "Right here, Addy. Not going anywhere. Just... slow your breathing. Try to match mine."

His chest rose and fell against her side, the steady rhythm finally easing the panicky feeling. "That's it. Just breathe. Everything's going to be okay."

"But what if it isn't?" She cursed the way her voice cracked on the last word. "What if I never regain my sight? If I'm...*blind* for the rest of my life?"

Kent sighed, easing out of her then rolling her against him, her smaller frame cocooned within his larger one. He placed her hand on his arm. "Whether you need me to guide you or just have your back, I'm right here. For as long as you'll have me. And yeah, I know how crazy that sounds, but... Ice was right. I jumped the moment I bumped into you. And I'm ready to land, now."

He dropped a gentle kiss on her lips—more of a brush of skin than anything else. But the simple act, his whispered words, prickled tears in her eyes.

Kent chuckled. "I'm hoping those are happy tears."

She gave him a watery laugh. "They are."

"Good. Now, how about I go warm up the shower, then I'll come and grab you. We can clean up—get something to eat before the guys return."

She nodded, and he was gone. Vanished then was back before she could do more than make her body move—sit up on the bed. He leaned over her, scooped her in his arms then walked across the room in the direction of her bathroom. Water splashed in the background, growing louder as he moved toward the sound.

She tsked. "You do know I can walk, right?"

He shrugged, the powerful muscles in his shoulders flexing beneath her arms. God, the man was delicious. All hard planes and smooth skin. "Never said you couldn't. I just like having you in my arms. Safe."

Addison stared up at where she thought his face

would be once he'd set her on her feet. "I realize we're heading into unchartered territory, here, but... It's not your sole mission in life to keep me safe."

Silence. Not a breath. Not a sigh. Had he left without her realizing it?

"Kent?"

"You're right. It's not my *sole* mission."

But it *was* his mission. That's what he was saying.

A swirl of air, then his hands on her face, cupping each side. Drawing her closer. "I know you're a cop. That you can handle yourself. That you have Blade, but..." A strangled grunt, as if he was in pain. "I need you to let me do this. Protect you. I know I can't follow you around. That when you regain your sight, you'll be back chasing meth heads and drug dealers, but..."

He rested his forehead on hers. "I *need* to feel like I have some control over your well-being. That you're as safe, as protected, as humanly possible. And I need you to be okay with that."

More tears burned her eyes, and she tiptoed up—kissed his mouth. Thankful she hadn't missed. "You said when. *When* I get my sight back, not if."

"My girl's too damn badass not to kick this."

God, *his* girl.

"I think I can make that concession. As long as you allow me the same privilege. To have your back."

"You already do, sweetheart."

She snorted, taking a step back. "Again, currently blind, not deaf. I heard that tone."

"What tone?"

"The one that said I can have your back as long as it doesn't put my safety at risk."

He laughed. Not a forced one, but one that sounded rich and full, and she promised to do whatever it took to hear him laugh like that, again. "Damn, you're something else. Now, get that adorable ass in the shower before I remember that Ice and the others are coming back and pounce on you."

She smiled. "And what would happen if I pounced on you?"

She didn't have time to consider it. His arms wrapped around her, lifting her up—taking them both into the shower. Warm water cascaded over her skin as he plastered her to the wall, trapping her with his body. She gasped at the cold press of the tile, inhaling sharply when he cupped one ass cheek, tilted her pelvis, then pushed inside her.

She broke.

Just like that. One stroke. The whispered sound of her name, and her senses exploded. She clamped around his shaft, each contraction drawing a harsh grunt from him. He was rock hard inside her, balls deep. His breath washing over her face.

Then, he moved. Pounded into her. No semblance of the man who had touched her as if she'd break. This was lust. Hunger. Desperation. He claimed her mouth, kissing her as if he couldn't remember her taste, despite having just made love. Then, his hand wedged between. Flicked across her clit. And she came, again.

Harder than before. Crying his name against his lips.

Clawing at his back while he grunted then stilled, emptying inside her in a series of long spurts.

Addison slumped against him, hoping he could hold them up. She was drained. Exhausted in a way she hadn't experienced before. Sex had always been a means to an end. A quick tumble. An equally quick goodbye. She'd never lingered. Hadn't spent more time than necessary. So sleeping with Kent, showering together. Having him care for her... It meant more to her than the steamy sex. The pretty words.

Kent moaned, slowly easing free. "God, sweetheart. Are you okay? I..." He sighed, his hands trembling a bit as he trailed them along her arms.

She smiled. She did that to him. "Remind me to threaten to pounce on you more often."

He smiled against her lips. "I'm trying to remember you need to eat." He gave her a soft kiss. "Are you sure you're okay?"

"Positive. Though, if you wanted to check for yourself after everyone leaves, I wouldn't resist."

"Christ." His breath breezed over her face, his chest pushing against hers. "Addison..."

"I know. Me, too. Now, are you going to clean me up then feed me? Or was that all talk?"

"Sass like that won't get you a gentle loving, later."

"Who said that's what I wanted? Or needed?"

"Point noted. And no, it wasn't all talk. But... Can we stay like this? Just for a few minutes?"

Her throat thickened at the pleading tone of his voice. "For as long as you want. I've got nowhere else to be."

He kissed her, again, staying close. "I'm glad you don't have plans, because you do, now. With me. For as long as I can convince you I'm indispensable."

"Then, I guess you'll be here for the foreseeable future, because I already know how irreplaceable you are—clued in the moment you saved my life." She smiled against his skin—kissed his chest. "Now, about that food…"

CHAPTER 15

I THOUGHT you said you had scars?

And damn, she'd been serious.

Rigs had known the moment he'd glanced at her—her beautiful blue eyes fixed on his. Attentive. Focused—that she was in the midst of one of her flashes. That she could see everything.

But for once, he hadn't cared. Hadn't gotten the familiar tensing of his muscles. The chill down his spine at being on display. Then, she'd cupped his face—right over the marks—and told him he was breathtaking.

Him.

Breathtaking.

He'd been unrelenting after that. Pounding into her until she'd climaxed. He barely remembered his own, too caught in the sheer beauty of her as she pulsed around him, head thrown back, eyes squeezed shut. When she'd opened them and realized her sight was gone, again, his damn heart had hurt. Physically hurt watching pain shape her features—listening to the panic in her voice. The despair. He'd managed to calm her, but only after admitting what he'd been keeping to himself —that he was falling in love with her.

Belay that. He was already in love with her. He just didn't know how to say that without sounding as crazy as he felt. He'd never been one to believe in love at first sight. In magic or fate. That a couple of tumbles in the sheets would feel so different than all the other sex he'd had. That's when he'd realized how far gone he really was.

The thought should have scared him. Thirty-five years without getting attached, with having his life be all about the mission—his brothers—and he'd fallen the moment she'd smiled at him.

And now, all he could do was hold on. Pray she didn't suddenly come to her senes and realize she could do so much better than a scarred soldier. One who couldn't seem to keep his hands off of her. After he'd carried her to the shower, he'd been silently reminding himself she needed to be pampered. Fed. To pull back. Give her some time to recover. He hadn't wanted to come across as some sex-crazed asshole. Have her think he was only interested in her body—in using her.

Then, she'd teased him about making the first move, and he'd pinned her to the damn wall and pushed inside. He didn't know if it was the years of abstinence or just because once he'd admitted he loved her—even to himself—he'd wanted to spend every moment with her. Holding her. Loving her. Make up for not finding her sooner. That only Addison could affect him this way. But... Fuck. He was lucky she hadn't told him to leave. Or slapped his face.

He'd been prepared for both. Had been working through a number of scenarios. Ones he'd hoped would keep him in her house—in her bed. Because, simply holding her had quieted the voices in his head. And for the first time since Ice had saved his ass, Rigs had forgotten about the marks.

She did that to him. Broke him down then built him back up. Stronger than before. As if she'd found his missing pieces and secured them in place. Hell, maybe she had. Given him back what the IED had taken. His confidence. His humanity.

His life.

Not that he'd done anything to deserve it. Sure, he'd dealt with a few threats against her. But he would have done that for anyone. It was in his blood. An essential part of his genetic makeup. She deserved to know what she meant to him. That she was special.

Too damn bad he didn't have a clue how to do that. He'd never been romantic. And spending a dozen years in the Marines hadn't helped the situation. If anything, he was more emotionally removed than before he'd enlisted. Special Forces soldiers didn't let their feelings dictate their actions. They were focused on the outcome. On taking whatever measures were necessary to guarantee the success of their mission. On making hard decisions. Exactly the opposite of what Addy deserved.

Which meant, he needed to change tactics. Be less the hardcore ordinance soldier Rigs, and more the man she'd brought back to life. More Kent. Surely, he could figure out a way to make that a reality. To stop looking for trouble every second of every day.

After he'd unearthed who was after her and disposed of the fucker. Permanently. Because putting her stalker in jail didn't feel like enough. Wouldn't completely eliminate the chance of more men being sent in the future.

Damn, how would he deal with her rejoining the force? Hunting down drug dealers? Because he knew, without a doubt, that she'd be back on duty the moment her sight returned for good.

Rigs took a calming breath. He could deal with that. No problem. He'd just have to make sure he wasn't on an assignment whenever she went on a raid. That he could find himself in the vicinity—just in case. Or... Maybe he could convince her to join the bomb squad—have Blade at her side. While most people thought bomb disposal officers were crazy, he considered it a calculated risk. One far better than dealing with men with nothing to lose. Who'd rather kill everyone than get taken into custody. And Rigs could definitely help her out—give her pointers. Have an excuse to hang around her work more often.

Fuck. He was thinking like a possessive asshole. Not the kind of ideas that would keep Addy in his life. Maybe if he—

Footsteps sounded in the hall, then she was standing there. Blonde hair gleaming in the sunlight. She was dressed in jean shorts and a tank, her adorable sandaled feet shifting on the wooden floors. Those beautiful blue eyes searching the area, not that she could see, right now. The way she tilted her head, trying to zero in on any sound. How one hand was palmed against the wall —whether for balance or to keep herself oriented he wasn't sure—but it all spoke to her being back in the darkness.

She smiled, and his heart kicked over. Left a sore spot right in the center, again. Confirmed all the thoughts running through his head—that she was his. That he'd find a way to be the man she needed—the one she'd resurrected. Only better.

He forced himself to breathe, to do anything other than stare at her in utter silence. "Damn, you're beautiful."

She laughed at his words—at the raspy tone of his voice. The one he'd used when they were making love. "I'm not the only one."

Christ. She was serious. Again. It didn't make any sense, but Rigs wasn't going to question his good fortune.

He stepped out from behind the counter, finally realizing she wasn't holding her cane. "Shit, did I move your cane? Forget it someplace?"

She shook her head, blonde hair swishing about her shoulders. "I thought maybe I could just use your arm." She toed at the floor with one delicate foot. "If you don't mind?"

Mind? She wanted to let him *care* for her. *Guide* her. Spend the rest of the evening with her *touching* him, even if it was just his arm. While his teammates were there. A visible declaration that they were a couple.

He made a noise—part grunt, part moan. Did she know what that meant to him?

Addison laughed louder, holding out one hand. "I'll take that as a yes. Of course, once Blade's recovered, you'll have to share that duty. Though, I'm sure you two can come to some sort of understanding."

Damn straight they would. He didn't have much experience with dogs, but he'd make sure he became an expert. Or at least, Blade's best friend.

Rigs stepped toward her, heart hammering, his hands clammy, when a red dot flashed on the corner of the wall behind her, then shifted to her shoulder.

His training kicked in before he'd even finished processing the situation. Had him diving across the space, catching her in his arms and taking her to the floor. Glass shattered in the living room, chunks of wall spraying across them as he rolled them into the hallway. Another dull thud, and the light next to the kitchen exploded, raining down glass and bits of filament.

Rigs glanced up, Addison's body pinned beneath his —as much of her as possible shielded from the debris. From another attack. Another bullet cracked through the wall—far too close to their heads for his liking— then punched through the drywall across from them.

"Shit."

Why hadn't he thought about a sniper? That maybe the person or people hunting her might be done trying to make it look like a random murder? That they would come at her with every resource at their disposal? He had measures in place—more than what he'd admitted to—but they wouldn't be much help unless the shooter tried to access the property—come inside the damn house.

Another shot. Closer than the last. Lower.

Rigs slid off Addison, grabbing her hand as he leaned down. "Whoever wants you dead isn't stopping. And your walls aren't going to offer much protection. Bastard's slicing through them like butter. We need to get out here."

"I have a Beretta in a lockbox in my bedroom."

"I'm fully loaded already, but your window might be the exit point we need. We can grab your weapon in the process." He helped her onto her knees. "Stick to me like glue, sweetheart. And stay low."

She nodded, then they were off, crouching low, staying out of any sight lines from the windows. More bullets tracked their progress—had they gotten close enough to use a Range-R? Maybe a drone overhead beaming them information—and he had to grab her and launch them both through the doorway when one nearly clipped her arm.

Rigs cushioned her fall as much as possible, ensuring her head didn't hit the floor. "Stay here a second."

He darted to the dresser, tipped it over then angled it in front of them. It wasn't much, but it might be enough to prevent full penetration.

She turned toward him when he ducked down next to her. "Not sure the dresser will be enough."

Damn, she was good at reading his actions by sound. "Might make any hit non-fatal. Where's your Beretta?"

"Closet, top shelf on the right."

"Wait here."

He raced over, grabbed the box then returned, hitting hard when another bullet crashed through one of the walls. "Shit. There're just too many external walls. What's the code?"

She rattled it off, and he opened the box, loading in a magazine then handing her the gun. She arched a brow, but he merely touched her hand.

"You'll have more accuracy with a weapon you're familiar with. And after the way you took that creep down at the auction, I'll trust you to have my back any day."

Her mouth hinged open, but she didn't answer, cocking the gun then nodding at him.

He looked at the window. It opened onto the opposite side of the house. Would hopefully give them enough time to get around to the front and in sight of his truck.

He took her hand, again. "Okay, we'll go out the window. You'll focus on listening for anything behind us. We'll head straight for the driveway. My truck's not that far, and I can give us enough cover we should be able to reach it."

"Cover?"

"I'll explain once we're there, just... Don't stop moving, and do exactly what I say, when I say it. Understand?"

"Crystal clear."

"That's my girl. Okay. Let's go."

He tugged her against his back, then he was moving. Five steps, and they were at the window, off to one side, bodies low. He checked the area then opened it, kicking out the screen and scanning the yard before lifting Addison and jumping through with her still in her arms. She gasped but didn't resist, quickly gaining her balance once he'd placed her on his feet.

He squeezed her hand, then they were off, again. Six seconds, and they'd reached the corner, backs against the wall, her body trapped behind his. He surveyed the walkway up the side of the house then started along it, already working through the steps he'd take if someone jumped out at them.

Addison followed behind him, silent. Her body moving with ease despite the death grip he had on her hand. The quick pace. He silently reminded himself to praise her later as they made their way to a gate. He lifted the latch when she inhaled.

He didn't wait for her to warn him—spinning them both around, catching the guy racing across the back-yard—the one who'd obviously disarmed Rigs' trip wire. Who was quickly narrowing in on the walkway—pistol tucked at his shoulder, mask covering his face. The guy jerked, feet flying forward as he landed on his back. Motionless.

Rigs took a step, searching for more tangos, when the gate flung open behind him. He tried to turn, but Addison was already moving—ducking low then step-ping into the guy—swinging her arm up then around, knocking the guy off-balance. A quick sweep of one leg, and she had him onto his hands and knees, startled gasp sounding around him. She kicked the guy in the ass, landing on his back and smashing the butt of her Beretta across the back of his neck.

Rigs moved in beside her, snagging her arm then helping her up. "Remind me not to piss you off. Let's go."

He guided her through the gate, knocking the guy back down with a firm boot to the head when he tried to push onto his elbows. The bastard stilled.

Another few seconds, and they'd made it to the front corner of the house. Rigs checked the area—nothing sounding around them but the wind blowing through the trees—rustling the leaves.

No birds. No crickets.

That was never a good sign. He'd been tracking time —twenty seconds. That's how long it had been since the last shot. Which meant the fucker was probably on the move, too. Had figured out they were fleeing and was actively hunting them. And when his buddies didn't check in...

Not a problem. Getting to the driveway had been the hard part, but now... Now, the bastards were in Rigs' playground. And Rigs didn't play nice.

He pulled out his phone, tugging Addison closer. "It's about thirty feet to my truck. I'll activate some countermeasures, then we'll run. We'll get in my side. Once I toss you in, you get low and stay low, got it? I'll tell you when it's clear."

"Countermeasures? I thought you only wired the place for visual effects?"

"I may have forgotten to mention *every* detail."

"You didn't forget."

"No. I didn't. Ready?"

He hit the number, pocked the cell, then waited.

Two seconds, and a series of smoke grenades ignited along the driveway, quickly covering the area in a green haze.

Four seconds, and the small charges he'd planted around the yard exploded, shooting chunks of dirt and rock into the air. Shouts rose above the other noises, followed by sirens blaring in the backyard as lights flashed in the setting sun.

"Movement behind us. Run, now."

He took off, still staying low, gun at the ready, Addison's hand firm in his. He followed a zigzagging pattern, unlocking the door several feet back. They hit the truck as shots rang out behind them, ricocheting off the grill.

Rigs opened the door then bodily threw Addison in, ensuring her head was down before starting the truck. More bullets cracked the windshield, one breaking through and impacting the seat rest next to his head.

He hit the gas pedal, squealing the tires as the truck shot backwards, smoke billowing out from the friction. He spun the wheel, executing a full one-eighty, then accelerated forward, jumping onto the road as the truck fishtailed to the left.

The street was deserted, nothing but the setting sun glinting off the hood of the truck. He floored it, rounded the next bend then kept on going. This stretch was long. Nothing in the way of cover. He reached for Addison when a truck squealed out behind him, skidding onto the pavement in a spray of mud from some dirt path off to the left.

He glanced in the rearview. The vehicle was black, tinted windows obscuring his view of the interior. The front bumper was bare, which meant the bastards had either stolen it or it wasn't licensed.

Had to be at cleanup crew—a second set of hired thugs sent to ensure no one survived. Or maybe for this exact situation. If they knew Rigs was shadowing Addison—that he hadn't left her side. That he was ex-Special Forces. It might have changed their strategy. Might be the reason they'd disposed of the stealthy route—were attacking head on.

It also meant it there was at least one mole in her department—someone who was privy to information that hadn't been made public.

A ping, then a shower of glass as the rear window shattered. Had to be at least two people in the truck—armed with a rifle if Rigs was correct.

He glanced at Addy. "Bastards are persistent. I'll grant them that much. Addison. I need you to take the wheel for a moment."

Addy shot up beside him, eyes wide, mouth hinged open. "You want me to what?"

"I need you to hold it steady. So I can take out one of their tires."

"Great idea. Let the blind girl drive."

"Just for a few seconds. The road's straight for at least a mile." He squeezed her hand. "You've got this."

"Wait. Kent."

He placed her hands on the wheel then turned,

lowering his window. Leaning out. Addison gasped, her knuckles blanching white around the leather wrapping. The truck shimmied, veering left then shifting back over.

He ignored the motion. As long as she didn't steer them into a ditch, he could adapt. And she wouldn't. She might doubt herself, but he didn't.

Addy mumbled something in the background— probably cursing at him—the truck shimmying, again, before steadying. Rigs focused on the other truck. On the tires spinning across the pavement. The direction the wind tipped the bushes over on the other side of the road. Anticipating any possible redirection as he lined up his target.

The bastards kept firing, hitting his tailgate. The mirror just off to his right. A couple more flying through the cabin. God, if one of them hit Addison…

Rigs steadied his hand then fired. Hit wide the first time when the driver veered right—sending a chunk of dirt into the air. The next shot blew a hole in the grill, tendrils of steam rising out of the hood.

"Kent."

Damn, he hated the hint of fear in her voice, not that he could blame her. He'd be shitting his pants if their positions were reversed. Which just made him love her more. "You're doing great. Just another couple of seconds, sweetheart."

Rigs aimed, again—waiting for the bastard behind him to shift in anticipation—then squeezed the trigger. The front tire popped then flattened, careening the truck off the side and across a stretch of gravel.

Kent didn't waste time watching. Didn't entertain the thought of stopping—confronting the men here. Now. Not when he couldn't guarantee Addison's safety. When others could be on the way—trailing behind. Ready to attack as soon as he turned around.

Instead, he slipped back in, taking the wheel from Addison. Her fingers stayed locked beside his, her harsh pants filling the cabin.

Rigs placed one hand over hers. "It's okay, Addy. You can let go."

She sucked in a few gasping breaths then uncurled her fingers. It seemed to take her a few tries before she finally let go, clasping her hands in her lap.

He reached for her. "You did great."

"You're lucky I didn't tip the damn truck over." She focused on him, color high on her cheekbones. "Don't do that, again. I could have leaned out the window. Taken a few shots. At least, I wouldn't have risked your life."

"Not chancing they would fire directly at you."

"Right, because killing us both was a much better plan. And what the hell happened to Russel's theory that my survival instincts kicked in whenever I was in mortal danger? How was this not life-threatening enough to make me see?"

"Guess you were more confident than you thought." He frowned when she huffed, then hissed as she grabbed her side. "You okay?"

"Fine. My side just stings a bit."

Dread settled in his stomach as he looked down. "Lift your arm."

"Kent. I'm fine. Concentrate on the road."

"Addison. Please, lift your arm."

He considered it a miracle he'd kept his tone even. That he hadn't yelled—pulled the truck over—because if his suspicions were right...

Addison grunted but obeyed, revealing a slash of red against her blue tank.

"Fuck."

"What?"

"You're hit. Lift your tank."

"Hit? I don't remember..." Her breath left as a raspy curse. "Damn."

Rigs stared at the long line across her ribs—the one oozing blood down her creamy skin—and had to fight not to scream. Not to turn around—finish off the bastards in the truck because he was going to make them pay.

Addison touched the area. "It's just a graze."

"It's a fucking bullet wound. Shit!"

"I barely feel it. Honestly."

"Don't care. I swore you wouldn't get a scratch, and..." And he'd fucking failed.

Her hand settled on his. "You were incredible."

He grunted, knowing if he answered he'd say all the wrong things. Instead, he pulled out his phone—hit Ice's number.

His buddy answered on the second ring. "We were just heading out. Wanted to give you and Addison a bit of alone time." Ice cleared his throat. "You *did* make up, right?"

"They've switched tactics. They're using snipers. A crew of men."

"Report." Any lightness had left the man's voice.

"Got pinned down inside her house. We managed to make it to the truck. Left a couple on the ground at her place. A few more on the side of the road in an unmarked black truck, but Addison's been hit."

"Lay it out for me, Rigs."

"Left side. Doesn't look life-threatening, but…" But he'd allowed her to get hurt. And that ate at him.

Addison found his hand—took his phone. "Russel? It's Addison. I'm fine, just a scratch down my ribs. I'm not even sure it's from a bullet. I probably cut myself on some glass."

Rigs huffed, easing the phone out of her hand. "It's a bullet wound. She's just being…stubborn."

Russel sighed. "Where are you guys?"

"Headed your way. I'll make sure no one's following us, but… We need intel. Something to go on. I can adapt, keep eliminating the threats, but…" But her getting grazed was a direct result of having to constantly shift gears. And with her not being able to see anything coming until it was on top of her… Like it or not, she was at greater risk. Despite taking the guy out. Holding her own.

He blew out an exasperated breath. "Whoever's after her has far more resources than we thought. First, C4. Now, sniper rifles and suspected thermal or UWB imaging resources. Probable drones. Vehicles I'm betting can't be traced. And they've obviously been watching her place. Waited until there were only the two of us there—gave us just enough time to get cocky."

"Cannon's on his way. Hank and Sam are already here. We'll figure this out. But either way, we'll find you someplace safe. You risked your ass for Harlequin. For me. We've got your back. In the meantime, keep pressure on the wound. I'll take care of everything once you get here. How long?"

"Twenty minutes. But I'll make it in just over ten."

"Roger. And Rigs… We'll keep Addison safe."

Rigs cut off the call. He didn't want to be reminded how he'd already let Addison down.

"Kent. Stop."

He frowned, glancing over at her, before removing his shirt. He never bared his chest outside, but Addison's welfare was more important than someone seeing his scars. Reacting to them.

He wadded it up, pressing it against her wound. "Hold that tight. And we can't stop."

She hissed out a breath as she took the shirt from him. "I meant stop blaming yourself. We're both fine—"

"You were shot."

She sighed, then slid over, resting her head on his shoulder. "And I thought cops were stubborn. You were amazing. But you can't cover every angle, every second we're at risk. If my damn sight had just kicked in—"

"You took that bastard down without missing a beat. Couldn't be prouder, sweetheart." He dropped a kiss on the top of her head. "Keep the pressure on. We'll be at Russel's soon. And he's real good."

"Thank you."

"I'm the lucky one. Rest, like Ice said. We'll figure this out."

If it took Rigs venturing out—taking the fight to them, he was ready. They'd made it personal. And not just for him. Russel. Sam. Hank. Even Cannon. They were brothers. Family that went deeper than blood. And they wouldn't stop until the men were caught—dead or alive.

CHAPTER 16

ADDISON SAT IN A CHAIR, one arm braced on Russel's kitchen counter, the other snugged to her chest. Kent had insisted on carrying her inside—muttering something about blood loss. About her saving her strength. Despite the fact it wasn't even that bad. After being shot three times—getting caught in an explosion—a four-inch groove down her side barely registered. Sure, it stung, but not the way Kent had worked it up inside his head.

Though, she suspected he would have reacted like that to *any* kind of injury. A bump on the head. A bruised elbow. A damn splinter. Somehow, he would have found a way to take the blame. To find fault in his actions. When in reality, he'd saved her ass.

Again.

Addison groaned inwardly. The situation had quickly gotten out-of-hand. How she'd ended up on someone's hit list, she wasn't sure. She stuck to her original argument. She still didn't remember what had happened the night of the raid. Couldn't have outed anyone, even if there was a fellow officer or group of people abusing their power—acting as if they were above the law. It would have made more sense if she'd been targeted shortly afterwards—when the chances of regaining her memory, her vision, had been fairly high. But after all this time...

Despite the flashes, the possibility of a full recovery, she was losing faith. If Russel was right, her damn vision should have kicked in while they were running to Kent's truck. Or at least, when he'd asked her to take the wheel. Over fifteen years of driving under her belt, and she'd never been so terrified trying to steer a vehicle. Though she'd locked her arms as best she could, lest she risk inadvertently redirecting the truck, all she'd been able to do was picture what would happen if she drove off the road. All the ways Kent could die.

The air swirled next to her, and she knew he'd returned. He'd gone to grab another shirt after he'd placed her in the chair—told her not to move until Russel had fixed her. She hadn't realized he'd had to come in bare chested. Show off the scars he'd been hiding because he'd used his shirt to stem the bleeding. And she'd secretly wondered if maybe, as a result, he'd changed his mind—decided having to guard someone who was an obvious liability was too much. That she hadn't lived up to the fantasies inside his head.

If he'd really had them.

She had. And he'd surpassed everything she'd imagined. The way he tasted, how well he kissed. The gravelly tones of his voice that could make her cream her shorts from nothing more than her name. A random word. And his body—the man could be on the cover of a magazine he was so ripped. Why he'd want to tie himself to someone like her—someone incapable of truly having his back. Being a teammate—still mystified her.

A sigh, then Kent curled in close, his body touching hers. "Must be losing my touch if you're having this many doubts after only five minutes apart, sweetheart."

She concentrated on where his face would be—those luscious lips of his that were likely pursed together. Begging to be kissed. "You're not losing your touch. Trust me. And it's not crazy of me to question why you're still hanging around. Why you're *all* still hanging around instead of handing this off to the police. Or the Feds. Someone. Especially, when I'm not exactly up to your qualifications. Besides, how did you even know?"

"Facial expressions. It was written across your forehead. The fine lines around your mouth and eyes. And you already know why I'm here. What you do to me—*mean* to me. That I have no intentions of leaving. Which makes you family to everyone else in the room, so…" He dropped a kiss on her mouth. "Get used to having a team. That's not going to change anytime soon."

Addison stilled, certain her face betrayed her shock. Kent had just outed himself—outed them—to his friends. Announced that they were together. Kissed her. Right there. In front of Russel and whoever else was in the room. She'd been too preoccupied by Kent's obvious distress when he'd carried her in—by the play of his muscles, the feel of his skin beneath her palms—to properly sense how many other people were in the room. On the phone, Russel had said Sam and Hank were there, but... It was impossible to tell. Not with how silent they all were.

Not that she minded being outed. Now that she'd jumped—had decided she couldn't go back to simply existing. To a future that was darker than the one she faced still blind—she didn't want to hide their relationship. What woman would, with Kent on her arm? And she'd already assumed his friends had clued in to her feelings for him. The way her skin heated whenever he was close was sure to show on her face. But hearing him say the words—give everyone a visual display—blew her away.

Russel tapped her on the arm, drawing her attention. "Okay, honey. You're all set. The laceration wasn't that bad. You should be fine in a few days. I'm sure Rigs will stay on top of you…it."

Kent grunted. "Must you always be such an ass?"

Russel gave her hand a squeeze, his breath on her cheek alerting her that he'd moved in close. "Curious how he thought it was funny when it was me and Harlequin."

"I've never thought you were funny, Ice."

"Right. Anyway, Cannon should be here any minute. In the meantime, I'll grab you something to drink. You lost a fair amount of blood. You should keep yourself hydrated."

Kent grumbled beside her at Russel's words, staying close when she felt Russel stand—sensed him leave.

She turned, homing in on Kent's face. "Again, this wasn't your fault."

"Thinking we'll have to agree to disagree on this one. You're under my protection. That means every bruise, every scratch is on me."

She arched a brow. "I'm going to get hurt sometimes. It's called life."

"Not on my watch."

"You're a born protector. As long as you're alive and breathing and hanging around, you're going to insist it's your watch."

He chuckled, then kissed her cheek. "Touché. And yeah, it is. I just..."

She reached for him—drew him closer with a finger on his chin. "How about we go for staying alive on your watch?"

"Already a given. Anyone gunning for you will have to kill me, first. That's just the way it is. Today. Tomorrow. Whether you're a cop, again, or not. Only way I know how to function. How to get it straight in my head."

"This ties into that 'letting you protect me' thing, doesn't it?" She smiled when she heard him inhale. Felt his muscles tense beneath hers.

Did he think she'd deny him that? He'd saved her life three times. Had put himself in the line of fire. Had been willing to get shot, killed, just to keep her safe. And he was worried she'd balk at allowing him to have a say over her safety? When she knew it stemmed from his injuries—from the demons he'd faced in war. The ones she suspected he hadn't quite vanquished.

Kent blew out a breath—somehow got closer. "I know you're not helpless. I do, but—"

"But it's in your blood. The same way Blade must have pegged you as an ordinance soldier. Which means I'll just have to let you do what you need to do. Just don't get mad when my vision comes back, and my captain tries to recruit you."

"Or maybe Hank will recruit you? You'd be one hell of an addition."

"Are you always going to have a comeback?"

"If it involves your safety? You bet. Besides, you already have far more power over me than I'd care to admit. This might be the only avenue where I actually win an argument."

"Ah, don't give up too easily. I'm betting the makeup sex would be phenomenal."

He grunted. "You did that on purpose, didn't you? Reminded me how damn desperate I am to touch you, again."

"Maybe after—"

A knock, followed by a swirl of air. She turned toward the doorway, then froze. Breath held. One hand fisted against Kent's thigh, the other at her side. While she hadn't put much stock in the whole sixth sense thing blind people seemed to develop. Hadn't really believed she'd done more than focus her hearing better, increase her ability to feel the air. She was willing to believe it all, now. Because despite being locked in the dark. Unable to see whoever had just entered the room

—hadn't Russel called him Cannon—she knew, without a doubt, that the man was dangerous.

And not in the way Kent and his buddies were. Men who'd face any threat without blinking an eye. Worrying about the odds. Men who had honor shoved up their asses. Who bled red, white, and blue.

This guy *was* the threat. The personification of the bogey man. He didn't just eliminate his enemies. He decimated them. Escorted their souls straight to hell. And he was good at it.

She wasn't sure how she knew. But there was something in the air—an energy that made every inch of her exposed skin bead. Made it feel as if the room had suddenly dropped ten degrees. And there was a scent. She wasn't sure what it was, but it kicked her heart rate into triple digits. Made her pulse throb inside her head, and for a moment, she thought she might pass out.

Or run.

That seemed like the best scenario. Grab Kent's hand and leave. Get as far away from the other man as possible. Hide until the overwhelming sense of doom left her system. Until she could breathe.

Hushed voices. A few soft footsteps, then he was there. In front of her. She knew it. Felt it. Breathed it in through every pore. She was in the presence of a true predator. The kind that never lost.

"Addison? Shit. Ice!"

Hands on her arms, tugging her toward the chair, again. But she wouldn't budge. Couldn't. Not until she was somewhere else. Anywhere else.

"Breathe for me, Addison." Russel's voice. Close, but somehow distant.

A hushed curse in front of her, then audible steps back. "It's okay. Ice. Just…give her some space."

The movement stopped. Russel and Kent's hands grazing down her arms then off. Everything stilled. Went silent.

"It's Addison, right?" God, his voice was so deep— was there something below *basso profondo*? And so far above her. Far higher than Kent's or Hank's. Even Russel seemed small compared to how the air moved around this guy. He must be massive.

"You've been blind for a while, haven't you? Long enough to hone your senses. To get a read on people the moment they walk in the room. But… What you're sensing…"

He moved toward her, and she hated that she unconsciously stood then matched his step sideways. Bumped into Kent before he wrapped his arm around her waist. Tugged her against his chest.

She reached for his arms, covering his hands with hers. He couldn't let go. Not without her fearing she'd fly apart. Completely unravel.

A sigh. "Sorry, guys. I didn't realize…"

"Realize what?" Kent's voice. Close. Soothing. "Addison. Sweetheart. This is Cannon—Master Sergeant Rick Sloan. The guy we called to help us out. He's a fellow soldier. One of the good guys."

She shook her head.

"Sweetheart. I promise. He'd never hurt you. He—"

"It's okay, Rigs. The girl has excellent instincts.

Knows danger when it's staring her in the face." The guy —Cannon—sighed, again. "Look, Addison. I have a feeling I know what you're sensing. But... It's not me. Not really. I—"

"Death." She barely whispered the word, but it cut the guy off. Spread silence through the room. "*That's* what I smell. Death. On you."

Another sigh. "Yeah. Killed a room full of insurgents less than seventy-two hours, ago. It wasn't pretty. Probably one of the messiest takedowns I've ever been involved in. The whole op went sideways. It's part of the reason I'm back—on mandated leave. I won't lie. I'm still feeling the adrenaline dump. But..."

She frowned. There was something in his voice. Regret. Or maybe sadness. But it loosened the tight feeling in her chest. Took the edge of fear off. She tilted her head to the side. "You've been undercover, haven't you? And not for just a week or two. You've been living like them for months. Maybe a year."

That's what else she was sensing. The restlessness that came from being pulled out. Having to reintegrate into his old life. She'd watched colleagues go through it countless times. Had even done a short stint, herself, just before the raid. It left a mark—one that didn't wash off with a hot shower and some soap.

He chuckled. "We should have you screen possible informants. You're better than any profiler I've ever met. And yeah. Almost two years."

Christ, six months felt like forever. How had he done two years and not lost his sanity? Gotten in so deep there wasn't any coming back? No way to separate the two lives? Resurrect the part of him he'd neglected in order to maintain his ruse?

She nodded. "Russel said you're Delta Force. What squadron?"

"Got recruited to Alpha Squadron ten years ago. I was an Army Ranger before that. I've worked several missions with Midnight. Had Ice haul my ass out of a few places I'm still trying to forget. Teamed up with Hank and Rigs in Afghanistan. But I haven't had much contact since I went under."

"And you're here to...help?" She cringed when her voice rose, sounding like more of a hiccup.

"Russel mentioned Rigs found some C4 at your place. That you just escaped from a crew armed with sniper rifles. Advanced weaponry. Sounds organized. Not to mention military. So, yeah. I'd like to help... If you're comfortable with that?"

She swallowed, managed not to choke, then nodded, again. Not that his energy had changed. More that it had eased. Lightened a bit.

"All right. Why don't you all grab a drink and have a seat? If it's okay, Ice, I'll have a quick shower. Try to wash more of the death stench off me." Cannon snorted. "Forth damn shower I've had in the past two days. But it obviously isn't enough, yet."

Russel muttered something, then they were gone. The heavy feeling lifted off her chest, and she relaxed against Kent.

He sat, handing her a drink after pulling her into his lap. He waited until she'd had a few sips of the tea

Russel must have given him, then gave her a squeeze. "Better?"

"I'm sorry I overreacted. But—"

"No apologies. Not when it comes to your safety. If your spider sense told you Cannon was a threat, then you go with it."

"He's dangerous. That's what I sensed. But not in the way you and your buddies are." She sighed. "I don't know how to explain it. Wouldn't have believed I could feel something like that, until now."

"He *is* dangerous. But not to you. Regardless, I'm not letting anyone hurt you. Period. Not even a fellow soldier."

A chuckle, then the energy was back. Weaker than before. More of a push against her than the suffocating weight she'd experienced. "Easy, Rigs. I just got back. Would rather not have to throw down with you. Not when I know you'd wire my shit so it blew up the next time I sneezed. That's if I made it out of here alive." Footsteps closer. "Any better, Addison?"

"Less like death. More like a mercenary, now."

He laughed louder. "I can live with that. Okay, let's talk about these men who are after you."

She snorted. "I'll have better luck explaining what just happened than who's after me."

"That's why we're here. Let's move over to the living room. Get you more comfortable. Then, we'll start."

Kent rose with her still in his arms then started walking. She clung to his neck, wondering what everyone must think, until he lowered onto a chair, sliding her to his left. It was tight, but they fit. If having half her ass on his thigh counted as fitting.

She waited for his friends to tease them. For Russel to make some comment, but other than the soft press of fabric against cushions, the room remained silent. She reached for Kent's hand, relaxing when his fingers wove through hers.

While she wasn't sure how the conversation would progress, she suspected it would involve talking about the raid. The one topic that sent her into a tailspin. Hadn't they been discussing that when she'd passed out here before? When she'd been unable to give them any concrete intel to go on?

Kent squeezed her fingers. "Breathe, Addy."

She turned to tell him she was breathing—when she realized her lungs were burning. Her throat closed tight. Apparently, just thinking about the raid affected her, now.

He sighed then lifted his arm—wrapped it around her shoulders. Practically pulled her back onto his lap. It seemed childish, but it soothed the raw feeling in her chest. The jumpy sensation making her stomach roil as if she was sitting on a roller coaster.

Addison drew in a deep breath, held it for a moment then blew it out. She'd spent twelve years facing armed men. Surely, she could talk about one raid and not pass out. Let her team down.

"Okay, let's walk through what we know." Cannon, again. "I understand you were a narcotics detective. That you were involved in a raid to gather evidence against a man named Alexander Stevens. You were targeting a gang called the Raptors. But the raid went sideways. Your task force was hit hard, resulting in a few deaths. And you were gravely injured. Is that accurate?"

A twinge of pain. A few flickering images, but she managed to hold it together. "That's what I've been told. I don't remember anything from a few hours before the raid until I woke up in the hospital."

Silence, then air by her left side. Russel's hand on her thigh. "But you're having flashbacks. About that night. The raid. What happened to your partner."

Don't die on me... Kill her, too.

She winced at the harsh voices. The pulse of pain through her temples.

"Easy, Addison. I know it's hard, but… Anything you can tell us…"

Kent huffed. Drew her closer. "I'm right here, sweetheart. Nothing can hurt you. But if this is too much—"

"No." She breathed through the throbbing in her head. "I can't keep hiding. I need to remember. Will died, and I haven't even caught the bastard who shot him. He never would have let me down like that if our positions had been reversed."

A press of boots on the floor then another hand on hers. "Addison? It's Sam. I had Bridgette check the reports. They all say Detective O'Toole died from injuries sustained when the meth lab blew—knocked a wall down on him."

Echoed gunshots sounded around her, and she whipped her head to the side, hoping to hone in on them before she realized they weren't real. She focused on Sam. "What did you say?"

A moment of silence, then he squeezed her hand. "I said, the police and DEA reports say your partner died due to crushing injuries sustained when the meth lab in the next room blew. A wall fell on him."

She shook her head. "I don't understand. He was right there. Above me, then..."

More shots, followed by the ghosted image of a figure silhouetted by a bright light. She tried to see the person's face, when the room appeared around her. No flash of light, this time, just a quick fade into colors. Into brick walls and hardwood floors. The men gathered around her. Kent's tanned hands against her shirt. There was a hint of vanilla in the air from the tea Russel had made her. A stronger scent of coffee from the pot still steaming on the counter.

Addison pushed to her feet, stumbling against Kent when he rose beside her. She turned to look at him—get another glimpse of the blue in his eyes. The handsome lines of his face. No doubt she'd be back into the darkness in a matter of seconds. She couldn't pass up this opportunity to drink in every detail. Put all the dips and curves into memory.

Kent's eyes widened, then he was leaning in—cupping her cheek with one hand. "You're having a flash, aren't you? Right now."

She lifted one hand—traced the line of his jaw. She didn't care about the scars. All she wanted was to feel his skin. See his reaction when she touched him. See her need mirrored in his eyes.

Kent pushed into her touch, and his smile nearly took her to her knees. God, everything he'd said had been true. Because what she saw staring back at her...

She smiled. "Kent..."

She gasped as the images shifted, Kent's face fading into a smoky haze. Gunfire popped in the distance, the acrid smell of propellant heavy in the air. It mixed with something else—some kind of flowery scent that made her stomach threaten to empty. Right there on Russel's floor. Her name sounded from somewhere, but it was crushed beneath the weight pushing her down. She blinked, and Will was above her—hands on her chest. Her blood splattered up his arms. He was telling her to hold on, not to die, then he was falling—covering her. Voices all around her. A face behind his shoulder. A gun...

"Addison!"

Kent called her name, again, and she sucked in a deep breath, realizing she was on her knees, Kent's face level with hers. Russel was on the other side, taking her vitals, his bag opened beside him.

How long had she been lost? Reliving that night while everyone watched?

Her vision started fading—little black dots slowly slipping in from the sides. She pushed everything away, willing the light to stay. The darkness paused—held steady as she made eye contact with Kent. His eyes were so blue. So bright amidst the encroaching shadows.

She wet her lips, still fighting to see. "Will was shot. I saw it. He was over top of me, trying to stem the bleeding. He was fine, then...then..."

Pain had her closing her eyes, grabbing her head in order to stop the unrelenting pounding. It stole her breath, constricted her chest. Kept pushing on her until she finally let the memories die—crumble around her like the warehouse had done.

"Addison. Come on, sweetheart, talk to me."

She groaned, palming one temple as she blinked—knowing the instant nothing changed that the flash was gone. She lifted her hand off her head. Held it out, relaxing when Kent sandwiched it between his. As if he'd been waiting for an opportunity to hold it.

His breath caressed her cheek. "You back with us?"

She nodded, too drained to voice the words. Kent sighed, then gently scooped her into his arms, once again, lowering onto a chair. She wasn't sure if it was the same one or if they'd moved her. But feeling his body hugging hers eased the unsettling sensation in the pit of her stomach—the one that usually had her clutching at the blankets, or wrapping her arms around Blade's neck.

Kent stroked her hair, brushing a soft kiss across her forehead. "Flashbacks are a bitch. Just try to breathe while Russel gets you some more tea."

She burrowed against him. "This feels pretty great just the way it is."

His heart kicked up against her cheek, the increased rhythm making her smile. The guy was hardcore. Had made a living by blowing up bridges. Disarming trip wires and IEDs. He hadn't shown any kind of reaction to danger. No increased breath. No shaky voice. Yet, her admitting that his arms soothed her had his heart tapping wildly in his chest. His breath fluttering the hairs around her face.

Kent exhaled. "You're determined to be the death of me, aren't you?"

"Not a bad way to go."

"Nope. But I'd prefer it to be after we spend the next fifty years together." He smiled against her head at her gasp. "Okay, we'll make it sixty."

Addison eased forward, thankful when Kent helped her sit upright. She opened her mouth to question him when footsteps sounded beside her followed by the press of a mug in her hand.

"Drink." Russel. And she hadn't missed the commanding tone. The one he'd probably used as a PJ whenever he expected compliance.

But the mug felt warm, and her hands were cold, despite the summer temperatures. So, she lifted the cup and took a cautious sip before arching a brow at him. "Is there any tea with my whiskey?"

Russel chuckled. "Very little. Just...trust me. It'll help."

She smiled her thanks, taking another sip. It went down warm and smooth. She relaxed against Kent, only to have him give her a gentle shake.

"I know you're probably exhausted, Addy, but... If there's anything else you can tell us. Anything to go on. You said Will was over you, then..."

A shiver shot across her skin as a few of the memories shuffled through her head, but she kept them distant. Used her grip on Kent's hand to keep her grounded.

"Then… He fell on top of me. There was blood—his blood. I remember voices. Smelling some kind of sickeningly sweet fragrance. Seeing someone over his shoulder, then…" She shook her head. "Maybe that's when the lab exploded. It's like a flash of white light."

That heavy energy pressed in on her, again, and she knew Cannon was standing close. Then, his voice at her level—he must be crouching. "So, he was dead before the place blew?"

She nodded, grimacing against the resulting pain through her temples. "I couldn't move. Couldn't do anything other than lie there."

"You said you heard voices. Do you remember what they said?"

Kill her too… The whole place is gonna blow…

The words looped in her head, the malicious tone settling with unforgiving clarity. Most of the other stuff was still muddled—echoed voices that didn't quite make sense outside of the moment. But those phrases stuck.

She straightened, still holding Kent's hand. "There were two people. One of them said to kill me, too, but the other guy knew the place was going to blow. I think he thought I'd die in the explosion. And I know I've heard their voices before, I just can't place them. It's still…mixed up. Like I'm listening through a filter."

Silence.

Then, Kent's harsh breath. "I'll kill them."

"Kent—"

"Don't even suggest otherwise. Bastards will pay."

She turned toward him when Cannon moved closer, his sheer size disturbing the air around them.

"Rigs? You're our expert." It was Cannon, again. "Is it possible her partner falling on her is what saved her from the explosion?"

Kent's body stiffened, and Addison was certain she felt a low rumble through his chest. "Explosions are tricky. Using the wrong amount, even just a slight miscalculation, can have dramatically different results. Not anticipating the way the heat will fill the building, how the walls will react, can alter the explosive pattern. Decimate areas you thought would be fine. Save others. Or if they had to improvise on the spot—use different chemicals to create the blast than what they were used to... A thousand ways it could go wrong. How about I paint a picture for us?

"Let's assume the people in question are cops or feds or DEA agents from the task force Addison was on. That they're on Stevens' payroll. They'd want to make it look like a takedown gone wrong. People getting shot? Nothing new. They alert the gang they're coming, and anyone not involved meets a tragic end."

He released a slow breath. "But on the off-chance some of them die from friendly fire, or just to reduce the chances of leaving any damning evidence behind, they've rigged the place to blow. No one's going to question a meth explosion—which rules out using C4 as the charge, by the way. Chances are the ME won't even dig that deep when they have the reports—obvious burn and crushing injuries. Even if they find evidence of bullet wounds, they were involved in a shootout. No bullet, and they assume it was from one of the bad guys. They just make sure everyone uses the same caliber.

"But Will and Addison survive the shootout, then Will falls on top of her too close to when things are going to get ugly. They can't move him in time, and he shields Addison, just like you suggested. Takes the brunt of any burn or impact injuries. Either way…they weren't planning on anyone coming out of there alive."

Addison inhaled. "Oh god. I think I know why this is all happening, now. I was added as a backup witness to the Stevens' trial about a month ago. It's very unlikely I'll testify—not like this—but the US Attorney's office wanted me and Joe Wilson put on the official docket so they had the option to call us. Obviously, in my current condition, they wouldn't consider my testimony reliable, which is why I didn't even think about it. It's a remote possibility, at best, but…"

"But these people aren't taking any chances. Figured they'd eliminate any possibility of you or Joe saying something you shouldn't. Something that would have the attorney's office digging deeper. Which is why they staged that burglary." Kent groaned. "Damn. I knew I'd forgotten to ask you something. You mentioned at the auction that you had a new phone. Was that just weird timing or…"

She shook her head. "I was getting odd calls. Either no one on the line or voices that didn't quite make sense. They sometimes gave me headaches. Triggered flashbacks. I tried blocking the number, but they kept coming, so I finally opted to get a new phone number." She groaned. "You think it's all connected. I mean, of course, it's all connected. I should have considered that before. Told you straight off. Maybe then, we wouldn't be continually adapting. And I would have before the raid—when I was at the top of my game. Before I became this version of myself."

"Hey..." Kent's hands wrapped around hers. "You've had a bit to deal with besides trying to adapt to losing your sight—the robbery. Blade getting shot. Attempts on your life." He cleared his throat. "Me being an ass for a while. I'm not sure any of us here would be as well put together as you are."

She smiled at him, wishing she could look him in the eyes. "I like the way you turned out."

Russel chuckled. "Who's making all the goo goo eyes, now, Rigs?"

Kent snorted. "Unless you want your Tacoma to end up in a million pieces, I wouldn't be too cocky."

"You'd never blow up that truck. You love it, too."

"Just keep putting that theory to the test, bro." His breath caressed her cheek, and she knew he was focused on her, again. "Okay, we have a working theory. But that's all it is. What we need is more intel. A plan."

"Addison?" It was Cannon. "Can you give me a list of who was on the task force? I'd like to investigate if any of them have a military connection. Maybe they're ex-military themselves or have friends. Family. Might help narrow down possible suspects because my gut's telling me there's definitely a soldier or two involved."

"Of course, but... I worked with some of them for years. No one ever mentioned being in the military."

"Might not be common knowledge. I can't talk about the past ten years of my life without worrying about accidentally giving something away. So, it's easier to just pretend it didn't exist to anyone who hasn't been part of the Teams."

"I hadn't really considered that. Though, I was thinking…" She paused, giving Kent's hands a squeeze. "I have an idea. One that might shift the balance of power to us."

Kent snorted. "Am I going to like your idea?"

"Probably not."

CHAPTER 17

NO WAY. No *fucking* way. Not happening. Over his dead body. Or worse—Addison's.

Rigs clenched his jaw, looking around the table at the men gathered in chairs, gazes fixed on Addison. They'd reconvened after dispersing last night—giving Cannon, Hank, and Sam more time to investigate the members of Addison's task force. To consider her idea —the one that put her in the crosshairs. Made her even more of a target. The plan Rigs was about to crush until it was nothing more than a dim memory.

Because he would not put her life in jeopardy, again.

"Rigs?"

Rigs pulled himself out of his thoughts—from the plan of hiking Addison up over his shoulder and disappearing. Going so far off-grid no one—including his teammates—would ever find them. And he would. He'd lift her in his arms, walk out to his truck, and drive. Except, she'd never leave Blade behind, nor would he, and the dog wasn't fit to travel, yet.

Then, there were his buddies. No way they'd stand idly by while he ran. That's not how teams functioned, and he owed every man at the table his life. Had saved theirs. They were in this together. Which meant talking calmly. Rationally. Not glaring at his buddies before he'd explained his concerns.

He turned to stare at Ice. Convey his displeasure with nothing more than eye contact. "Ice."

The man winced. Actually winced at Rigs' tone. "Obviously, you're not happy with what's being discussed, so… Might as well get it all out in the open."

He glanced at Addison when she swung her head his way, that beautiful sightless gaze staring at him—all bright blue eyes and pink lips. It was the same expression she'd had when she'd woken up in his arms, after spending the night together in Russel's spare room. They hadn't even had sex—how could he when her fucking side was still raw. Still likely oozing beneath the bandages. All because he'd allowed her to get hurt.

Instead, he'd simply held her. Counted every second of her body pressed against his, her heart tapping against his palm. Listened to her steady breath. Assured himself that she was still alive. Still there with him.

It had been one of the best nights of his life.

And it had scared him shitless.

Because he knew. He knew as sure as the damn sun would rise, that his face would still be scarred, that she wouldn't back down. Wouldn't stop at anything less than what it took to bring these monsters in. Put the bastards who'd killed her partner behind bars.

She didn't seem to care about the risks. The real chance she would get killed, because despite his determination, his crew, shit happened. It had happened to his MARSOC unit, and it could easily happen here. Now. And he'd lose her. Lose himself.

He took a deep breath, once again, reminding himself to keep his voice even. "Not sure there's much to say other than I can't get behind a plan that has Addison front and center. Out in the open where these bastards want her. We're at a distinct disadvantage. Have no idea how deep Stevens' pockets really are. For all we know, Addison is the only cop in her precinct *not* on the take."

To his credit, Ice didn't roll his eyes. Didn't snort or laugh. Instead, he nodded, looking around the table at the rest of their team. "You're right. We don't know for sure that our suspicions are correct. But before we rule anything out, let's hear what Cannon has to say. He should be here any minute."

Rigs clenched his jaw in response. It was the best he could do without pounding his fists on the table—looking like a complete ass. Because he knew what the others were thinking—that Rigs had fully supported the plan when Harlequin had been willing to face her enemy. Had convinced Russel to trust him. It made sense to allow the other man the same privilege.

Except for the part where Rigs knew—firsthand—how even the best plans went up in smoke. How Ice had nearly lost Harlequin to a lack of intel, and how this could go so much worse. Granted, Addison was a trained officer. Had proven she could hold her own. Wouldn't go down without a fight.

But that didn't sooth the burning sensation under his skin. The nervous energy that was making it hard to sit there when he wanted to pace. He never paced. Never let any doubts show. Feeling like this—it was new and not something he enjoyed.

Addison reached over—placed her hand on top of his. And bam, everything slid into focus. That he'd do anything to protect her. Starting with eliminating everyone gunning for her.

A knock, followed by Cannon walking into the room. Addison inhaled, tightening her grip on his hand. Rigs shifted closer. While he couldn't stop her from sensing how dangerous Cannon was, the least he could do was offer her the comforting support of his body close to hers. A subconscious signal to her brain that assured her nothing bad would happen as long as he was beside her. That he was primed and ready to strike.

Cannon stopped a few steps back, studying Addison before releasing a weary breath, then taking a seat next to Ice. He offered Rigs an apologetic smile. "Still sensing that mercenary vibe, Addison?"

She snorted, visibly pushing her shoulders down. "How big are you?"

"Six four. Two fifty."

"Wow. Okay, that accounts for the shifting of air whenever you're around. As for the mercenary vibe—I know you're not a threat. At least, not to me. I do. It's just…" She sighed. "Maybe it's all the sensory input over the past few days. The flashes of vision. I'm hyper aware of everything. Though, having a mercenary vibe when it's directed at the people targeting me isn't a bad thing. And Kent has assured me—repeatedly—that you're one of the good guys."

She twisted to face Cannon. "I can't imagine how hard it must be reintegrating after two years. Even if it's just some forced R&R. I've seen veteran cops go sideways after several months of deep undercover work. After all your time, and in unimaginable conditions…"

He shrugged, even though she couldn't see him. Though, maybe she could feel the other man move. Rigs wasn't a small guy. He matched Ice for height at six feet, though his buddy probably had a good thirty pounds on him. Still, size had never really mattered. Someone was either a threat or not. But even he had to admit, Cannon was large—beyond that, really. Not someone Rigs would choose to go up against unless it was necessary. And he was pretty damn glad the other man was on their side.

Still, for Addison, Rigs would challenge anyone. Eliminate any threat.

Cannon leaned back in his chair. "I'll do my best to direct that energy at the shitheads after you. Because any soldier who'd betray a fellow officer. Sell out his soul for blood money deserves everything we throw at them."

Rigs straightened. "You've got leads?"

"A few too many for my liking. Seems there were three ex-military personnel on the task force, and another two who have ties. Our ex-soldiers are Detective Trent Seymour, and DEA agents Shawn Townsend and the recently deceased Joseph Wilson. His partner, Grace Sanchez, has a brother in the service, as does the medical examiner, one José Pedro, who signed off on the findings for both Agent Sanchez and Detective O'Toole."

Addison's mouth gaped open. "Trent's ex-military? What branch?"

Cannon laughed. "That wasn't easy to unearth. Had to call in a few favors. The kind that were forged from blood. Turns out he spent a very short time in Black Ops. Rumored former Delta, as well, but was then recruited to the CIA. He was only with them two years before joining your precinct. A rather...odd career change. And all my time with Delta, and I've never heard of the guy. Sam? Anything on the Ranger front for him?"

Sam huffed. "If the guy was ever a Ranger, no one I know ever served with him. He's a ghost."

Cannon grunted. "Which leads me to think he might have been CIA all along. Gets a phoney military record made to cover his tracks. Then, he goes more mainstream Agency until he joins the Seattle Police Department. Makes it look all above board."

Hank whistled. "Is it just me, or is everyone else's spider sense tingling? Because that screams plant to me."

"You and me both, brother. If I had to guess, I'd say he's been reporting back to someone. I suppose there's a chance he's one of the good guys. Sent to investigate some obvious moles in the PD, who have ties to organized crime, likely a military connection, but..."

Rigs tapped the table with his fist. "But why hasn't he made any arrests? Seems like he's had plenty of time and lots of opportunities to gather evidence. And why not come clean, at least, to Addison when bullets started flying her way? Once Wilson got capped, Seymour should have made a move. Offered to protect Addy."

"If he's clean. Hank? You get anything else on our DEA friends? My contacts couldn't unearth anything after they left the service. And there's nothing in their records to suggest they were involved with drugs or organized crime."

Hank sighed. "All my buddy would say is that there isn't anything usual about them. Clean records. No huge purchases that would flag a sudden influx of money. Which would be stupid on their part. Though, it's obvious they wanted to shut Wilson up. Thinking the guy might have been part of it but was having...regrets."

"Best way to keep a secret is to kill everyone involved but yourself. Maybe one trustworthy partner." Cannon reached out and touched Addison's hand. "Have you worked with those agents before?"

"Wilson was on a couple of other task forces, but I wasn't ever on his crew. And Townsend's new. He transferred from another department. That was my first time working with Grace Sanchez. She spent most of her free time with Will. She didn't strike me as dirty. And, while Trent can be an ass, he's a decent cop. Always had mine or Will's back in a takedown over the past couple years. That's all I can really tell you."

"Which leaves us with a lot of conjecture and no real direction." Cannon raised his gaze to Rigs'. "Unless we go forward with Addison's suggestion. Have her walk in there—find a way to let them think she's recovered her memory. Could bring everyone involved down."

Addison must have felt his muscles tense. Maybe the way the air around him changed because she twisted toward him, tilting her head to either side as if trying to read him through her pores. Through any minute sound or breeze.

He glanced at his buddies, but they all just sat there, faces stone cold, elbows resting on the table, their hands clasped together. The universal sign for him to take lead. To voice his concerns. He drew a deep breath, only to have Addison arch a brow.

She gave his hand a squeeze. "I know you're worried—"

"Worried? I was worried when I bumped into you. That maybe I'd hurt you. That you wouldn't agree to have coffee with me. This..." He pulled back the anger he knew colored his voice. "This is defcon two, sweetheart, because the only reason it would ever reach one is if you were dead. Which is what could very well happen if we go through with this."

He pushed out the chair then stood, pacing over to the counter then turning and leaning against it. He knew he was likely overreacting but... Damn it. He'd only just found her after spending the last two years trying to make peace with the fact she couldn't exist. That no one could ever look at him the way she did— blind or sighted. That he'd be the one forever lost in the darkness—afraid to step into the light.

She'd given that back to him. The sun. A world beyond skeezy motels and backwoods cabins. Something more valuable than his life. She'd saved his soul. And now, she wanted him to just stand there and let her waltz into the precinct—a fucking viper's nest of tangos.

Nope. Cop training or not. Her vision a perfect twenty-twenty or completely blind. That just wasn't something he could do. Not and still look at himself in the mirror. Still see any form of honor staring back at him.

Addison swiveled to follow his progress across the room, starting at him with those beautiful sightless eyes for so long, he thought maybe she was caught in another flashback. A silent one where she couldn't move. Couldn't speak. But just when he went to move—call her name—she nodded.

"All right. If Plan A bothers you, how about we switch a few things up? Get to a place where you *are* comfortable."

"Oh, so you're going to stay locked up with Ice while Cannon, Sam, Hank, and I flush these bastards out then eliminate them? Because that's the only plan where I'll ever be *comfortable*."

Rigs had to give her credit. She didn't stand up, yell then tell everyone to leave. Or make her way over to him and slap his face. Call him an overprotective asshole. She was a cop. Blind or not, she'd proven she could handle herself. Save his ass if needed. But...

How did he explain that it had nothing to do with her abilities and everything to do with his fears? That the one thing he wouldn't survive—would never come back from—was knowing he'd gotten her hurt. Killed.

Instead, she smiled, patting the seat next to her. He tamped down the urge to pick her up—return to his fallback plan of driving off and getting lost—then walked back to the table, sliding in beside her.

She waited until he was sitting, then held out her hand, knowing he'd take it in his. That he'd never leave her hanging. "Actually, I was thinking that you're right. I shouldn't go in there alone. That's...foolish. I wouldn't chase an armed perp alone if I could help it. Wouldn't walk into a raid without backup, so... I should take the same precautions, here. Especially, when I have my own Black Ops squad just itching to cap the bad guys. And since Blade is still at the vet's, I could walk in on someone's arm without anyone batting an eye."

"On someone's arm? And who were you thinking you'd walk in with?"

Her smile dimmed the room. Made his damn stomach do somersaults. "You, of course. They already met you at the auction. And whoever is in on this knows you've been at my place. That you haven't left my side. No sense outing anyone else." She winked at him. "Besides, you'd probably pop a blood vessel if I said I wanted Cannon or Russel to take me in."

"You're on my watch, sweetheart. It only makes sense." He glanced at his buddies, again, noting their smug smirks. Not that they'd say anything, but damn, it made him want to smack a few off.

He relaxed back. "Okay. Let's say we go through with this—still, insane, by the way. Still a million ways it could get ugly if it turns out your precinct is crawling with Stevens' puppets. You can't just walk in there and say... Oh hey, I got my memory back. Not without them suspecting something. Because if our hunches are right, and you know who's been bought—what really went down that night—there's no way you wouldn't show up without the US Attorney's office and the Feds in tow."

Her smile widened. "Damn straight. Which is why I'm going to have a flashback. And you're going to carry me out."

HOW THE HELL had he let Addison talk him into this?

Rigs was still mulling it over as he led Addison up the front steps then into the lobby of the station. He matched his pace to hers, though she moved considerably fast for only having his arm to guide her. She'd mentioned something about knowing the layout intimately, but with all the people mulling about, he wasn't sure how she could decipher anything. The noise level equaled that of a rock concert, and it was like trying to maneuver through a minefield, only one full of cops and perps and people reporting stolen purses and jacked cars.

But Addison barely seemed to notice. She walked confidently at his side, her arm tucked through his, her hand resting on his forearm. All he had to do was tense his muscle and shift his elbow, and she moved in the direction he wanted her to go. She even stopped on her own when some shithead lunged toward her before an officer yanked him back.

And just a moment before Rigs punched the asshole in the face—knocked him down for good.

At least, no one seemed to notice them. Notice him. The scars on his face. Whether it was nothing new, or that everyone was walking around with blinders, he didn't know. But it suited him just fine.

Except where the mass of people made it extremely hard to keep Addison out of the line of fire. Normally, he'd have already cleared behind him and would position his body in front of hers—whatever angle he needed to put himself between her and a possible bullet. But here...

Here, he wasn't supposed to be dancing around her in an attempt to keep her safe. She was supposed to *be* safe. Just walking at his side while Seattle's finest kept any threat beyond the doors.

Didn't help that the biggest threat was already in the building—armed and licensed to kill. That there was a chance the bastards would simply open fire—blow all of Rigs' team's plans to hell.

His earpiece buzzed.

"Rigs. Cannon. Got you in sight. If anyone so much as twitches wrong toward Addison, I'm on it. Hank, you ready?"

Another buzz, then Hank's voice. Low. Calm. "Second story in view. I can follow you all the way to the stairs."

"I'm on the third. Over by the water cooler." Sam,

this time. "I'll be here until after Addison puts on her show."

Rigs didn't speak, just nodded, making a small gesture with his hand. His buddies would understand the signal—that the mission was a go.

Mission. Addison putting her life on the line, and it was somehow his mission. Damn, he should have just run —spent the rest of his life with her on some tropical beach. Sipping drinks out of coconuts with tiny umbrellas.

Addison tilted her head slightly toward him. "It's going to be fine. I can't get hurt as long as you're with me."

God, he hoped she was right. Because for the first time in his life, he was scared. Though he thought he'd been scared before—when that fucker had been ready to shoot her. When the bullets had been flying through the walls—he realized it had been a cakewalk compared to the clammy slide of fear down his back, now. The sick feeling in the pit of his stomach or the icy shiver of regret already beading his skin.

Not that he'd let her know. She was depending on him, and he had *not* spent all those years in the Marine Corps to fail the one person who meant more to him than life, itself.

Which was how he managed to whisper encouraging words as they made their way to the narcotics floor, heading straight for her colleagues' desks. Both men looked up from their paperwork, eyes going wide— their mouths opening slightly in shock. One of the agents he'd met at the auction—Townsend—had a hip on one of the edges, and barely managed not to tumble onto the floor when they stopped in front of the trio.

Trent Seymour recovered first. "Addison? This is a surprise. And it's Walker, right? The MARSOC guy. What brings you two over?"

Rigs kept his face slack, his expression even. Nothing to even hint that this was anything other than a visit.

Addison did that wobbling thing with her head—homing in on the voice he suspected—before smiling. "I thought you knew?"

Trent frowned, even though the prick knew Addison couldn't see him. "Knew what?"

"About the meeting? With the US Attorney's office? They called and asked me to meet them here. I guess they want to go over my testimony. And since Blade is still recovering, Kent offered to help me out. Be my guide before he has to go back to work tonight."

All three men glanced at each other, mouths pinched tight. Eyes narrowed.

Agent Townsend coughed. "Your testimony?"

She swiveled to face him. "Shawn?"

"That's right, Addison. Sorry, I should have let you know I was here."

"That's okay. Where's David?"

"Out grabbing some burgers. If Walker's your guide, I guess that means you're still…"

"Blind. Yeah. Still that. And yes, my testimony. On the off-chance they call me to the stand. You know how lawyers are…always prepared. I just figured they were meeting with everyone. Isn't that why you're here?"

"No. We're in the midst of another investigation. I hadn't realized you'd been put on the docket."

"Just a technicality, I'm sure."

"So, how are you feeling? Having any more of those flashes you mentioned?"

She beamed. Actually beamed. Christ, she was convincing. "A lot, actually. The doctor thinks I'll make a full recovery once I get more of my memory back. That it's probably what's causing the blindness."

"*More* of your memory?" Trent, again. "You remember stuff, already?"

"Not a lot, and nothing important, but… I've been seeing things. Odd things. About Will. Which is why I'm glad the attorney's office called. Now, I can check up on some facts. Try to figure out what the images mean."

Paul Johnson stood, palming the desk. "What kind of images, Addy?"

She kicked at the floor, looking lost. "It's hard to explain. It's like I keep hearing his voice. He keeps telling me not to die."

"Will told you not to die? Wasn't he killed in the shootout?"

"No, you got it all wrong, Paul." It was Townsend. "O'Toole died going back in to try and find Addison. He didn't get more than a few feet inside when the meth lab blew. I tried to go after him, but…it was too late. But there's no way he could have talked to you."

Addison shook her head. "But…that's not what I remember. I swear he's there, over me, telling me not to die, then…then…"

She gasped, palming her head then falling to her

knees, just like she'd done the other times Rigs had been unable to help her during a flashback. She groaned, mumbling incoherently as she sank even lower to the floor.

Rigs crouched beside her, telling her he was there. That she'd be okay before she gasped, again, then went limp. Splayed out across the floor. Motionless. Her colleagues gathered round, breathing heavily, faces pale. Rigs scooped her up in his arms, rolling her into his chest when Townsend grabbed his arm.

"What the hell are you doing? You're supposed to put victims in the recovery position after a seizure while you wait for the paramedics."

Rigs managed to knock the guy back without jostling Addy. "She didn't have a seizure, you jerk. She had a flashback. And I'm more than aware of how you treat those. She needs to rest. Can you do her a favor? Let that Jeremy guy from the Attorney's office know I'm taking her home. He can drop by or call later. I'll be with her until I have to go."

"Will do. Hey…" He snagged Rig's shirt. "What time are you heading out?"

"Around ten. I want to get her settled. But I'll be back tomorrow afternoon. I can bring her back, then, if the lawyers still want to meet here."

"I'll let them know. Just… Take care of her. I hate seeing her like this. She used to be one hell of a detective."

"She still is. And she'll be back soon. The flashbacks are getting worse. Only a matter of time before her memories follow."

With that, Rigs left, still cradling Addison against his chest. Other than a slight smile against his neck, she didn't move. Didn't give anything away. His buddies chirped in his ear, giving Rigs the "all clear" as he headed for the exit. Phase one was complete. Now, all they had to do was wait and see who tried to bust down her door. Because whoever it was, however many people there were, they were dead men walking. Rigs would see to it, personally.

CHAPTER 18

"This isn't what we agreed to."

Addison sighed, listening to Kent discuss the current situation. Or more correctly—voice all the ways their sting could go wrong. How he couldn't guarantee her safety. How she'd end up dead.

She'd opened her mouth to correct him on several occasions, only to snap it shut when she'd heard the underlying fear in his voice. Fear for her, because she knew, without a doubt, that he'd willingly step in front of a train for her. Wouldn't suffer from a moment's worth of hesitation or be at all scared that he'd die. If it saved her life, he'd do it.

Yet, letting her take a risk reduced him to the man he'd been before the Marine Corps had beaten any sense of self-preservation out of him, filling the empty space with unyielding honor. With duty. Rigs had left, leaving Kent to take his place.

And Kent was scared.

Addison waited until there was a lull in the conversation—the one-sided one Kent had been having with the other men in the room. His team. Men he respected but was willing to go head to head with if it meant keeping her on the sidelines. There was just one problem...

She was the bait. No way these men—who apparently had thermal scopes, and drones, and were possibly highly trained Special Ops soldiers, just like Kent and his team—would bite if she wasn't in the house. If her body signature was missing.

So, once Kent had paused to catch a breath—probably think up another dozen reasons why she needed to be sequestered away to some kind of safehouse—she cleared her throat. Gained everyone's attention.

At least, she assumed she had. All the men were in prime soldier mode—silent. Doing that vanishing act she'd felt before. For all she knew, they'd left the room, and she was sitting there, alone.

Then, Kent touched her hand, and she relaxed. She wasn't alone, and if Kent was still there, chances were the other were, too.

She placed her hand over his, orienting herself. "If you're all done talking around me—about me—while I sit here as if I'm invisible, I'd like to say something."

Kent grunted. It sounded painful, but she pushed aside the part of her that wanted to comfort him. He needed to listen to her, not just acknowledge that she'd spoken. Actually listen.

She drew herself up. "I realize all of you have more... extensive training than I do. That you've trained for the kind of battles I can't even imagine. But at the end of the day, I'm still a cop. Still took an oath. And if you're all right—if these flashbacks I'm having are actually the truth slowly bleeding through the cracks—then someone I worked with. Some bastard I trusted my life to, killed my partner. Tried to kill me. Now, you can put as much security as you want around me. Kent can wire this entire place to blow, if he hasn't already. But I'm staying. End of discussion."

She whirled on Kent when he huffed. "I'm not helpless. I appreciate that everything you're saying is coming from a place of caring. That you don't want me to get hurt. And I'll admit, a part of me loves you for that. But—and you really need to listen to this part—if I ever manage to get my sight back, I'll never be able to look myself in the mirror if I bow out. Will was more than a partner. He was my best friend. Saved my ass more times than I can count. Even took a bullet for me once. And I've let him down. Well, that stops. Now."

She stood, took a few steps to the side, then crossed her arms. Kent wasn't the only one who could be stubborn.

A chorus of sighs, then a round of chuckles.

"I gotta hand it to you Rigs. You sure know how to pick 'em." Russel, off to her left. "Sounds like she's made up her mind."

A growl. No other way to describe it. Kent was pissed. "We're talking about having her sit in the middle of the damn room. The same one they put bullets through not twenty-four hours, ago. That I'm sure they have satellite imagining on or drones patrolling the area, gathering intel. How is that remotely sane?"

"You're right. It's not. But it's also the best we've got. And she won't be alone, buddy. We'll all be here. Hidden, but here. All we need is for her to stay visible long enough to get the bastards here. Get them to out themselves. Then..."

"Then, we'll be outlining her body in chalk when they decide talking is overrated and they send an RPG through the house, instead. Or pick her off with a sniper. If there's even enough left to outline."

"Do all MARSOC guys think in terms of worst case scenario? Or is it just you?" Cannon. From somewhere off to her right. And Addy didn't miss the humor in his voice.

"I'm not gambling with her life. Ask anything else of me, and I'll do it. But not that."

Addison sighed and held out her hand, smiling when Kent was there instantly. Taking her fingers in his. Placing them on his forearm. Her rock. "Surely, there's a way we can compromise. One you can live with."

"There is." Cannon, again, moving closer. His energy washed over her—just as deadly as before, but now, she sensed the difference. How it wasn't directed at her. More like a permanent part of his DNA. "When we first discussed this, I made a few inquiries. I wasn't sure if I could get my hands on what we needed, but..."

He paused, and Addison bet her ass he was smiling. One of those big, authentic ones that men got when they were looking at a new car. Or in this case, weaponry. Because she was sure these guys turned into kids at Christmas when a new gun or knife came their way.

"But…" she pressed.

"Let's just say, it's good to have a few friends in low places. And I think I have just what we need." He placed a small device in her hand. "Picked this up after that great show you put on this morning. Seeing as our friends are relying heavily on electronics, seems only fair we take them down a peg or two."

She used both hands, gliding her fingertips over the surface. "Is this a…a…an EMP?" Electro-magnetic pulse that would disable anything electronic for god knew how far.

"It's fairly compact. Concentrated. Enough to scramble a drone or any kind of device relying on a charge to drive it that might be in the immediate vicinity. Thinking that will level the field if they decide to come at us armed for bear like Rigs fears. Guarantee that no one will be able to see you—see us—until they come through that door. By then…"

He snorted, and she imagined him shrugging those massive shoulders she'd gotten a glimpse of the other night. "But just to be sure, I have a few blankets that will lower our heat signatures. Make it hard to detect. If we coordinate that with Rigs tripping some smoke grenades, or blinding them with a flashbang… They won't stand a chance. Besides, I figure Rigs will be close enough he'll have you off the couch and under him before anyone could take a shot. Ain't that right, buddy?"

"Joke all you want, Cannon, because you're right. I won't be more than a breath away. Period. Not if everyone insists on going through with this."

Addison smiled. She heard the tone of Rigs' voice. The slightly reduced tension. Obviously, Cannon's precautions had eased some of his worry.

Defcon two.

That's what he'd called it.

Either way, it meant they'd end this. Tonight.

Of course, she hadn't anticipated how much work was involved in getting the place—getting her—ready. Though, all she'd done was sit at the table, listening to Hank go over the plan. Step by step, multiple times, until she thought her head would explode. And all around her, noises. Nothing concrete she could pinpoint, but the men were doing…something. Moving stuff. Changing the layout, maybe.

She suspected they were installing cameras and motion detectors. That Kent was wiring *everything*. If she'd learned anything about him it was that he didn't feel truly secure unless he had explosives in the mix. Had rigged her home to his satisfaction. And after intruders had managed to break through his defenses the other day, she suspected he wouldn't worry about whether the charges were lethal. Only that they stopped whoever tripped them.

People she'd worked with. Trusted. That's who would trip them. Men she would have taken a bullet for.

A hand on her shoulder. It wasn't Kent or Russel. She'd recognize the feel. The shape. And there wasn't any oppressive energy sending her system into overdrive, which only left one other guy, besides Hank sitting across from her. "Yes, Sam?"

He laughed. "Guessed me by default?"

"Is that a bad thing?"

"Nope. Still impressive. Okay, we're just about ready. We've got everything wired for sound, too. If our hunches are right, whoever's coming for you isn't going to break down the door. They're going to knock. Have you invite them in. Make it all seem innocent. Build a backstory that will account for you dying. Personally, I suspect they'll have their forces barge in after they're here—most likely outfitted like gang members. Say they tried to help, but you got caught in the crossfire. Couldn't see to help yourself. And Bridgette wants everything on tape so she can crucify them—or at least have Jeremy do it.

"Also, the Bureau still owed Hank a favor from when we unearthed a few moles in their ranks—back when Harlequin was being hunted. They've got a small crew down the street. Far enough away the EMP won't affect them should we need to use it, but ready to bust in. We'd like this to go down with as little bloodshed as possible."

"Fat chance." It was Kent. She could tell even before he spoke. By the way he moved in beside her. The soft brush of his hand over hers. "They've got nothing to lose, here. That makes them more than dangerous. It makes them desperate."

"True. But with Addison showing up at the precinct... It might look too suspicious if her house gets attacked like that, again. Thankfully, most of the damage was on the outside. Easy to hide." Sam squeezed her shoulder. "You ready? Any questions?"

"I'm ready. Though, my job is pretty simple."

Sam sighed. "Okay, we're going to make a show of leaving, in case they're already watching. They were expecting Rigs to stay until ten. It's nine thirty. We'll all head out, then double back. Take our positions. Ice will hang with Bridgette, Jeremy, and the Feds—in case anyone needs his expertise. He doesn't like it, but...he knows the score as the only medic among us. Rigs will see himself out at ten. Drive off until he can make his way, back, too. He'll come in through one of the rear windows, then take up a position not too far from your living room. Clear?"

She nodded, turning to hopefully take in everyone. "Thank you. All of you. I don't know what I would have done if you hadn't..." She choked on the rest of the words. The ones that felt like lumps stuck in her throat.

The others came over—making enough noise she could hear them. Pinpoint their location. They took turns giving her arm a squeeze, then made their way to the door. It seemed surreal as they joked and laughed, chatting about poker and who would win next time. Like this had been nothing more than a friendly night with buddies. Then, they were gone. Nothing but an eerie void in the house.

Kent took her arm, walked her back to the couch. He didn't speak, just wrapped his arms around her—held her close. His heartbeat strummed against her cheek— slow. Steady. Only the occasional breath that belayed his worry.

He was putting on his own show for her. And she knew why. If he wasn't concerned, wasn't anxious, then it meant things would be okay. Or maybe he'd just changed into soldier mode early. Become Rigs—ordinance soldier and stone cold operative.

She didn't care, clinging to him until it was time for him to leave. To start the entire ball rolling. He dropped a kiss on her head then pushed to his feet. She went to follow him, but he held her shoulder—keeping her seated.

"I'll see myself out. You..." He huffed, but she heard the tremble in his voice. The way he swallowed with effort.

"It's going to be okay."

He chuckled. "That's my line, sweetheart. But yeah. It will, because I can't think about it any other way. You're going to live. Period."

"You, too. Don't go getting any crazy ideas that sacrificing yourself for me is an acceptable countermeasure. Losing you..."

"We're quite the pair." Another kiss. Soft. His lips barely brushing hers. "Stay vigilant. And when the shit starts flying, get down."

Then, he vanished. Just like that. Standing in front of her one moment, gone the next. She didn't even hear the door open and close, just the subtle growl of his truck as it started, then pulled away. And she was alone.

Completely.

Sure, the house was wired. Explosives. Cameras. Bugs. But that feeling—the sense of no one else around her—it hit home. And she realized how lonely she'd been before Kent. Having Blade had helped. Had taken away the overwhelming pain of loss. But Kent had banished it. Obliterated it as if it had been an enemy force he'd secretly been sent to destroy.

And now, it was back. In her face. Making her acutely aware of what she had to lose. That if things went badly—if Kent sacrificed himself for her like she knew he would if the situation warranted it—she'd be smothered, this time. Lost in the grief. In the never-ending darkness that had nothing to do with conversion disorder or trauma or her fucked-up mind. That he was the source of light she'd been searching for. The only part of her she needed to keep whole.

The doorbell rang.

Showtime.

Addison rose from the couch, gripping the cane Kent had left by her side, then made her way to the door. She'd wondered why he'd insisted she use it—her home was the one place she could navigate on her own —only to realize the men had moved things around. Not a lot. Just minor shifts in her chairs. In a small table in the hallway by the door.

Probably opening up different sight lines.

Or maybe Kent had moved the pieces in order to wire her house. Not that it mattered. Using her cane would make whoever was at her door feel as if they had the upper hand. That she wasn't a threat.

She reached the entrance after the second chime of the bell. "Yes? Hello?"

"Addison? It's Shawn. I'm here with Dave, Paul and Trent. Can we come in?"

All of them?

She hadn't counted on that. Were they all in on it?

All dirty? Or had she gotten the visions from her flash-backs wrong? Implicating people who had nothing to do with Will's death. The attempts on her life.

She forced herself to swallow, to remove any emotion from her face as she turned the lock then opened the door. They were standing there. Close. She felt the weight of the air pushing on her, the combined heat of their bodies. They took a step forward, the sound of fabric sliding over metal reaching her.

They were armed. No doubt. Not that it was highly unusual. But it made her feel at a disadvantage. A part of her had hoped they'd count on overpowering her—using their hands. That, she could have countered. But guns—she'd have to rely on hearing them draw. Maybe the click of the safety going off. But if they had Glocks —and that was definitely Paul's choice of weapon—they didn't switch off like her Beretta. She'd never hear anything before it was too late.

Addison waved them in, closing the door behind them, then following them back to the living room. The two chairs the guys had moved slightly creaked, as did one of the cushions on the love seat. She took her place on the couch, feeling the cushion next to her dip.

That meant two of the men were across from her. One on her right in the love seat and one beside her on the couch. Virtually surrounded by people she suspected had shot her. Killed Will then hoped they'd both get lost in the explosion.

"So, Addy, are you feeling better?"

It was Trent. Beside her on the couch. Shit. He was the one that was CIA. Might have been a Black Ops soldier. Delta, like Cannon. Though, she didn't get the same sense from him. No overwhelming death vibe. And while she *knew* they were dangerous, they didn't compare to what she'd felt from Cannon or any of Kent's friends. God, she hoped that meant they weren't a match for them.

She twisted to face him, plastering on her best smile. "Much. I'm...sorry you guys had to see that. I never know when an episode is going to hit me, or how hard. They've been getting...worse, since the incident at the auction."

"No apologies needed. We were just a bit...shocked." He snickered. "Townsend thought you'd had a seizure until your...friend said it was a flashback." The cushion shifted, and she knew he was looking around. Searching for Kent. "Is Walker gone?"

There was something in his voice. It sounded like regret—frustration that Kent wasn't there—but it faded. Replaced by the sense of being watched. That all the men were staring at her, judging her response by the way she tilted her head. How she looked at them. Even if she couldn't *see*, she could out herself. Give away their plan by a careless shift of her eyes.

"He left about ten minutes, ago. Had a security issue he needed to tend to. He hopes to be back tomorrow."

"You two seem to be hitting it off." It was Paul. And she didn't miss the sarcastic tone. She just wasn't sure if he was amazed that Kent wanted to be with her, or the other way 'round.

She forced herself to turn in his direction. Smile, again. "He's...one of the good guys."

"Right. MARSOC. Those guys are pretty hardcore. Not really known for being...soft. Emotional."

"No, they're not. So, what brings you guys by? Did I miss the meeting? Is the US Attorney's office upset?"

"Walker must have called them. They didn't show up. Though, that is why we're here. We thought maybe we should go over what happened. Talk it out. *If* you remember."

This was it. The part where she needed to get them to spill something damning. One slip up, and the feds would storm in—avoid what she knew would be a bloody shootout.

"That's the hard part. I remember...bits. Walking into the warehouse. Gun shots. Will over me before arching back. I know this sounds crazy, but...I think he was shot. Killed. Are you sure he died in the explosion?"

Silence. They didn't vanish like Kent and his team, but it was unnerving, just the same. Sitting there. Being the only one who *couldn't* see. Who didn't know what was happening around them. They could be drawing their weapons. Signaling each other who would fire, and she wouldn't have a clue. Would simply sit there, waiting for one of them to cap her in the head unless they made a noise. Gave themselves away.

Was that a rustle of cloth? A muted scrape of one of their feet across the floor? She heard a ping. Not the kind of a bullet ricocheting or someone removing a safety. It sounded like an incoming text. The same noise Kent's phone had made just before he'd set off his countermeasures. Bought them enough time to escape.

God, had they wired something to blow? She wasn't

sure Kent's team had considered that. Someone using explosives close up. Was there a contingency plan? Had Hank mentioned something, but she'd been too busy being stubborn to hear?

A slight dip of the cushion next to her. Trent had moved closer. Not a lot. So little no one might have even noticed. Just him rearranging his legs. Then, the cushion behind her. He'd laid his arm across the back. Caging her in. Close enough she was sure he could grab her if he wanted. One move, and she'd be in his arms. Or dead.

Did he have a knife? She was sure Kent had one. Maybe several stashed on his body. Between his shoulder blades or at his ankle. Maybe both. She remembered hearing what seemed like an endless array of weapons hit the side table when they'd made love that first day.

How long ago had it been? A day? Two? Half her life? Because it felt as if he'd been in it forever. Or maybe it was simply that she hadn't started living— really living—until he'd bumped into her. Filled some hole inside her she hadn't know was there. Just waiting to be fixed.

Warning bells went off in her head. She needed to adapt. Or get them to confess. Something before Murphy's Law kicked in and blood started flowing.

She shifted forward on the seat, gripping her cane. Wondering if she could use it as a form of defense. "Can I get you guys something to drink? Water? Maybe a beer? You're off-duty, right?"

Trent's hand on her shoulder, holding her in place.

"We're fine. But...tell us more. You said you think Will was shot. Do you know by who?"

And just like that, she knew. Knew her visions had been right. That Will had been killed by one of the men sitting in this room. That they were just waiting for her to admit how much she knew—if she'd told anyone— then they were going to kill her.

"Shit. She knows."

Townsend. From her right. She felt the air stir, heard the floor creak, and knew he'd gotten out the chair. A click, and a light breeze, and she was sure she was staring down the barrel of his gun. The one she couldn't see.

And, in that instant, it all came rushing back. His voice. Townsend. Telling someone to kill her, too, And it had been Paul's that had said she'd die in the explosion. Both men had been there. Had been standing next to her while Will had tried to save her, then died. She didn't know which one had shot him—only that theirs were the voices she'd heard in her head. The ones that never went away. That haunted her waking hours.

A sigh. Townsend was sighing. As if killing her was going to be an inconvenience. Going to mess up whatever plans he'd had tonight. The ones not revolving around her blood on the floor. A bullet between her eyes. Then, it happened. The window shattered, a soft thud breaking the relative silence. Townsend screamed as something clanked to the floor. His gun? His entire hand?

The door burst open, footsteps rushing forward before a series of explosions rocked the house. There was noise and coughing, then the hand on her shoulder was pulling her close, tipping her back.

She had the sensation of falling, of the couch rolling. Then, she was on her back, pinned beneath a heavy weight. Not Kent. She'd recognize his body. The feel of him over her. This was someone else.

"Stay low."

Trent Seymour. That's who was above her. Straddling her hips, firing his weapon. Another few seconds, then a thud beside her. A hand on her cheek.

Kent.

She knew it. The shape of his hand, the feel of his skin against hers. She turned to look at him, and the room burst into view. Kent crouched beside her, M4 at his shoulder. Dirt smeared his face, tinged with hints of blood. Trent was still kneeling over her, bloody patch on one shoulder, pistol in his right hand. He kept ducking, then firing, aiming beyond the couch.

Kent glanced at her, narrowing his eyes. "Hey, beautiful. Do me a favor and stay still. Fuckers had a crew waiting. Had to eliminate four out back before I could even access the property. Far more than we'd imagined. I swear they had an entire SWAT team. They sent two guys in to trip my grenades, then sent in the rest. Gas masks. Goggles. Hank and Cannon have them pinned down, but... We're waiting on the Feds to make their move. That or for Sam to get his ass around to the front."

He cursed when a bullet ricocheted off the top of the couch. "Seymour. Cover her."

She shook her head—all she needed was a gun, and

she could cover herself, damn it—but it was too late. Trent was down low, obscuring her view. Hiding everything but the determined look on Kent's face before he darted out—vanished.

There were shots, shouts, then another explosion. This one sent bits of siding showering down on them. Left a smoky haze in the air. A splattering of blood across the ceiling.

Then silence.

Just like that, it all stopped. As if everyone had paused to breathe at the exact same time. She pushed against Trent, tried to shove him off of her, but he merely grunted, using more of his weight to keep her still.

Time ticked in the background, the eerie silence stretching out until she wondered if they'd all died. If this was what it was like in those moments between earth and heaven. Nothing but an empty silence.

Then, it came rushing back. Voices shouting in the distance. Men coughing. Feet pounding on the floor next to her. She was shuffled, then bam—Kent was there, again. Lifting her up. Tugging her into his arms. He smelled of sulfur and blood and sweat. Of propellant and dirt and life, and she wrapped her arms around him. Buried her face in his neck, content to stay there until the world stopped spinning. Until she could find a way to tell him she loved him.

Fingers in her hair. Lightly stroking. "Easy, sweetheart. It's over."

Over? But…didn't he feel the way she did?

Then, it hit her. Not them. The fight. The fight was

over, which meant they'd won. That she could finally have a future.

She opened her eyes. Looked into his. "I can see you."

He smiled, and her stomach clenched. God, he was stunning. "You've always seen me, Addy. Always."

Tears burned her eyes. "I…" She gasped as the darkness started pushing in. Tiny holes in his face that slowly dissolved it until there was nothing left but the ghosted image. "No!"

She cupped his jaw. Tried to will the vision back. They'd cracked the case. At least, started to. Surely that was enough to make her see? To end the torture?

Kent held her close, one hand holding the back of her head, the other her waist. He started rocking. "Easy, Addy. It's okay. Everything's okay."

"It's *gone*. How is that okay? How can I kick this if I don't even know why I'm blind? We've caught whoever killed Will. I remember, now. It was Townsend's voice telling Paul to kill me, too. And Paul who said I was already going to die. That the explosion would kill me. One of them must have pulled the trigger. Surely, that's enough? It needs to be enough."

"I'm sure it's just a matter of time, but either way, I'm here."

She fell against his chest, listening to his heart beat against her cheek. He would be enough. Having Kent for the rest of her life. She had to believe that. Blind or not, she'd make sure not to waste this chance.

CHAPTER 19

SHE WAS SHAKING. Shaking and crying and fucking alive, and that's all that matter to Rigs. All that registered. He didn't care if her sight ever came back, if she could look him in the eyes. See what she did to him. This—holding her. Knowing he could spend the rest of his life loving her—this was enough. More than he'd ever thought he'd have. And he wasn't going to let her go.

Rigs made soothing sounds as he held Addison close, a scattering of debris in her hair. Smoke still filling the room. What seemed like an entire squadron of men were moving through the house. Checking everything. Signaling to their superiors if medical attention was required.

Two of the fuckers were down. Dead. He'd seen to that personally. Jeremy and Bridgette might have wanted them alive, but Rigs hadn't. Dead was perma-nent. Meant he'd be able to sleep at night without worrying if others were on the way. If Addison would face some unknown threat from within if she ever went back to her precinct.

And there was the part where they'd hurt her. Shot her. Killed her partner. Her friend. *That* couldn't go unpunished.

"Shit, are you two okay?"

Ice plopped down beside him, oblivious to the shards of wood and glass, his focus on Addison. Rigs sighed, not sure he could let her go, yet. Not even for Ice to check her out. Then, the soldier part of his brain, the only part not still edged with fear, had him easing back—allowing Ice to move in. Give her a once-over.

His buddy took his time, checking every scratch or nick before finally smiling. "Just a few minor cuts. Nothing that a warm bath or shower won't fix. Though, I'll want to change that bandage on your side before you go to sleep tonight. Make sure you didn't reopen the wound. Okay?"

She nodded, finally taking a moment to scan the room. Not that she could see, but Rigs suspected she was doing her best to drink it all in. Gather information from the sounds and smells around her.

She tilted her head to the side. "So, what the hell happened? I was sure Townsend had pulled his gun, but then he was screaming, and I was falling backward. Over the couch, and Trent was on top of me. I thought he was one of them?"

"I'll let Rigs fill you in. Seymour took one to the shoulder. I'd like to have a look while we're waiting for the paramedics. But don't go anywhere."

Addy frowned as Ice darted off, relaxing in Rigs' arms when he drew her close, again. "Trent was shot?"

"Let's start closer to the beginning. You're right. That fucker Townsend did pull his gun. Asshole. But Cannon assures me he was on it the entire time. Only waited long enough to get a better angle. Shot the asshole's gun right out of his hand." Took a few fingers in the process, but she didn't need to know that.

She cringed then sighed. "What happened next?"

He grunted. It fucking hurt to talk about it. Not because he cared about the shitheads who'd been killed. But because he hadn't been there. Had gotten tied up dealing with the bastards out back, and he'd had to rely on his team to take the assholes down. When it should have been him.

He tightened his hold. Not because she was shaking, but because he was. Hands like a damn junkie as he drank in the sweet scent of her skin. "That's when things got tricky. They sent in a couple of men while outside forces laid down some suppressor fire. I'm betting they were planning on us still being here. Weren't taking any chances. Then, they charged the house. Set off a bunch of countermeasures, but there were too many of them. Cannon and Hank kept them from overrunning the room, while Sam flanked left— finally got in front of them."

He glanced over his shoulder, watching Ice treat Seymour's wound for a moment. "That's when Trent Seymour grabbed you—tipped the couch back and took cover. Fuck, Cannon nearly blew the guy's brains out before he realized he'd pulled his badge—CIA still, by the way—was signaling he was undercover and was there to protect you. And he did."

Kent didn't say where the other man had taken a bullet for her. A bullet Rigs would have taken. *Should* have taken. Because she was under his care.

Addison nodded. "Is that when he got shot?"

Damn, busted. "Yeah. He thinks it was David. Wasn't sure. Ballistics will tell us which of his supposed buddies tried to cap you but got him, instead."

"So, he was investigating the precinct."

"I guess so. We'll have to wait to hear all of it. Though, if the CIA is involved, I doubt we'll ever get the full picture. But from what I've overheard, he's been unearthing Stevens' payoffs for a couple of years, now. Something about a military connection. None of which matters because it's over."

"Over. I like that sound of that. As long as we're just talking about the threats on my life."

"What else would I be talking about?" He grunted. "Us? Not a fucking chance. Not as long as you want me in your life."

God, he hoped she wanted him in her life. Because ensuring her safety was going to get him arrested if he had to do it from afar. But he would. No matter what. For as long as he lived.

Addison swiveled in his lap, wrapping her arms around his neck. "You already mentioned something about fifty or sixty years. Can't go back on your word, now, soldier."

And just like that, the band around his chest eased. The one he thought was residual fear from the takedown. But was just, now, realizing it had been another kind of fear. The kind that went soul deep at the thought of having her walk away. He hadn't wanted to consider that their attraction might only last as long as the threat against her was real, but a part of him—a part he was ashamed to admit existed—had wondered.

Hearing her say the words out loud...

Fuck. It stopped the ringing in his ears, the frantic beating in his chest. She was his. That was clear. Nothing else mattered.

Footsteps, then his teammates were there. Standing in a circle around them. Silent. Waiting. He knew they'd stand there for hours. Give him whatever time he needed until he was ready to move. To share Addison with the rest of the world.

Addison glanced around, sightless gaze falling on each of his buddies. "I guess it's time, huh? To talk to everyone? Get debriefed?"

"Looks like it. But only if you're up to it. The feds can kiss my ass for all I care."

Hank laughed. "Now, Rigs. Sooner or later, you're gonna have to learn to play nice with others."

"I haven't blown up your chopper or trucks, yet, have I? I'd say I've been playing extremely nice."

"Still ornery. Look at it this way. The faster we get through this, the faster you can take Addison some-where safe. Give both of you a chance to recover. Pretty sure she could help make that cabin of yours a bit less depressing. Not to mention this place is gonna need a bit of work."

Addison tensed. "Safe? But I thought it was over?"

"It is. But I also know Rigs won't truly settle until he has you someplace he considers tactically sound. At least, for a few days. But after that, I have a job lined up for you, Rigs. Maybe Addison would consider staying in Montana for a while? I could use her help vetting prospective employees. There're a few who look great on paper, but none of us know them, personally. If you'd be willing?"

Addison laughed. "You want me to sense them out? Seriously?"

"You pegged Cannon pretty well."

"I got it backwards."

"Trust me, you really didn't. More of a misdirection, is all. So, is it a deal?"

She leaned her head against Rigs' chest, and he had to fight not to breathe her in. Sniff like a damn dog until her scent was all that remained. "I'd like that. But...I'll have to be back next week. To get Blade. Can't leave him a second longer at the vet's." She sat up straighter. "Will he be okay at your place? Do you even like dogs? Want us there?"

Kent grinned. "Love them. And yeah, I'll make sure it's safe for him, but seeing as he's an ex-bomb dog, he might enjoy revisiting that work. Just for fun. And I thought I just told you I was in your life until you kicked me out of it? Are you having trouble hearing?"

She slapped his shoulder. "My hearing is fine. I'm just..." She smiled. "I'd love to stay."

Hell yeah. She'd stay. Never come back if Rigs had his way. "Perfect. Now, let's get this talk with the feds over. Then, we'll go home."

Home.

He hadn't believed any place could feel like that. And hell, his place wasn't even close to being cozy. Or comfortable. But he'd see it got that way. Quick. Or, they could find somewhere else. *Their* place. Oh yeah, he could definitely get behind that.

RIGS WAS STILL GRINNING at the idea as he drove along the highway the following afternoon, Seattle long gone from his rearview—Montana on the horizon. They'd ended up staying the night at Ice's after enduring a few hour's worth of questions. Addison had fallen asleep on the drive over, and Rigs had carried her in, careful not to wake her. He still remembered the feel of her in his arms. How they'd gone to sleep holding each other, then woken the same way. His damn dick had been hard the entire time—adrenaline from the op coursing through his veins. Making him intimately aware of her skin. Her scent. How every breath caressed his neck—made him itch to touch her.

But she'd been exhausted. And, at that moment, her comfort had outweighed his desire to strip her bare and sink inside her. Besides, they had a lifetime of sex and heat and love ahead of them. He was tough enough to wait out one night.

Except where his damn dick was still hard. Still aching to be inside her. Hanging between his legs like a pipe. One that threatened to explode if she so much as touched him. He'd managed to keep it under wraps while making small talk with Ice and Harlequin—though they'd both clearly been amused by his unspoken state of arousal—before heading to the vet's. Blade had been conscious and had spent the entire time alternating his attention between the two of them. Rigs had thought the dog was going to lick the top layer of his skin off, but it was hard not to smile. Seeing the animal's obvious devotion to Addison touched that soft spot he hadn't known existed inside him. The one reserved for her and ragtag mutts. It had nearly killed him seeing the tears in Addy's eyes when it had been time to leave.

That's when the soldier part of him had kicked in. He'd asked Addison to give them a minute, then he'd used every intimidation tactic he'd learned to convince the good doctor to let them take Blade, now. Ice wasn't a veterinarian—hell, he wasn't even a doctor—but he knew more about bullet wounds and changing bandages than anyone Rigs had ever met. And he'd bet Blade's life on it, no hesitation.

The doctor hadn't been easy to sway, but with a bit more coaxing and a quick call to Ice—a personal guarantee the man would make daily visits. Would call if he suspected there was anything wrong—and the vet caved. Rigs could still see the overwhelming excitement and joy on Addison's face when he'd told her the news, then carried Blade to his truck.

Rigs had needed to put the dog's kennel in the back, but he was with them, just the same. Would most likely sleep the entire way. But despite the happy turn of events, Addison had been strangely quiet on the drive back to her place. Had barely spoken more than a few words as he'd helped her pack a bag then walked her back to his truck. Even now, she sat beside him, hands clasped in her lap, sightless gaze fixed on somewhere off to the right. He'd tried to start up a conversation a few times, but she'd answered in short, choppy sentences, and he'd decided to give her some space.

But that ended, now, because if he had to sit there for one more minute, agonizing over what she was thinking, he'd go insane. Instead, he pulled over on some dirt road, following it around a short bend to give them some privacy, then waited patiently for her to realize they weren't moving. That he was staring at her. It was eerie the way she sensed him, but in this instance, it was exactly what was needed. It took her about thirty seconds before her head wobbled—tilting left and right as she turned toward him, brow arched.

"Okay, sweetheart. Out with it."

She frowned, twisting in her seat as if, just now, realizing they weren't even on the highway. "Out with what? And where are we?"

"On some dirt road, just inside the Montana state lines. And you know what. This silent treatment. So, spill."

Her eyes widened, those beautiful blue irises staring right at him. Even without seeing him, he knew she was aware of him on a level that transcended sight. That was etched into their DNA. That she knew the minute his mouth pinched tight or his brow lifted.

Her neck muscles tensed as she swallowed, her gaze

finally dipping to somewhere on his chest. "I'm fine. Everything's...fine."

Did she honestly think he'd buy that? The strained voice, the waver in her pitch—as if she was fighting back tears.

He reached for her—cupped her jaw as he thumbed the corner of her mouth. Fuck, she was just so beautiful. It hurt his eyes to look at her. "Fine. You're fine?"

Her bottom lip trembled—her eyes welling with tears as she nodded, all the warm, healthy color draining from her face.

"Fuck this."

Rigs moved. Leaned forward, wrapped his arms around her, and bodily lifted her onto his lap. He shoved his seat back, giving her room to sit without her ass hugging the steering wheel, then waited. Addison seemed stunned, as if she hadn't thought him grabbing her had been a possibility. That it hadn't registered as a possible outcome to her answer. She remained stiff against him for nearly a minute before finally melting into his embrace.

He grunted, held her close then waited, again. It was coming. He knew it. It was there in the way she trembled in his arms, the awkward way she swallowed—as if having to force it down. She was only seconds away from...

Her chest constricted, then the tears came. Huge gut-wrenching sobs that shook her entire body. Rigs sighed, holding her close, gently rocking her. He didn't ask her to stop. To pull it together. This is what he'd been waiting for.

She buried her face in his neck, her tears hot against his skin then soaking through the neckline of his shirt. He didn't care. She could ruin every piece of clothing he owned if it made her feel better. Relieved the tension that had been straining her muscles since the raid. Since her sight had fled, once again.

He suspected that's what this was about. But he wanted her to tell him. Feel comfortable enough to lean on him. Expose herself. Only then, would she believe him. When she was raw. Vulnerable. That's when he'd convince her—prove to her—that he was there. Would be there. Always. He wasn't sure if he'd get the words, "I love you," out, but he'd make sure she knew.

Addison clung to him, the horrible tremors finally abating. Leaving her balled in his lap, her breath washing over his damp skin, her fingers biting into his neck. He smoothed a hand down her hair, leaving his fingers pressed on the small of her back when she finally eased away. She snagged her bottom lip between her teeth, her cheeks dotted with tears. God, she looked so lost. So damn gorgeous, he wasn't sure whether to sit there and stare at her or capture her lips in his.

A watery sniffle, then a sigh. "Sorry."

He grunted. "Nothing to be sorry about. It's been quite the week, though I have a feeling this isn't about the bad guys that were gunning for you."

She shook her head, blonde hair swaying across her shoulders, gleaming golden in the sun. She opened her mouth, then closed it, pursing those full lips together until they blanched white. She tried, again, having the same luck as before.

Rigs sighed. "You know you can tell me anything, right? Anything, and it won't change how I feel about you. Nothing will, not even death, so..."

Her eyes widened, her lips falling apart. He couldn't help himself. He pushed up, touched his mouth to hers. It was supposed to be soft. Just a physical reassurance that he really was there. That he'd stand by her. But it morphed into heat. Into tongues and lips and bodies writhing against each other.

He didn't know how she ended up with her shorts and panties on the seat beside them, his jeans shoved down over his knees. He swore he hadn't moved. Hadn't lifted his hands from her hair and back. Hadn't let her go long enough to breathe, let alone strip them halfway bare. But there they were. Her body above his, her warm wet sheath slowly sinking down his shaft.

He felt every inch. Every hot glide of her skin against his. The way her walls contracted with each tilt of her hips. The gravelly sound from deep inside her chest that clawed free, echoing around them until it consumed him. Blocked out every other noise. Everything but the frantic beating of his own heart.

It hammered inside his head, threatening to simply explode with every pass. She was moving faster, now. Up and down, riding him hard. Her hair fell in a curtain around his face, all that soft, silky mass running across his scars. He had a moment of fear—of the long tresses catching on his rough flesh—but it vanished the moment her lips touched his, again.

That kiss. Long. Desperate. As if her life depended on his response. On how hard he clung to her. On the raspy growl that sounded between them when she lifted just enough to reposition her mouth. Suck in some air. Then, she was back. Lips melding together, their bodies straining toward a pinnacle so high, he wasn't sure he'd ever hit the ground once he fell.

She did that to him. Took him someplace beyond his physical being. To where it was nothing but senses. Her heat. His strength. Their love.

Rigs thrust up into her, wanting to banish the last of her doubts. To prove this was exactly where she needed to be. Where she'd always belong as long as he was alive. Was breathing. Even after, his ghost would follow her. Be there to vanquish any threat. It was the only way he could justify what she did to him. How strongly he loved her.

Addison gasped, her head falling back as she arched over his arms. Then, she was coming. Hard, strong contractions around his shaft as she convulsed in his lap. Eyes squeezed shut. Muscles flexed. He pushed into three more times then exploded, just like one of his bombs. It shattered him, broke him apart. Leaving nothing of the hardened soldier behind.

Rigs was gone. But Kent was back. Holding her in his arms. Every part to him exposed. Her forehead fell to his, her arms limp at her sides as she collapsed on him. Their harsh breaths sounding in time to the thundering of his heart. Hers was thundering, too. Matching his beat for beat. In perfect sync.

He closed his eyes, content to sit there. Hold her until she was ready. A minute. Ten. All night. However long it took. Because she was his. Completely. He knew it. Sensed it all the way to his toes. This incredible woman belonged to him.

Addison took a few shuddering breaths, finally smiling against his lips. "God, Kent."

He chuckled. "I'll take that as an indication it was just as earth-shattering for you as it was for me."

"That went beyond earth-shattering. That was supernova. A complete obliteration of energy at the atomic level. Christ, I swear I saw stars…"

Her voice hitched. That word. Saw.

Rigs sighed, smoothed his hands down her hair, then moved them to cup her face. Prevent her from turning away. "Talk to me. Please, sweetheart. I can't help you if you don't tell me what's wrong."

Though, he knew. It was stamped across her face.

Addison stared sightlessly into his eyes, more tears pooling in hers. "It's…stupid. After everything we've been through, it seems…selfish to get so upset over one detail. We could have died. Hell, you and your friends risked everything to help me. I should be happy. I have you. I have Blade. I have everything I need, but…"

He swallowed. God, it hurt to see her like this. "But…"

She hiccupped, looking as if she was going to burst into tears, again, before nodding. Holding them at bay. "I'm…blind. God, I can barely say it. Before… I always believed that I'd beat this. Maybe not in the way you and your friends know you'll be successful on an op, but it was always in the back of my mind. That once I remembered who'd killed Will—made them pay—that

I'd open my eyes, and it would all be okay. That I'd be... whole."

She choked back a few sobs, swiping angrily at a few tears that broke free—cascaded down her cheeks. "But here I am. With everything to live for. With Will's killers, my fucking colleagues—men I would have died to protect—locked away or dead, and I'm still in the dark. Still...broken. And I can't help but wonder if it's too late. If I missed my opportunity to heal. That I'll be like this for the rest of my life. A liability to you. To your team. I—"

He kissed her. Shut her up, if he was honest, because she was going somewhere dark. Someplace she wouldn't come back from, and he wasn't going to let that happen. Let her slide into an abyss.

He'd been there. Had managed to claw his way out, and it was mostly because of her. Because she'd looked beyond the scars, beyond his own demons, and loved him anyway. Despite the barriers he'd put between them. Now... Now, it was his turn. To save her the way she'd saved him.

Addison pursed her lips when he pulled back, adorable lines creasing her brow. He took a moment to put her features into memory. To add to the ones he'd already created.

He breathed in her scent, smoothing out the bridge of her nose. "It's not selfish. And it's not stupid. What you've gone through... Christ, sweetheart. It would have killed a lesser person. But not you. You're strong and smart and caring, and so damn resilient, I can't believe you ever took a chance on me. I keep pinching myself to test if this is all just a dream. If maybe I died back in that rubble. That this has all just been my brain slowly dying. Living the most wonderful life before shutting down for good."

He moved his hands along her face, down her shoulders to cup her waist. "But it's not. You're real. What we have is real. Do I want you to see, again? Fuck yeah. But not because it's important to me. That it would change how I feel. But because it's important to you. To who you want to be. Either way, I'm here."

Silence.

Utter silence as she stared at him, eyes wide. Mouth slightly open. Then, she moved her hands to his chest—one over those hideous raised lines running across his flesh. She stayed that way for what felt like hours. Her body still above his, his damn dick still semi-hard inside her. He wasn't sure what she was searching for, but she smiled, and his heart thumped hard against his ribs.

"I *believe* you. I can...*feel* it. You really don't care if I'm blind. You don't see me as a burden. You..."

Love me.

That's what she was going to say. And damn, it was true. Though, even love felt like an inadequate word. What he felt for her went soul deep. Was burned into every cell, every neuron.

He kissed her. Again. This time to stop her from voicing what was pulsing through his veins. Likely glowing around him like a damn beacon. Yes, he loved her. But he wanted to be the one to say it. To see her reaction when he spoke words he'd never said to anyone. Ever.

But not like this. In the front seat of his damn truck. Still joined. Their clothes scattered around them. Not when she was this vulnerable, when she might think he was saying what she needed to hear.

No, he wanted to take her by surprise. When she least expected it. When she'd know it was real. Genuine. Unwavering.

Addison chuckled when he finally let her breathe. "Don't think I'm not aware what you're doing. I'm on to you, soldier."

Yeah, she was. But he didn't care because the light was back in her eyes. Light and warmth and fuck, love for him. Him!

"You're too smart for your own good. Now, can we get to my cabin, or are we spending the night here? Because once barely took the edge off. I need to spend hours touching you. Convincing myself you're okay. That I didn't damn near get you killed. And I'd rather have a bed for that. For the number of times I'm going to need to make love to you. But I can adapt if necessary."

A delightful blush crept into her cheeks then down her chest. Damn, she was adorable.

She looked about to answer when a low, playful bark sounded behind them. She blushed deeper—as if knowing Blade had heard them making love embarrassed her—before she sighed. "We can go to your cabin. Blade needs to have a nice place to sleep tonight. But you're not the only one with needs. I plan on running my tongue all over you. Tasting you, so…"

His dick filled. Made it hard for him to ease her off

him—zip up his jeans. Addison laughed the whole time, teasing him about flinging the metal teeth across the cab, before settling in close to him. Her head on his shoulder.

Rigs started the truck, rejoining the evening traffic. Just a few more hours, and he was turning onto the gravel road leading to his cabin. He hadn't thought to leave any lights on. Hadn't cared if he came home to complete darkness. Nothing to welcome him back. It had never been a home. Until now. Whether they stayed there or not, it was home as long as Addy was in it. And he'd do whatever it took to make her comfortable. Make a place she wanted to stay in. The two of them. Plus Blade.

Rigs was already going through what he'd need to do to make the place safe for Blade—even if the canine would be sidelined for a bit longer. Though, his previous thoughts still rang true. He was certain the canine would enjoy a little bomb-sniffing. Nothing that would hurt him, but something they could do together. A bond they could form. And he'd teach Addison, too. Being blind didn't matter because it was all about trust. Trusting Blade to do the work, and they already had that trust. So, this would be a cakewalk.

Addison wrapped her arm around his, following him to the back of the truck. He opened the gate, then eased Blade's kennel forward, stopping it parallel with the end of the flatbed. Addison unhooked the latch, laughing when the dog licked her palm, laying his snout out of the cage. He didn't seem overly anxious to leave, so Rigs decided to take Addy inside, first, then come back for

Blade. She could pick out a spot for his bed, though Rigs suspected the dog would eventually end up at the foot of theirs. Not that he minded. He'd share anything with Blade if it made Addy smile. Made her feel safe.

She seemed to get that he was lost in thought, remaining quiet, but content as he led her along the path, up the three short steps then toward the door. His phone pinged as he stopped on the porch, searching his pocket for the keys, while juggling the cell in his other hand—trying to read the screen without asking Addison to let go. She couldn't let go. He'd rather drop the damn phone, have it shatter, than have her fingers leave his arm. That's what it was for. Her hand.

He managed to get the key in the lock. Half open the door as he read the message.

Rigs. Cannon. They found that doctor—José Pedro—dead in his office. Time of death was 0600. Several hours after the takedown. Something's not right. I'm looking into it. I feel like I've missed something—something to do with that military connection. Watch your back. I'm on my way to Montana. We're meeting at Hank's place tomorrow—0800. Stay safe.

He frowned, stepping across the threshold, Addison still holding his arm, when his senses kicked in. The ones he'd honed over years in the Teams. That had saved his life and alerted him to the IED with just enough time to move—not get killed outright.

But his hands were full, his brain not quite firing on all cylinders—half his thoughts still focused on the color of Addison's skin, and how she'd felt wrapped around him. Pulsing as she orgasmed in his arms.

He moved, managed to shove her out of the way, not

really certain what the threat was, but feeling there was one. Standing there. Inside his house. She gasped, rocked sideways just as a flash lit the room, the report of the gun echoing around them. He had enough sense to feint left, prevent a shot to his heart, before he was blown back, skidding across the porch then down the stairs.

CHAPTER 20

HE'S DEAD.

That's the only thought that went through Addison's mind as she hit the wall, then stumbled against a small table. She managed to catch herself before tumbling to the floor, scrambling upright when the floor creaked in front of her.

She froze. Not out of fear, but to focus on the sounds around her. Follow the progression of whoever was in the house. Armed. Out for blood.

She could smell it. Kent's blood. Hanging in the air around her like a death shroud. Coppery. Metallic. He'd sensed the other person just a moment before she had, and had somehow managed to shove her aside—save her life. Take the bullet that had most likely been meant for her.

Or maybe this creep wanted to eliminate her protection, first. Make her suffer before finally killing her. And she was. Standing there, smelling Kent's blood, not hearing so much as a raspy breath from him—it sucked out any light she'd managed to get back. Crushed her soul.

A scuff.

Not much, but she'd heard it. Slowly getting closer. Moving off to her right. There was no sense trying to hide. She didn't know the layout of Kent's place. She hadn't even counted how far back his truck was, too caught up in the feel of his muscles beneath her fingers to care. Knowing he'd keep her safe. Make sure she didn't bump into anything, so she hadn't worried about counting.

Which had been fucking stupid, because now, she needed that information. Needed *all* the information. Why hadn't she asked him what his place was like? What kind of furniture he had? Where the bedroom and bathroom were? He'd have told her. Laid out a perfect picture of his interior for her. And he'd have been happy to do it.

Instead, she'd been basking in the afterglow of their love making. In knowing that Kent was a breath away from telling her he loved her.

That's why he'd kissed her. To stop her from saying it for him. She'd sensed that about him. That he wanted to be the one to say the words. To have her believe them. And that hadn't been the time or the place. She'd been raw. On the edge. And he'd wanted to wait until she'd be convinced of his sincerity.

And now, he was lying somewhere bleeding to death. If he wasn't already dead.

Kent.

Dead.

His body limp. Unmoving. His scars in sharp relief because there'd be no color in his skin. No warmth beneath it. Nothing but cold, unforgiving death. Just like Will.

Fuck that.

She'd never given up before, and she'd be damned if she'd give up, now. Whoever was in the room with her, obviously wanted to draw it out. Otherwise, she'd be dead. Lying on the floor beside Kent. Which meant there was still time. She couldn't outmaneuver her opponent, but she had other abilities. If she could get them to talk, maybe distract them long enough, she could do...

What?

A smug chuckle. Right in front of her. She hadn't even felt the air move, which meant the person wasn't large. Surely not like Cannon or Hank or Russel. Even Sam, though slightly shorter, not quite as thick, registered whenever he'd moved around her. This person... It was as if they weren't there, but not in a Special Forces kind of way. They were...small. Like her.

Kill her, too... The whole place is gonna blow...

It started as it usually did. The voices—Paul. Shawn. Voices she now recognized. Will was above her, pleading with her to stay with him. Stemming the bleeding. Then, he was falling—covering her body. Blocking out everything beyond his shoulder, but the flash of a hood. The hint of a smile. The glint of a gun. It wavered above her, muzzle pointed at her head, until flashes went off the in background. Streaks of yellow and white and orange as flames shot into the air.

This is where it ended. Where her memories faded just like Kent's life was fading. Only, this time, it continued. Someone was yelling—Paul, again. To get out. To leave them. That hooded face turned one last time—chestnut hair falling out from the edge. A flash of red lips and brown eyes. Of manicured nails—one just inside the trigger guard.

Then, it was gone. Just the lingering scent of smoke. Of burning flesh and chemicals. A sweet fragrance that didn't fit in.

Addison inhaled, coming back to herself as she slumped against the wall. Somehow, she'd managed to stay on her feet. Brace herself as the flashback took hold. Given herself one last chance to fight. If she'd been on her knees or passed out, like she often was, she'd be dead. A bullet cracked through her skull. But she was standing. Not straight, but upright. Strong.

The air moved next to her. How had she missed it before? It wasn't much, but it was there. The whisper of breath. The rustle of fabric. The scent of something fruity—just like in her flashbacks...

Perfume.

It all made sense. Why she'd blocked it out. Why she'd assumed it had been one of the three men who'd pulled the trigger. She hadn't wanted to believe it was true. That anyone could be that ruthless. Betray a person they cared about to that degree.

But there it was. Staring her in the face. So bright and strong, even she couldn't ignore it. See it through the curtain of darkness around her.

Addison straightened—turned to face the person she

knew was standing just off to her right. Anger burned across her skin, beading it with goosebumps. Will was dead. Her partner. Her best friend, and all because of the bitch standing behind her. The one who'd shot Kent. The love of her life. The only man who'd ever hold her heart. Ever feel like the other half of her soul.

She was going to pay, even if it killed Addison.

Addy kept her left hand curled around the rim of the small side table, her right on the wall for balance. "Hello, Grace."

A gasp. Yeah, she'd surprised the bitch. No doubt about it. Addison heard the woman exhale, take an involuntary step back, the slide of her arm lowering ever so slightly down her side.

That's all the opening Addy needed. All she knew she'd get. She swung her arm, taking the table with her. It connected with something hard—Grace's body—then crashed to the ground. But beneath the clatter of wood splintering, of something breaking—she heard the unmissable thud of flesh hitting the floor.

Grace was down.

Addy took off. She didn't remember much, but she remembered where the door was. That it had taken Kent two steps to reach it from the stairs. Three stairs, she thought he'd called out, though she wasn't certain. She bounced off the doorframe then out of the cabin, taking three of her steps before leaping forward. She hit the ground hard, slightly lower than she'd anticipated, and nearly tripped. But she caught herself—managed to limp to her left then head for the side of the house. It was dark. She knew that much. Which evened the odds marginally. Grace could still see—might even have NVGs, or some kind of night vision scope—but at least the other woman wouldn't be able to follow Addy without the aid of something.

God, she hoped Kent hadn't rigged a bunch of lights to switch on if someone ran down the side of his place. That she wasn't making all these assumptions only to get picked off because she was never truly hidden.

She couldn't think about that, now. Couldn't do anything other than concentrate on reaching the corner before the other woman made it out of the cabin. If she saw which way Addison had gone, there'd be little hope of escaping. Of helping Kent.

And she needed to help him. Needed to believe he wasn't dead. That there was still time. Time that was quickly ticking away as she finally reached the edge of the house, slipping quietly into some bushes as boots sounded on the porch. Pounded across the short space then down the stairs—there had been three—then stopped.

Grace was trying to determine which way Addy had gone. Had she left evidence? Footprints? Broken branches. Couldn't Spec Op soldiers tell if the grass had been touched? Something about dew patterns or pressure spots?

But Grace wasn't a Spec Op soldier. She was DEA. A fucking traitor. And for what? Money? Power? She'd killed her own lover without hesitation. That made her worse than any drug dealer Addison had busted.

But—Grace could see. Sure, it was night—thankfully a new moon, according to Kent—so there wouldn't be much ambient light. And if there was any kind of Karma at all, it would be overcast. Addy had heard distant rolls of thunder, but that didn't mean it was cloudy, here. The mountains were notorious for unpredictable weather. It could be clear skies and a thousand stars above her, and she'd never know. But Grace would eventually adjust to the darkness. Overcome it. Addy could, too. She'd been living in the dark for eighteen months. Was intimately connected to it—if she'd had her cane. If she knew even a fraction of the layout.

She stilled. She didn't know the layout, but she knew Kent. Knew he'd have the place wired. That Grace had probably gotten lucky—bypassed a few easier security measures on the doors. But she had no idea his yard would be riddled with explosives and trip wires. Even if they didn't kill her, they'd be enough to give Addy the upper hand. To get close enough to fight the woman hand to hand. And she'd bet her desire to save Kent outweighed Grace's desire to kill her. All Addy had to do was make her way through the traps. Get someplace she could hide until she could take the other woman by surprise when she undoubtedly went down.

Right. A blind woman walking through a minefield. Even with her cane, she wouldn't be able to traverse it without setting something off. Kent would have been too thorough. No question.

A curse, then footsteps…going away. Around to the other side. Addison released the breath she'd been holding when something went thump. Shit. Was there someone else? A backup? Maybe one of Stevens' men or another dirty agent?

She listened carefully, straining to pick up on any hint of sound. Or an unfamiliar fragrance. An overpowering energy.

Something cold nudged her hand, and she barely held back the scream clawing at her throat. She whipped her head down—not that she'd see what it was, but it made her *feel* as if she had control.

A lick this time, followed by a low growl.

Blade.

Against all odds, he'd jumped down out of the truck —made his way over. Found her. She wasn't sure how he was standing. Christ, it had only been a few days, and he'd lost so much blood. He'd been so deathly still when she'd first visited him. Sure, he seemed better today, more energetic. Had been able to walk. And the vet had let him come with them—though she suspected Kent had used some MARSOC intimidation technique on the guy. Convinced him it was in his best interest to let him and Russel look after Blade. And all because it made her happy.

And now Kent was…somewhere. Close to the house. Bleeding. Maybe dead, already.

Blade growled, again. Low. Throaty. Like at the foundation, only as if he knew he shouldn't make much noise.

Addy knelt down, hugged him, then wrapped her fingers around his collar. She wasn't sure how it would work without the harness, but damn it, they weren't going down without a fight.

She nudged him toward the rear of the property, and he started forward. Not fast. In fact, it felt painfully slow. But Blade kept moving, stopping occasionally as if deciding whether it was safe. She didn't question his judgment. He'd already proven he was far more than a guide dog. He was a soldier at heart. One that took protecting his handler to the extreme. He'd already bled for her, and she knew he'd do it, again. That he'd instinctively avoid Grace Sanchez without being told she was the enemy.

They walked for about thirty feet before he veered them to the right. Away from the house. She stumbled along beside him, wondering if they were in full view. If Grace would pop out at any moment and fire.

Was Blade limping?

It was impossible to tell. Maybe it was the ground. It felt uneven beneath her boots. Definitely Kent's yard. Or the forest. She didn't know. Blade seemed confident until he stopped.

He sniffed something. She heard it. Soft, fast pants as his head dipped toward the ground. Then, he was off, again, angling her to the left, then right. Zigzagging their way to god knew where.

The charges.

That's why he was weaving. He was steering her around Kent's countermeasures. Through his trip wires.

Blade stopped, gave a low yip. She reached out her hand, inhaling sharply when it connected with wood. Some kind of shed. She groped her way along it, found the corner then ducked behind it. She couldn't go inside. Didn't want to get trapped. Besides, she needed to be ready to move the moment an opportunity arose.

They couldn't have traveled more than twenty feet.

Twenty agonizing feet between her and Kent's cabin. What stood between her and a chance at saving Kent—if she could disarm Sanchez. Knock her out.

She should have insisted on having a weapon. An oversight she wouldn't make, again. If she lived. If Kent lived because if he didn't, she'd just have crawl up into his coffin with him. She couldn't picture life without him. And if she did, she knew it wouldn't be worth living. It would be dull. Two dimensional at best.

Footsteps. Soft. Slow.

Someone moving across the yard. Placing each foot carefully. Sanchez wasn't taking any chances. She was scouting the area before taking each step. A three-hundred and sixty degree check, then moving, again. Somehow she hadn't activated any of the charges. Had missed the trip wires. Unless she knew where they were. Could drones see beneath the ground? Source out explosives? Addy didn't think so, but then she never would have thought the men she worked with were dirty. That Grace Sanchez could kill Will—the man she'd claimed to be in love with.

Another curse, then a shot. Close to Addison's head. She felt the wake of the bullet. Heard the ping as it hit the wood. Had she been spotted? Was she somehow visible? Just a lucky shot? Or had Grace tripped? Depressed the trigger by accident?

God, what if she had thermal imagining at her disposal? Or some of that new tech that could sense a person breathing? And Addy was definitely breathing. Shallow fast pants as she stood there, waiting for one stroke of luck to come her way. Give her a single opening.

Was that a click? It sounded like—

The ground shook as the explosion rocked the small shed, nearly tripping Addison onto her ass. She felt the light, the heat against her face. Smelled the smoke from the blast as chunks of dirt and grass rained down around her.

She steadied herself then tapped Blade's collar. "Now, Blade. Forward."

Blade lunged ahead, dragging Addison along as he raced across the yard. He took a sharp turn right, then another left, then he was growling, tugging at Addison's hand.

"Leave it."

She didn't want him hurt, again. To take another bullet. Blade ignored her, pulled free. There was a second of silence, then he was attacking. That familiar growl, the sound of his mouth around flesh. Grace screamed, shouted for help. That was all Addison needed.

She took three steps, then the world appeared. Blade in front of her, his teeth locked around Sanchez's arm. Her gun on the ground beside her. Smoke blanketed the yard, some still curling up from a hole in the ground. Grace had blood running down her leg, more on her arm and cheek. But she wasn't dead. Far from it. Blade shook his head, pulled the woman off-balance. There was a glint of something silver.

A knife.

Addison dove. She didn't care about the risks. If her

sight decided to wink out. She'd claw the woman's eyes out if necessary. Rip her own arm off and beat Sanchez to death with it, if that's what it took. But she wasn't going to let the bitch hurt anyone else she loved.

She landed off to the left—one hand covering the knife, the other locked in Grace's hair. She yanked, smiled at the woman's cry, then slammed her hand on the ground.

Addy got lucky, hit a rock, clattering the knife to the ground. She didn't reach for it. Didn't waste time going for the gun, or the taser strapped to Sanchez's thigh. Instead, Addy grabbed the rock, then brought her hand down hard on the other woman's head.

She stilled.

Addison pushed to her knees, nudging Sanchez a few times before sitting back on her heels. Blood welled from a large laceration just below the woman's temple, a few lines trickling down her cheek. Addy placed one hand on Grace's neck. Pulse thready and weak. Each beat further apart than the last. Every breath lifting her chest a bit less. Chances were, Addy had killed her, but her body hadn't quite caught up with the fact, yet.

Good. She could burn in hell for all Addison cared.

Blade released Grace's arm, then sat, looking at Addy as if waiting for his next command. The bandage at his shoulder was spotted with blood. He'd probably pulled out a few stitches. Was most likely in pain. But he wasn't leaving her. Wasn't bailing.

She stumbled to her feet, once again, then grabbed Grace's weapons on the off-chance the woman wasn't alone. That Addy would need them, before reaching for

Blade—wrapping her fingers around his collar. Even if her vision stuck, she needed him to get around the charges. "Find, Kent."

Blade barked, then took off. Faster than before. He was definitely limping. Each stride a half stumble as he wove them back across the short expanse of yard. Her vision washed in and out. A flash of Kent's cabin. Then, nothing. Then, another snapshot of the side they'd traveled down. Shadows crossed in front of her, real or imagined she didn't know, but it didn't matter. Blade was taking her toward the driveway. Toward Kent.

Another few glimpses of her surroundings and there he was. Splayed out on the ground. Something dark beneath his side.

Blood. His blood. But not red. Black. Blending in with the darkness shrouding her vision. Threatening to plunge her back into the abyss.

She fell at his side, fingers pressed to his neck. Blade yipped, licked Kent's face, as Addy waited to feel any evidence that he was alive. That she hadn't lost him.

A pulse.

Weak. Weaker than Grace's had been and damn, he looked pale. White against the shadows. Against the dots slowly eating away her sight. She shook her head. She would *not* go down like this. His shirt ripped beneath her fingers as she yanked at the seams, desperate to get a look at his wound. The puckered hole glared up at her. It looked big. Bigger than she'd expected. She watched him take a labored breath.

No bubbles.

No obvious wheezing.

No arterial spurting.

Though, she knew if he'd been hit in the heart, in the artery, he'd already be dead. It had been too long—precious minutes she'd spent running. Hiding. Fighting. Minutes he couldn't spare. That might be the reason he died.

He coughed, flecks of blood spraying from his lips as his eyelids fluttered. Once. Twice. Finally staying open.

She cupped his face, his blood smearing across his skin from her hands. "Easy, Kent. I need you to stay with me, okay? Stay awake."

He coughed, again, and damn, it looked as if it drained half his energy. As if his battery had gone from full to fifty percent just like that. Then, he was looking around, trying to push onto his elbows.

"Stay still. You'll make the bleeding worse. I need to get some pressure on it."

She ripped off her own shirt, balling it up then holding it tight against his side. He inhaled, eyelids fluttering, again, before he forced them open.

He shook his head, trying to bat her hand away. "What the fuck are you doing? Run. Hide. Before—"

"It's over. She's... She can't hurt us." She pushed on the wound. "We need to get you to a hospital. Where's your phone?"

"I..." He coughed, would have fallen back down if she hadn't managed to bridge his weight. Damn, he was heavy.

She shushed him. "It's okay. Blade. Phone."

The dog barked, then hobbled off, returning a few moments later with Kent's phone in his mouth. She turned it over, feeling her heart stop. It was broken. A hole right through the center as if the bullet had hit it, too, before punching through Kent's chest.

She gave Blade a quick pat. "Good, boy. Truck, Blade."

She didn't know if he could jump in. Hell, if he could even make it there. The patch on his shoulder was larger. Redder. But he stood, limped toward Kent's truck.

Addison studied Kent's form. No way she could carry him, but she might be able to drag him. Pray he had enough strength to help her lift him onto the seat.

Kent grunted, still trying to bat her hand away. "You can't lift me. I'll walk."

"Like hell you will. Just, save your strength until we reach your truck."

He growled, then groaned, falling against her as she wrapped her arms around his chest from behind, then slowly started dragging him. Her vision flickered, went dark, then came back, again. She didn't stop, knowing she'd eventually hit the wheel if her sight failed. That she'd, at least, make it to the door.

It felt like hours. Days, as she placed one foot after the other, gradually cutting down the distance between them and his only chance at surviving. She was sweating, breathing harder than she ever had, by the time she reached his truck. Kent was panting, each breath taking a toll. But he managed to palm the seat, heave his body upright.

He swayed, and she had a moment of panic. Imagined him falling down, dying right there. But between them he managed to catch his balance—crawl onto the seat.

Blade waited beside them, tail wagging. She tapped her thigh, and he fell in beside her, jumping into the truck with a boost from her. He wormed his way behind the seats, laying his head across Kent's thigh. The dog whimpered, gaze locked on Kent.

Kent managed a smile, coughing up more blood before shaking his head. "That dog's as stubborn as you are. You're certainly a pair."

"We've got nothing on you. Okay, where's the nearest hospital."

He coughed, again, swayed, only opening his eyes when she shook him.

"Kent! Hospital! Which way? And you need to stay awake. My vision…it's too risky. Kent!"

He blinked. Slowly. Like it hurt, then nodded. "Hank's place is programmed into the GPS. He's got a chopper. Head there. Out of the driveway, then turn left."

"You'll have to put a hand on the wheel. Help me steer. I can't… Fuck, it's going. Dots in from the side. Please, Kent!"

He stared at her, looked as if it took a few moments just to process her words, then he lifted one bloody hand to the wheel. It slide down, but he repositioned it. Helped her make her way out of the driveway.

She spun the wheel, starting down the road, when everything went black. She panicked, hit the brakes, everything spinning around her.

Kent grunted, his hand landing on her thigh. "Easy, sweetheart. It's gonna be…okay."

Shit, he was coughing. No doubt spraying more blood across his perfect lips. She pounded her fist on the wheel, staring at where she knew he was. "It's gone. Completely gone."

"It's okay. I'll…direct you."

Tears threatened then fell, but she nodded, hitting the gas then heading down the road. Kent called out directions—gentle right turn. Sweeping left. Hold it steady. Her heart hammered in her chest, the sheer weight of possible failure nearly crushing her. They'd traveled for ten minutes when his voice faded. His hand slipping from the wheel.

She skidded to a halt, frantic hands reaching for him. "Kent! Kent! Damn it, talk to me."

Nothing. Just the raspy sound of his next labored breath. Blade's low whimper.

Addison groped for him, cupping his head—crying out when it lolled to one side after she let go.

"No. No, please don't do this. Please, I need…I need you to help me see. Please, Kent, I can't… Fuck!"

She slammed her hands on the steering wheel, again, Kent's blood sticky beneath her palms. This couldn't be happening. It couldn't end this way.

Addison closed her eyes. "Okay, Addy. Time's up. You can't wallow in this…this darkness any more. Not now."

Her voice sounded around her. She was talking to no one. But she needed to hear the words. Feel them.

Have them vibrate the air around her until they rang true.

"All this time, you've been waiting for a reason to come back into the light. Something worth abandoning the darkness. This isn't about being a cop. About Will. About anything other than your own fears. But there's no reason to be afraid. Not as long as Kent's by your side. So…this is what you're going to do. You're going to take a deep breath, count to three, then open your eyes. And when you do, you're going to see. Because Kent is depending on you. He's saved your life. He's all you need. And you're going to do this. For him. Because you love him."

Her hands shook as she took a deep breath, counted to three, then opened her eyes. It happened slowly. Like a veil being lifted. First a few shapes, then muted colors, until the road stood out before her—the headlights cutting a path through the darkness.

She didn't glance at Kent. Couldn't. If she saw he wasn't breathing, if she thought for a second she was too late, she'd lose it. So, she focused on the gravel road. On the map directing her to Hank's. How the dot was drawing closer. The mileage counting down.

She thought she heard Kent groan. Breathe, then drift off, but she just kept driving. Her vision wavered, blinked a few times, but she pushed through it. Never taking her eyes of her destination—the small red dot on the map.

She was sure she'd taken hours to reach the last road —the one that held salvation. She hit the gas, kicking up dirt and stones as she barreled down the path, skidding into Hank's ranch in a cloud of dust.

She was screaming Hank's name before she'd jumped out of the truck, racing around to Kent's side. She tripped when her vision cut out for a second, quickly recovering when she forced it back. It flickered but held. She reefed open the door, catching Kent when he nearly tumbled out. God, he looked so pale. So still.

She was too late. She knew it. Was he breathing? Normally she perceived all those small noises, but nothing registered above her pulse thundering inside her head.

Footsteps, then they were there. Hank, Russel. Some blonde guy she'd never met. Lifting Kent up, carrying him inside. She helped Blade down, then darted after them, tripping into the house and against the wall. The new guy reached for her, but she was already pushing off the wall, dropping to her knees beside Kent. Russel had him on the floor in the kitchen, a big black bag spread out beside him.

Russel looked at her, squinted, then nodded at Kent. "Tell me what happened, Addison."

"It was Sanchez. Grace Sanchez. She was waiting for us at Kent's place."

"Sanchez? I thought she was dead?"

"I did, too, but... Can you save him? God, you have to save him, I can't... I haven't even told him I love him, yet."

"Bastard's too stubborn to die. Hank, ready the chopper. Swede... Call ahead. They'll need four units of

O neg on hand. Have a team standing by. He'll need surgery. Bullet's still in his chest cavity."

Her damn chest clenched at his words, and she felt the darkness closing in. *No. Not, again. Never, again.* She steadied her hands, nodding at Russel. "I'm going with you."

The guy—Swede—took her hands. Stopped them from shaking. "We'll take my truck. Bring your buddy along. I swear we'll get there right behind them."

She wanted to argue, but he was already ushering her out. Helping her and Blade into his truck. A helicopter sounded nearby, and she watched as Russel carried Kent out, jumping inside the waiting chopper then disappearing into the night.

Blade settled next to her, his head on her lap. She scratched at his ears, a chilling numbness washing over her as the truck lurched forward, the miles passing like a gray blur beyond the window. Kent was going to make. He had to.

CHAPTER 21

Fᴜᴄᴋ. He *hurt*!

Everywhere. His head. His chest. Even his damn toes burned when he took a breath. One big searing pain eclipsing everything but the underlying thought that he was alive.

Somehow. Because pain meant life. They went hand in hand. It also meant he wasn't going anywhere. Not that he even knew where he was. He blinked, coming back to himself in a wash of more pain. Only, it wasn't quite as red hot. Not the crushing force he'd felt…

How long had it been? A minute? An hour? Weeks? He tried to open his eyes, assess his situation, but the signals weren't getting through.

"Don't try to move. Just…rest. I'm here."

That voice. Soft. Soothing. Like lying in a cool pond on a hot summer's day. It lulled him back. Eased the tight feeling in his chest.

Another blink. Another time shift. He knew that

much. He was blacking out. Barely coming out of unconsciousness enough to register he was awake.

"Sleep, Kent."

Kent. His name. It sounded odd. As if he wasn't used to hearing it. As if it belonged to someone else. And why did the voice keep telling him to rest? He wasn't supposed to rest. He needed to...do something. Go somewhere. Protect...her.

What was her name?

Darkness. Closing in around him. A hand on his cheek, gently stroking his skin. Something twigged in the back of his mind. Warning him she shouldn't be touching him. That *no one* touched him. But it faded beneath her fingers. The soft press of her lips on his forehead. It felt good. Felt right.

More darkness. He wasn't sure where it came from. It just slowly slid over him—dragged him under before spitting him back out. Into... He wasn't sure. He sensed the light against his eyelids. Felt something warm his face. The sun? A lamp?

No, a hand. *Her* hand. He wasn't sure how he knew, just that it was true. The kind of truth that came from deep inside. That you didn't question. She was there. And she was his.

What the fuck was her name?

He needed to remember. She was in danger. That much he remembered. A sense of being watched. A flash of light, then—bam.

He'd left her. Not on purpose. He was pretty sure he'd passed out after being knocked across the room. Maybe out the door. But that didn't change the fact he

hadn't been there for her. To keep her safe. To be her...
guide.

Guide.

Guide dog. Blade.

Addison!

Rigs bolted upright, groaning at the pull of tubes
against his skin. The flash of pain through his chest,
across his ribs then up the other side. Christ, it felt as if
his entire torso was being crushed. Trampled on by a
ten-ton elephant.

He tried to breathe through the pain, realized
breathing was pretty much beyond him, then collapsed
back, chest heaving, lungs fighting to inflate. He closed
his eyes. Sitting up shouldn't be that hard. *Breathing*,
shouldn't be that hard.

But, at least, he was awake. Mostly. He pried his
eyelids apart, again. Took stock. The room wasn't
overly big, though not small, either. A collection of
balloons and flowers were crowded onto a small table
on the far side, the words "Get Well Soon," scribbled
across most of the cards. A dingy beige curtain hung
from a rod that circled the bed, the bulk of it pushed off
to one side. He managed to twist his head to the right,
then froze.

Fucking froze because she was there.

His Addison.

Her eyes were closed, one small hand nestled under
her chin. She had her legs tucked underneath her, her
body curled onto a cushioned chair. Her blonde hair
gathered around her like a wave of gold, spilling over
her shoulders then disappearing down her back.

She was breathtaking.

Not that he had any breath to spare, but seeing her—knowing she was there. That she'd been there all along —it eased the pressure in his chest. Lessened the pain still throbbing beneath his skin.

Something cold and wet touched his hand, and he jerked a bit—instantly regretting the way the tubes pulled against his skin, again—then looked down. Soulful brown eyes stared up at him, the animal's tongue hanging off to one side. The canine gave a low, playful yip, licking his hand before settling back on its haunches.

Blade.

The animal tilted its head to the side, and Rigs wondered if he'd said the name or just thought it. He couldn't tell. Couldn't do much more than lie against the bed, alternating his gaze between Blade and Addison.

Her eyes fluttered, opened and closed, then opened, again. Wider. Blinking a few times before shifting toward him. Her gaze found his and stuck. Just stayed there, pinned to him, her mouth opening on a rough inhalation.

She seemed as frozen as he was. Sitting there, legs still crossed beneath her, her chest rising and falling rapidly—as if she'd just run ten miles uphill. That's how he felt, only he'd done it carrying a thousand pounds. The weight of the world.

But for her, he knew he'd do just that. Any obstacle, any cost.

Addison came out of the trance first, uncurled her

legs then leaned forward. He watched her move, every action full of beauty and grace, when it struck him that something was…off. Something about her was… different.

He swept his gaze the length of her. From her perfect feet hidden beneath canvas shoes to the long blonde tresses he wanted to wrap around his hand. Fist between his fingers as he tasted those luscious lips. Lips curved into the kind of smile that stopped traffic. Stopped the damn Earth from spinning.

But he still couldn't place what was different, until he focused on her eyes. Beautiful blue orbs that made the rest of the world look ordinary. Plain. Big, focused eyes.

Focused.

She could see. Was staring directly at him, without tilting her head—trying to pinpoint his location. Because god knew he wasn't making any sound. Okay, maybe he was breathing hard or grunting. He didn't think so, couldn't really tell over the constant beep of his heart in the background, but when she'd been blind, she might have picked up on those cues. Sourced him out.

But she didn't need to because she moved to the edge of her seat, reached her hand up and cupped his cheek. Touched him right over the long jagged scars on his face. The ones he normally hid, but not from her. It all came rushing back with that gentle touch.

Bumping into her in the garden. Armed men trying to kill her. Making love to her in her bed. The shower. The truck. Letting her see inside his soul.

Some fuckhead shooting him then gunning for her.

Shit. He'd dropped like a fucking pussy. One hit, and he'd been out.

Addison smiled, laughed, tears gathering then falling. She shifted forward—touched her lips to his in a kiss so fucking soft, it made his chest hurt. Right there in the center.

"Welcome back."

He smiled. Tried to, but the scars on his face tugged at his skin—and he was sure it came off as more of a snarl. But she didn't seem to care, laughing, again, more tears spilling down her cheeks.

He frowned. Managed to lift one hand to her cheek. Catch the next tear on his finger. He watched it waver over his skin, then fall to the floor. "Don't...cry."

God, it hurt to *talk*. How was that possible? He'd been shot before—hell, not that long ago. Three bullets, and he'd managed to drag his ass out of the hospital room and down three flights of stairs before crumpling. And he'd woken up ready to wage war.

This—this was bone-numbing pain. Exhaustion. He'd only been awake a few minutes, and he already felt drained. Barely able to keep his eyes open. What the hell was wrong with him?

Addison shook her head, face pinching tight. He blinked, and she was holding a glass, a striped straw pointed toward him.

He opened for her, took a cautious sip, then another. The cool water slid down his throat.

She smiled. "Better?"

He nodded, not certain his voice would work.

She brushed some hair out of his eyes. "Don't try to talk. It's still early." She laughed. A bit forced, but it still eased his muscles. "The doctors swore you wouldn't wake up for another few days. I told them you were stubborn. Are you in pain?"

Sure, but looking at her, feeling her hand in his, it didn't matter. She was there. Alive, despite him.

She tsked. "You're barely awake for more than a minute and already you're going into soldier mode. I'm fine. You're… Well, you're alive. Not sure how. A lesser man would have died, but you…"

Fuck, more tears. The kind that made her lip tremble. Her shoulders shake. He reached for her, and she curled into him. Not all her weight, but enough he could wrap his arms around her. Breathe her in.

He closed his eyes. He didn't know what had happened. How she'd managed to stay alive—save his ass in the process. If she'd called for help or done it all herself. It didn't matter because the end result was the same. She was there. Alive. With him.

Another playful bark and a lick. He chuckled, cursed at the jolt of pain. Apparently, laughing hurt, too.

Addison smiled, wiping at the tears dotting her cheeks as she gave Blade's head a scratch. She glanced around then leaned in close. "Don't tell anyone. They think he's still my guide dog. But…" She sniffed. "I couldn't leave him behind. Not after he saved my life. Saved *our* lives."

Rigs lowered his hand, gave the dog a pat. "Atta boy."

Soldier to the end. No doubt about it. It also meant

he'd have a hard time saying no when the dog decided his place was on their bed.

He took Addison's hand. Squeezed it. "You can... see?"

Her face lit up. Like a fucking Christmas tree, all golden and bright. "Turns out you nearly dying on me was just the motivation I needed. Though, I swear..." She leaned in closer. "If you ever, *ever*, scare me like that, again, Kent Walker, I'll tan your hide. Hardass Marine soldier or not. Are we clear?"

"Crystal." He relaxed back, didn't fight it when his eyes started closing. "You'll stay?"

"Try to kick me out." Soft lips on his. On his forehead. "Sleep. I'll be here when you wake up. I'll always be here, because...because I love you."

He snapped his eyes open, again, staring directly at her. Had he heard her right? He opened his mouth, but she laughed, held a soft finger over his lips.

"Not, now. Rest. You can pledge your undying love once you'll remember saying it. And I promise I'll tell you, again. As many times as you need until it's burned into your memory. So, sleep."

She loved him. He didn't need to hear it, again, to remember. It was seared into his brain. Echoing through every neuron. But...he wouldn't stop her from saying it. Not ever.

$\sim$

Six weeks later...

. . .

Rigs paced the length of Bridgette's clinic, constantly shifting his gaze to the door. She was late.

Not that she had given him an exact time. Interviews were hard to judge. Five minutes, ten. Three hours. It could go either way, and the last thing he wanted to do was rush her. Not after all she was giving up.

He moved back to the window, looking up the road. He couldn't quite see the sheriff's station from here, but he'd see her if she was on her way. Beautiful blonde hair lifting in the breeze. Her sexy hips swaying as she walked. Blade by her side.

He smiled. The dog had made the transition back to bomb disposal in a heartbeat. Not that he'd necessarily be needed for that on a constant basis, but the addition of a canine approved for that line of work—who guarded Addison as if it was a mission handed down from God—was a definite plus. And the reason she'd agreed to meet with local law enforcement.

He chuckled then cursed. His damn chest still hurt when he laughed. Fuck, when he breathed too deeply. Turned out Grace Sanchez had been Stevens' primary contact within the DEA—the one who'd hidden Stevens' drug dealings for the past few years. Who'd falsified documents and undermined the work of her fellow agents by alerting local gangs whenever a raid was imminent.

But that wasn't the worst of it. She'd joined up with a few key service members—her brother being one of them. They'd been using military routes to distribute the drugs worldwide—an arrangement that was in danger of being unearthed. Apparently, José Pedro had gotten antsy, and been killed because of it.

Sanchez had also been the one who'd killed Detective William O'Toole.

That's what really stung. Addy had gone into great detail about how the two of them had been inseparable for the few months before the raid. How they'd talked about marriage. Kids. Only to have her kill the very man she'd said she was in love with.

It blew Rigs away. Just like the shot had. Fucking forty-five point blank. He'd been lucky he hadn't died instantly. That Addison and Blade had managed to outsmart the bitch—take her out. She hadn't made it. Had died in the yard. Rigs hadn't lost a minute of sleep over that.

Addy had. Had battled with how to make peace with what had happened. The betrayal. She'd hidden it well, submersing herself in making him better. Helping him through the first few weeks of recovery. It had been a bitch. Between her and Ice—he wasn't sure which had hurt more. Getting shot or relearning how to function.

He smiled. Definitely the latter.

"Fuck, Bridg. Take a picture. Rigs is...smiling. Might never happen, again."

Rigs groaned then turned, scowling at Midnight as he leaned against Bridgette's desk, a smug smirk on his face. "I keep telling you guys to watch your sass, lest you end up with metal filings where your truck used to be."

Midnight snorted. "Right. Like you'd ever hold true to one of those threats. You're too honorable. Besides,

Addy likes us. And she'd have your balls if you behaved poorly."

"Have his balls for what?"

Rigs inhaled then spun. And there she was. Standing there. Larger than life. So fucking beautiful he wasn't sure if he could keep looking at her without having to rub his eyes. His chest—right there in the center where it hurt.

He held out his hand, and she came to him—wrapped her arms around his back and placed her head on his chest. And everything slid into place. All the pieces fitting together. Midnight could tease him all he wanted. Rigs didn't care. Not as long as he had Addison.

She dropped a kiss on his pec, then eased back, looking between the two. "Are you two boys arguing, again?"

Rigs shook his head. "Wouldn't dream of it. How did it go?"

She smiled, and his heart did that skipping thing. "You're looking at Eagle Rock's newest deputy."

"Seriously? You said yes?"

"Let's just say they made me an offer I couldn't refuse."

"Really? What was it? A retirement package? More vacation time?"

She shook her head. "A job in town, so I can be close to the man I love."

Fuck.

She'd said it, again. After her confession in the hospital, Rigs had been planning the perfect date. He wanted to make his pledge to her memorable. More than memorable. He wanted to make her swoon. A guaranteed setting to make her say yes.

To him. To spending the rest of her life with him.

And she'd gotten the jump on him, again.

He swallowed, opened his mouth, then closed it. God, how could he ever top that? The look on her face. The pure joy and love she felt for him.

He sucked in a breath, ran over all the sweet words he'd planned to say, then blurted out the first thing that popped into his mind. "Fuck, I love you. Marry me."

Shit. He hadn't given her the ring. Gotten down on one knee. Hadn't said a single poetic word.

But she was laughing. Crying. Kissing him right there in front of Midnight. Bridgette. Not an ounce of self-consciousness in her. He answered in kind, eating at her mouth, holding her close. It wasn't until Midnight cleared his throat behind them that Rigs finally let her come up for air. She could breathe through him as far as he was concerned.

But he managed to pull back—glance over at his buddy. "You got something to say, Midnight?"

"We were just wondering if we should make the wedding a double one? Or if you're going to follow in Ice and Harlequin's footsteps and run off to Vegas?"

Christ. Rigs hadn't thought about that. About the actual ceremony. That there'd be dancing and people and a photographer. That he'd have to be out in the open. The center of attention—

Then, he looked at Addison and sighed. If that's what she wanted, he'd do it. A thousand people, rolls of film. It didn't matter. As long as she was his, he could suck it up.

He took a deep breath. Faced her. "Whatever you want, sweetheart. Just say the word."

Addison looked at Midnight and Bridgette then back to him. "I'm free. now."

"Now?"

"Today. Montana doesn't have a waiting period, and we have two witnesses right here…"

Blade barked, and she laughed.

"Make that three. So… Why wait?"

"But…" He stood there, mouth gaping open. Stunned. "Don't you want a fancy dress? A party?"

"All I need is you. With me. For the rest of our lives." She held out her hand. "What do you say, soldier? Ready to land?"

Rigs shook his head, took her hand in his then tugged her tight to his chest. "Already have. But let's make it official."

MIDNIGHT RANGER

Kris Norris

Midnight
RANGER

BROTHERHOOD PROTECTORS

KRIS NORRIS

CHAPTER 1

Seattle. Ten months later...

"Don't you ever keep regular hours?"

Bridgette Hayward looked up from her desk, smiling at the man standing in her doorway. Tall, dark, handsome, dressed in Armani with his hair perfectly styled—Jeremy Brenner was the classic image of an assistant US attorney. In the two years she'd been working for the United States Attorney's Office, she'd never once seen the guy sweat or lose the calm demeanor he wore like a shield, regardless of the circumstances. And the man had gone up against some intimidating clients.

Bridgette leaned back, twirling her pen around her fingers. "Says the man standing in my doorway at...oh, nine o'clock on a Friday night."

"I just came back because I forgot a brief I needed. You, on the other hand, haven't left, yet."

"Big case means extra time, and I can't afford to screw this one up."

Jeremy's eyes narrowed, and he glanced around as if looking for others despite the fact the office had been closed for hours, before stepping through the doorway. "You know I think you're one of the best lawyers we've had come through here, right?"

She frowned. "Why do I sense a 'but' at the end of that statement?"

"Not a 'but'. I'm just…worried about you."

"That's sweet."

"Seriously, Bridgette. Alexander Stevens has been heading his family's drug business for longer than you've been alive. It's taken that many years to make a case against him, and it was essentially a fluke. Which means he's got more connections than anyone knows. The kind that's kept him out of jail and gotten other people killed." He nodded at her. "You still getting threats? Calls? Letters?"

A chill beaded her skin, the ghostly echo of a gravelly voice on her cell sounding inside her head before she shoved it aside. "Nothing I haven't gotten before. And, as usual, I'm being cautious."

"If you were being cautious, you'd either have a bodyguard or you'd be working remotely until the trial starts, and we can petition for police protection."

"I'm fine, Jeremy. Promise."

He shook his head. "I realize this is a huge leap forward in your career, and you deserve every bit of it. Your record here is more than impressive. I'd just hate to see you get hurt over it."

"I promise I'll be more vigilant. And if things escalate—"

"If things escalate, it'll be too damn late." He huffed, running his fingers through his hair. "You *are* stubborn. Anyway, I'm heading out. You ready to go? I'll walk you to your car like a perfect gentleman." He winked. "Or not, if you'd prefer."

She smiled—the guy had been trying to get into her pants for months. "Thanks, but I have a few things left. I'll be out of here soon, though."

"All right. Be careful."

"Always."

He shook his head then left, his footsteps fading down the hallway. Bridgette focused on the written testimonies, again, noting any concerns or questions she wanted to discuss, until the words started blurring together. She sat back and glanced at the clock—nine forty-five. She closed her eyes for a moment, rubbing the bridge of her nose in the hopes of lessening the ache building between her eyes. Jeremy was right about one thing. She needed a break. She could look at the files, again, in the morning, but reading the same paragraph over and over wasn't helping.

She stood and stretched, hoping to ease the tight press between her shoulder blades. A few more weeks like this and her colleagues would start calling her Quasimodo. Maybe she'd take a hot bath. Spend the night curled up on the couch watching a movie. Anything not related to Alexander Stevens or this case.

The thought made her smile as she packed some folders into her briefcase then placed it on her desk. She filed any remaining papers then grabbed her case and her purse. A quick trip to the ladies' room, and she could head out.

The building was eerily quiet as she walked down the hallway then into the bathroom. Usually, she enjoyed the silence after everyone else had left, but tonight felt different. Whether it was the storm raging outside or Jeremy's words, she wasn't sure. But she'd be happy to get home—lock herself inside.

Her boots clicked across the floor as she made her way back to grab her jacket. If she'd been thinking clearly, she would have taken it with her and locked up, already, saving her the return trip. But the long days were definitely taking a toll, and it seemed as if she forgot simple things more often, lately.

She sighed, stepping inside, before coming to a halt. A large yellow envelope sat kitty-corner on her desk, her name scribbled across the front. She glanced around, staring at the shadows lining the hallway. She'd been gone less than ten minutes.

Her heart rate kicked up as she walked over to her desk, staring down at the offering. No return address. No mail stamp. She thumbed the corner, debating on whether to open it or call the cops. Though, if it turned out to be nothing, she'd never live it down. And she hadn't been there long enough to bring that kind of attention to herself.

Bridgette took a breath then gently lifted the tab. It hadn't even been sealed, which hopefully meant it didn't contain any kind of deadly virus. Her pulse thundered in her head as she slipped her hand inside and removed a collection of photographs. A small note was stuck to the front, the same handwriting scrawled across it.

I'm coming for you.

The words glared up at her, the simple statement making her stomach roil. She bit her bottom lip then flipped through the images. Whoever had taken them had followed her from her apartment to her office. There were even a few of her at the boxing club—her hands in gloves as she moved around the ring. They'd obviously been taken over a few days, which meant someone was stalking her. *Had* been stalking her for some time, and she hadn't even noticed.

Memories surfaced in the background. Distant like a clock ticking in another room. But there, just the same. She pursed her lips then stuffed the photos back into the envelope. If Alex Stevens thought some creepy phone calls and a few pictures would be enough to intimidate her, the man had a hard lesson ahead of him.

First, she'd go home. Lock up. Double check her alarm system. Then, she'd make copies of everything. She knew firsthand that evidence had a way of "disappearing" with the right amount of motivation. And Stevens had more than enough motivation at his disposal.

In the morning, she'd head to the police station. She'd give them the envelope and half of the photos. Have them add the images to her growing file of harassment since she'd first been handed the case months ago. But she'd send the note and the other pictures to her friend, Special Agent Jack Taylor. See if the Bureau could match the handwriting or get some kind of DNA off the paper. It wasn't that she didn't trust the local precinct, she just trusted Jack more.

Her briefcase felt heavy as she slipped the envelope inside then headed for the bank of elevators at the opposite end of the hallway. Different scenarios bounced around in her head, trying to take shape, when a distant noise stopped her. She paused, trying to pinpoint it when the dull echo sounded, again.

Footsteps. Behind her.

Bridgette swallowed against the punch of fear cooling her skin and began walking. Faster this time. The footsteps followed her—two for every one of hers. She reached the elevator and hit the button. The arrow lit up, accompanied by the hum of machinery as the unit began moving.

She glanced down the hallway. Had she only imagined the footsteps? Wouldn't the person have rounded the corner by now? Was it another coworker returning to their office?

No. There hadn't been any other lights on. All the doors had been closed. She looked at the number pad click off the floors then made for the stairwell. At least she'd have some control by taking the stairs. No surprises when the silver doors opened, and she could easily detour to another floor if she heard someone approaching from below.

The heavy metal fire door clicked shut behind her as she bustled through, descending as fast as she could without making too much noise. She'd gotten two floors down when another click resonated through the air above her, followed by hurried steps.

Bridgette raced down the stairs, sticking to the outer wall in case anyone tried to see her over the railing. She didn't stop, winding her way down to the bottom level. Why had she decided to park in the damn garage today? It was like asking to become a victim. But the rain had been falling in steady sheets, and she'd been too rushed to try and find a spot on the road or in a neighboring lot. So, she'd opted for the staff parking. A key-activated sensor and garage door were supposed to make the area secure. But no such thing existed. There were always ways in, and if someone wanted her bad enough, they would have found one.

The exit door squeaked as she shoved on it, darting to her right once she'd cleared the small glass enclosure. Only a scattering of cars dotted the large space, a patchwork of shadows masking the glare of the overhead lights. She headed for the wall, keeping herself between it and the front of a few vehicles in case she needed to disappear. She'd made it halfway to her Jeep when the inner door bounced open.

Bridgette hit the concrete, crouching behind the grill of a large Suburban. The plate caught on her pants, ripping a line across her hip. She cursed under her breath, yanking the fabric free then slowing peering around the left side of the SUV. A dark figure moved down the outer edge of the parking stalls, head swiveling from side to side.

A man. No question. Wide, thick shoulders with a broad chest and narrow waist, the guy looked athletic beneath the snug black clothing and matching ski mask. As if he could chase her for hours and never get tired.

Judging by the size of his biceps, she had no doubts that he packed one hell of a punch. The kind that would knock her out with only a single blow. Something glinted off one of the lights, the silver gleam winking at her.

He had a gun, though the barrel looked strangely thick—shit. A suppressor. This guy meant business. He wasn't there to threaten her. To beat a warning into her. He was there to kill her. Period.

Bridgette weighed her options. She could call for help, but with the garage so empty, her voice was sure to echo. And the police wouldn't be able to reach her before her stalker would.

She could make a run for her Jeep. She was quick.

Not faster than a bullet, girl. Think!

It wouldn't take the man long to figure out she'd hidden behind one of the available cars. All he'd have to do was systematically check. Her best bet was to double back. Wait until she had enough distance to dash inside the building. She could head upstairs and find another way out. Or hide in a bathroom while she called for help. Anything but sit there and wait for the asshole to shoot her.

Footsteps.

He was moving. Each step carefully orchestrated as if he'd done this a hundred times before. He stopped at every vehicle, checked underneath then moved on.

Shit. He'd see her feet unless she could somehow balance on the bumper with her boots pressed to the wall. Sweat slicked her palms as she tried to judge how to bridge her weight, when a noise sounded from across the lot.

The guy turned, staring into the deep shadows, his body rigid. Alert. She didn't know how long he'd stay focused on other side of the garage. A second. Five. All night. She chanced it and quickly scrambled over to the bank of cars he'd already checked, doing her best to hide her feet behind the wheel on the left side.

Silence stretched out, the utter nothingness making her heart pound. Could he hear it? She could. Frantically beating inside her chest—making it hard to breathe.

A step.

Continuing in the same direction. She matched his movements, shuffling toward the doorway every time he took a step—hoping to mask her sounds in his. He kept going, kept allowing her to get closer to the door, until she'd reached the last car. Bridgette crept to the tail end, stealing a look beneath the vehicle. Black boots faced away from her, the guy's shadow stretching out like a snake behind him.

She glanced at the doorway. Nothing but an oversized pillar stood between her and the glass. If he caught her movement, she'd be wide open. Bile crested her throat, burning at her resolve. One chance.

She moved as soon as he took another step, surging to her feet then dashing behind the column. Her boots scuffed the cement, the dull sound echoing off the walls.

He stopped.

Damn. He'd heard her. She knew he had. Were those

his footsteps toward her, now? Getting closer? Louder. She couldn't check. Couldn't risk he'd see her. She was pretty sure her body fit behind the pillar, but it wouldn't keep her safe. And soon, he'd be there. Beside her. Nothing but a couple feet of concrete between her and a bullet.

The steady click of his boots stopped on the other side of the column, his harsh breath whispering close by. She held hers, inching around the column as he slowly picked his way toward the wall, keeping the pillar between them. What happened once he'd checked behind the cars? If he headed toward the door, she'd never be able to stay hidden. It nothing else, he'd see her shadow.

A cold sweat broke out across her skin, dripping down her forehead despite the near freezing temperature. He was on the other side, about to move past the edge of the column. Bridgette clenched her jaw, waiting for him to suddenly jump out at her, when the garage door started rolling. She startled, barely stopping the scream clawing at her throat from joining the grating sound of metal chains moving along a pulley as the door rose, exposing a flash of light from the street beyond.

The man stopped, quickly walking back the way he'd come. Bridgette moved with him, once again, darting behind the car. Headlights cut through the shadows as the approaching vehicle rounded the corner, pulling into an empty stall just down from where she was crouched against the wall. Music blared through the closed windows then cut off, easy laughter filling the void.

A couple stepped out, still engrossed in conversation

as they talked over the top of the car. Bridgette glanced at where she'd last seen the man, but he was gone. Most likely out through the employee door beside the exit ramp.

Her hands shook as she straightened then leaned against the wall, bracing her palms on her knees. A dull roar sounded inside her head, blocking out everything until a hand landed on her shoulder. She jumped, tripping sideways as she swung toward the person, her fist glancing off a torso.

"Whoa, Bridgette. Easy. Christ, it's just me."

Air wheezed through her lungs, the steady supply finally clearing her vision. Jeremy stood off to her right, brow furrowed, his lips turned into a frown.

He glanced around then looked back at her. "Are you okay?"

"I thought you'd left?"

The words rushed out, all melding together to form one long incoherent word.

"I got halfway home before I realized I'd left my damn cell on the counter in the men's room." He leaned a bit closer. "Did something happen? You look like a damn ghost."

She opened her mouth, but nothing made it past the lump in her throat. She scanned the garage, again, but it looked like it always had. Deserted. Safe. One of the overhead lights buzzed then winked out, blanketing them in dull gray.

Jeremy reached into his pocket, retrieving his phone. "I'm calling an ambulance."

"No." She managed to grasp his wrist—draw his attention. "I'm fine, I'm…"

Just terrified. Nearly died at the hands of a gunman. But I'm fine.

"You don't look fine."

She snorted, the aftermath of adrenaline making her shake. "I…"

She paused. While she didn't think there was any chance Jeremy had been bought—that he *could* be bought—she'd been fooled before. Betrayed. And she'd promised herself she'd never fall victim to that, again. Better to play it safe until she could talk to Jack. Jack couldn't be bought, and he wouldn't ever betray her. It was a given. A knowledge that ran soul deep.

She cleared her throat. "I thought I heard something. Saw someone. But…I must have been imagining it."

"Do yourself a favor and take a couple of days off. Or a week. But get some rest. You keep going like this and you'll burn yourself out." He motioned toward her Jeep. "Can I walk you to your car, now?"

"That would be great. Thanks."

She moved in beside him as he headed toward her vehicle, still searching the area. But they were definitely alone. Though for how long…

She stopped when his hand shot out and grabbed her arm, dragging her back a step. She snapped out of her thoughts, following his gaze until it landed on her Jeep. Two perfectly round holes were punched through the windshield, both front tires flat against the concrete.

"Shit." Jeremy turned toward her. "You still think this is nothing you haven't dealt with before?"

She opened her mouth to answer, but he was already on his phone, talking to the cops. Bridgette looked toward the exit door, wondering if the guy was on the other side. Waiting. Planning.

It didn't matter. She'd been given a second chance to get her head out of her ass and make better decisions. Jeremy was right. She needed to distance herself for a while. Stop giving Stevens' men an easy target. And she knew just where to go.

Montana.

The house her grandmother had left her.

The one still registered in her father's name. The last place anyone would ever look for her, and the only place she might be safe.

OTHER BOOKS BY KRIS NORRIS

SINGLES

Centerfold

Keeping Faith

Iron Will

My Soul to Keep

Ricochet

Rope's End

SERIES

'TIL DEATH

1 - Deadly Vision

2 - Deadly Obsession

3 - Deadly Deception

BROTHERHOOD PROTECTORS ~ Elle James

1 - Midnight Ranger

2 – Carved in Ice

3 - Going in Blind

4 - Delta Force: Colt

5 - Delta Force: Crow

6 - Delta Force: Phoenix

TEAM EAGLE

ORIGINAL BROTHERHOOD PROTECTORS SERIES

BY ELLE JAMES

ABOUT ELLE JAMES

ELLE JAMES also writing as MYLA JACKSON is a *New York Times* and *USA Today* Bestselling author of books including cowboys, intrigues and paranormal adventures that keep her readers on the edges of their seats. With over eighty works in a variety of sub-genres and lengths she has published with Harlequin, Samhain, Ellora's Cave, Kensington, Cleis Press, and Avon. When she's not at her computer, she's traveling, snow skiing, boating, or riding her ATV, dreaming up new stories. Learn more about Elle James at www.ellejames.com

Website | Facebook | Twitter | GoodReads | Newsletter | BookBub | Amazon

Follow Elle!
www.ellejames.com
ellejames@ellejames.com

f facebook.com/ellejamesauthor
𝕏 x.com/ElleJamesAuthor